THE GLASS MASK

THE GLASS
MASK

Lenore Glen Offord

FELONY & MAYHEM PRESS • NEW YORK

All the characters and events portrayed in this work are fictitious.

THE GLASS MASK

A Felony & Mayhem mystery

PRINTING HISTORY
First U.S. edition (Duell, Sloan and Pearce): 1944
Felony & Mayhem edition: 2016

ISBN: 978-1-63194-028-6

Manufactured in the United States of America

Library of Congress Cataloging-in-Publication Data

Offord, Lenore Glen, 1905-1991
The glass mask / Lenore Glen Offord. -- Felony & Mayhem edition.
   pages ; cm
"A Felony & Mayhem mystery."
ISBN 978-1-63194-028-6
I. Title.
PS3529.F42G58 2016
813'.54--dc23
                          2015032342

The icon above says you're holding a copy of a book in the Felony & Mayhem "Vintage" category. These books were originally published prior to about 1965, and feature the kind of twisty, ingenious puzzles beloved by fans of Agatha Christie and John Dickson Carr. If you enjoy this book, you may well like other "Vintage" titles from Felony & Mayhem Press.

For more about these books, and other Felony & Mayhem titles, or to place an order, please visit our website at:

www.FelonyAndMayhem.com

Other "Vintage" titles from

FELONY&MAYHEM

Other "Vintage" titles from

FELONY&MAYHEM

THE GLASS MASK

CHAPTER ONE

TODD MCKINNON'S car could easily have done seventy miles an hour on this broad and tempting road down the Sacramento Valley, but wartime restrictions held its speed to a sedate thirty-five. The spring-green curves of hill rising on either side of the road seemed never to change from one mile to the next.

There were three silent persons in the front seat of the car, each subduing his own particular brand of impatience. Todd was exercising rigid control over the foot that rested so lightly on the accelerator, and thinking longingly of letting her out. Georgine Wyeth, beside him, could almost sense this emotion through the shoulder which companionably touched hers, although what could be seen of his face under the tilt of his soft hat betrayed no visible strain. The flat plane of cheek, the sharply cut jaw and firm mouth with its glint of sandy mustache, added up to their usual sum of impassive good nature. She hoped her own appearance was as relaxed. The one thing she wanted was to get home as soon as possible after one of the most exhausting days she could remember.

Todd glanced beyond her at her daughter Barby, wedged in by the window, and then met Georgine's eyes in amusement. The child's slender little nape, framed in tow-colored pigtails, was still tense with excitement, bliss, and the desire to talk.

This had been Barby's day. She was exactly eight years old, and the celebration, specified by herself, had embraced not only a day off from school but a visit to the army camp at Sacramento where Todd's eldest nephew was stationed. Sergeant Dyke McKinnon, twenty-one years old, was a redheaded charmer and well used to making rapid conquests; but Barby's instant adoration, when he had first spent a weekend leave in Berkeley, had been of a character to turn any man's head. To most adults she seemed a plain, silent child, with a remote gravity that was very nearly formidable. When she got one of her rare crushes she lit up like a pinball game. The sergeant, who had small sisters of his own, had fallen with an almost audible thud.

Barby's silence for the past half hour was not from choice. For the first few miles out of Sacramento she had jabbered so incessantly that she was now under orders not to speak again until she had counted five large red objects, nothing smaller than a motorcycle accepted. Therefore, Barby's eyes were now diligently searching the countryside. She was dressed in a miniature WAVES hat and coat, her birthday gift from Todd. In one hand she clutched a flashlight, her favorite among Dyke's lavish assortment of presents. Georgine thought, I must remember this; it's something to have seen a perfectly happy person.

Todd McKinnon said, after a glance at his watch, "H'm, nearly five-thirty. What do you think, Georgine? Shall we stop off for a minute to see those friends of Dyke's?"

"What friends?" Georgine said hazily. She had only the vaguest memory of the sergeant's parting words, something about a girl and her charming aunt.

"They live at Valleyville. We'd have to turn off the main highway for a few miles."

"Isn't it a bit late for a call? And when we're eager to get home—"

"I've been figuring. We'd have to stop somewhere for supper, it'll be after seven before we get to Berkeley—at this rate of speed," Mr. McKinnon put in with venomous inflection. "We might as well drop in at this place for a fifteen-minute call, and then be on our way again. Wouldn't lose much time."

It was an effort to make decisions, but Georgine considered the plan. "On the whole, I should think not," she began.

"And a red barn and a red house," Barby shrieked. "That's five. Now can I talk, Mamma? Look, we haff to stop in that town Cousin Dyke told us about. We *haff* to."

"No, we don't, darling. What makes you think that?"

"Well, it was the very last thing he said, to stop there on our way home if we got a chance because his girlfriend lived there, and if she wasn't home her aunt would be, and he thought Toddy would be interested."

"But that was only if we felt like it, Barby, and we're all tired. You've been running your legs off since eight this morning. I think we'd better go straight home."

Barby said nothing, but her chin went in slowly and she looked at the floor of the car. The back of her neck was completely heartrending.

Todd and Georgine exchanged a swift look. Georgine thought, Oh, dear, I'm spoiling her. I'm going to be one of those soft fools who can't refuse her child anything... Just the same, it was evident that the glory had gone out of the day for Barby, and Barby's mother couldn't bear it.

"Then let's turn off and stop in Valleyville," she said swiftly. Barby's head came up, and the radiance returned to her face. "If it means so much to you, darling. I can't quite see why you want to stop there."

"Well, because Cousin Dyke said to."

" 'Whereon thy feet have trod,' " Georgine murmured. "Thank heaven you asked me for a doll, anyway."

Mr. McKinnon chuckled quietly to himself, and swung the car to the right. He thought, How easy it is to make a child happy. Why do we ever hesitate?

It was an enchanting small town. Georgine didn't know quite what she had been expecting; perhaps only the nice, undistinguished white or buff stucco of the newer valley towns; but she had not visualized anything like this gentle period piece, its cottages and narrow two-story frame houses set sociably close to each other and to the streets, its lilac bushes springing from neatly kept lawns, its huge trees, newly green with the approach of April, arching the pavement. She thought it must resemble New England. And how exactly like those early settlers in the seventies and eighties, with a whole broad valley to build in, to crowd their houses together in the smallest possible space! Just the same, there was something inexpressibly cozy about it, like a Victorian sitting room.

Todd seemed to be talking to himself. "The end of Walnut Street, wasn't that what he said? The last old house, and the biggest."

"Great heavens, Todd," said Georgine, leaning forward as the car stopped, "it's the town mansion!"

"Or was," McKinnon amended. He shut off the ignition and turned for a good look. "Suffering cats," he added.

There it stood, what remained of a magnificent monstrosity of the eighties; weathered white paint on boards, faded dark green paint on old-fashioned hinged shutters; a flight of front steps worthy of a summer hotel; a front door surrounded with colored panes of glass; corners truncated and then enlarged into square bay windows; tottering upper porches, and dim side porches, and porches inexplicably surrounding the whole third story. The house towered incredibly past the skyline of the enclosing hills, and on every possible inch of its surface there was, or had been, wooden lace.

Todd said he would spy out the land, and left them sitting in the car while he ascended the impressive front steps. Georgine watched him with frank pleasure. She thought, These slim, narrowly built men seem to be hard-surfaced, dust doesn't stick to them and their clothes don't wrinkle... If we're going to pay a call I'd better put on some powder and lipstick. There, the door's opening; I hoped there wouldn't be anybody home.

When she looked up from her mirror Todd was still standing in the doorway talking, his back to her. She glanced once more along the façade of the old house. That stuff at the lower windows must be Nottingham lace. Quite nice plain net or scrim curtained the second floor. There were no curtains at all for the third story, set back a little behind its railed balcony, but the windows were shining clean. The afternoon sun slanted into them just enough so that she could see some object, white or light colored, near the window. Was it someone standing very still, looking down at the car? Nothing was visible but the curve of a shoulder.

"Mamma," Barby said, "lookit across the street, there's a chimney standing up all by itself in the middle of that lot."

"Maybe somebody's house burned down. Some of those trees on the edge of the lot are still brown, it couldn't have been so very long ago." Georgine's eyes returned, after this brief interruption, to the uncurtained windows. The person was still there, unmoving.

Todd came running down the steps. "Young Mrs. Crane isn't home," he said from the sidewalk, "but her aunt Mrs. Peabody is. She very much wants us to come in. Okay for a few minutes?"

"I'll admit I'd love to see the inside of that place," Georgine murmured. "Come on, Barby, at least you can put your feet where Cousin Dyke's have stood."

She observed as they approached the steps that this house boasted a broader side yard than any other on the street. There was some distance between it and the nearest dwelling to the north, a space taken up by a tangle of garden and some dilapidated wooden outbuildings, to which a weedy carriage drive led from the street. The south side was enclosed by a line of beautiful maples, old and huge, their branches sweeping downward like willows. They made an effective screen for those side windows, Georgine thought, but the lower rooms must be very dark with all that shade. The porch creaked a little as she and Todd and Barby crossed it. She reflected that nothing took on the look and feel and smell of age as wood did; even outdoors her nostrils caught its sweetish scent.

"Mrs. Peabody went to take off her apron," Todd said in her ear. "She'll be right out to meet us." The three of them crossed the threshold, and met an even more perceptible odor of the Victorian: carpets that had been swept with tea leaves and wet newspaper, old fabric hangings and furniture polish, and wood again; but there was also a fragrance of hyacinth from a bowl on the table, and a hint of baking cookies, and the hall that stretched before them, nearly the depth of the house, was exquisitely clean. The slanting sun illuminated it. There were double doors on the right, a single one on the left, and in the depths of the hall more doors; at least three of them.

"Oh, lovely," Georgine said under her breath, looking at the staircase. It was on the right of the hall, starting halfway back, and rose in a beautiful, flying curve through the high ceiling.

One of the doors at the rear opened, and a small slim woman came hurrying through. "But I'm so pleased that you would come in," she was saying, both hands outstretched to Georgine and Barby. "I can't tell you how much pleasure it gives me to meet Sergeant McKinnon's family."

Georgine took her in with a quick glance as Todd performed introductions. Mrs. Peabody must be in her late thirties, but her sort of attractiveness did not depend on youth. She had the only really heart-shaped face Georgine had ever seen, its widely set gray eyes and delicate hollows under the high cheekbones giving her a look of great sweetness. Georgine thought, She plays it up well too; that soft bang cut to a point in the middle of her forehead. That dress is homemade, but it fits her perfectly...and how nice of her to shake hands with Barby in that grown-up way.

She held her breath for a moment. Normally at such a time Barby, though mannerly, turned into an unresponsive clod of childhood; but this time some of the magic must still be about her. Barby held out a paw which her mother devoutly hoped was not sticky. "How do you do," she said carefully, and added in an awed tone, "Do you know our Cousin Dyke?"

"Yes, I do. He was here to dinner once, and stayed the night."

"Oh, isn't he a lovely man?" Barby said, her voice faint with emotion. "He took me for *a ride in a jeep.*"

"Why, you darling," said Mrs. Peabody under her breath. "When was that, today? I must hear all about it. Come into the sitting room, won't you all?" She gave the adults a brief conspiratorial smile, and opened the door to the left.

Everything about this house seemed to provoke exclamations, either of joy or horror. Georgine sank down on a red plush chair, buttoned into rigid hillocks. For a minute she averted her eyes from the fireplace with its mantelpiece and surround of tortured golden oak, wondering how on earth the same person who had put in that heavenly stair-rail could have tolerated this room: the bamboo table, the jar of pampas grass in the corner—if there was one thing she hated, it was pampas grass!—the woolly chromos on figured wallpaper and the Nottingham lace. Would it be safe to look at Todd?

She glanced at him where he still stood in the doorway, and received a small tingling shock. He was motionless; his eyes were fixed on the fireplace, but he wasn't seeing it. His face, his whole body, wore an attentive look with which she was very familiar. To herself, she called it, "Todd with his aerial extended."

He caught her eye, smiled and came to sit near her. "So," Georgine said in an undertone, "George Washington slept here, too. I wonder if there's a home in the whole Sacramento Valley that hasn't entertained Dyke?"

"The boy gets around," Todd replied absently. "What's he got that I haven't?"

"Nothing," said Georgine. "That's what worries me sometimes." She looked at him speculatively. Two clichés in one breath was too high an average for Todd; there was no doubt of it, he was preoccupied with something more than the fascinating horrors of the room. His eyes kept resting on one bit of furniture after another, as if he were trying to remember something.

"And we met a lot of soldiers, Cousin Dyke knows them all," said Barby, seated on a sofa beside Mrs. Peabody. "Some of them wanted to buy me Popsicles, too, but Mamma wouldn't let 'em."

"I should think not," Georgine remarked. "I had my hands full with Dyke alone." She felt almost dizzy herself, thinking of the milk shakes, popcorn and candy bars pressed on her daughter by the infatuated sergeant; but Barby's cheeks were healthily colored, perhaps she was not going to be sick after all.

"We're in perfect agreement about your nephew, Mr. McKinnon," Mrs. Peabody said. "He really is charming. I can see that Mary Helen—that's Mrs. Crane—has some dangerous competition here."

The conversation became general, full of pleasant nothings to which Georgine could contribute without real attention. She glanced at an amazing marble clock which ornamented the mantel; in about three minutes one could decently suggest leaving...

"Oh, no, you *mustn't*," said Mrs. Peabody. "Couldn't you stay just for a pick-up supper? It would be such a pleasure to me, I don't really expect the children tonight and it does get very lonely for me, eating by myself."

She was alone, then? There hadn't been another member of the household on the third floor, looking at the car that had driven up?

Georgine made one more effort. "Truly, we must be getting on. It's so hospitable of you, Mrs. Peabody, but it's been a long day—and anyway, I don't see how Barby could eat anything."

"Well, I think I could. Bread and butter, and meat and potatoes, things like that," said Barby carefully.

I ruined my case with that last remark, thought Georgine despairingly. Now we'll never get away; she acts as if she really wanted us to stay, and Todd would like to, I know.

"It won't take a minute," Mrs. Peabody said with real pleasure, getting up and moving toward the rear of the house. "I have some chicken I canned myself last summer, so if you'll just entertain yourselves for a few minutes—no, no, of course you're not to help, Mrs. Wyeth! Won't you just rest, or look around if you care to?" Her voice floated back to them through the adjoining dining room, and was lost as a door closed.

Immediately Todd said, "Barby, play a game with me, will you? Go stand in the dining room, facing me, and don't tell me what you see; let me tell you."

Barby complied, interested and quietly giggling.

"Is there," said Todd portentously, "on each side of that archway which I can't see through from here—is there a whatnot?"

"What's a whatnot?"

"A sort of cabinet made of open shelves. You see them? H'm. Is there a picture hanging up over each one—a very cross-looking gentleman on the left, and a pie-faced lady on the right?"

Barby looked at her hands, figuring out which was which, and then nodded delightedly.

"Has one of the whatnots got a huge shell sitting on it? And do the shelves have bobbles hanging along the edges?"

"*Yes.* How'd you know that, Toddy? I didn't see you come in here. Have you been here before?"

"No," Todd said, "that I know for sure. I only feel as if I had."

"Darling, that just means your brain has fallen in half, or something like that." Georgine grinned at him.

"Maybe. Thanks, cricket, you can come in now. The game's over." He got up and began prowling with his light step about the room. His deep-set gray eyes were narrowed against the level evening light, and he bit his lip reflectively. "No, Georgine, this is something more than the I-have-been-here-before feeling. That only lasts a minute. I might have deduced the whatnots, but I've really seen that shell somewhere, and the portraits. I knew it as soon as we stepped into the house, though I wasn't sure until I saw the mantelpiece." His lean face looked actually troubled. "It's like something that oughtn't to be familiar, and yet is; as if—well, damn it, as if I were in Fall River, and walked down Second Street and went into a totally undistinguished house, and everything in it had been left the same for fifty-one years."

His glance at Barby, now quietly sitting in the upholstered niche of the bay window, seemed to say that he couldn't elucidate now. Georgine knew she ought to remember something about Fall River, but what it was eluded her.

She closed her eyes. This was rather pleasant; once having overcome her reluctance to impose on a stranger, she had to admit that it was better than getting home late and cooking supper in a tired hurry—certainly better than a crowded restaurant. Perhaps she could get Todd to leave before eight. He was sweet with Barby, as solicitous about her care as if he were already her stepfather.

"Bless her heart," said Mrs. Peabody's soft voice, "I believe she's gone to sleep sitting up."

Georgine opened her eyes to deny it, but saw that her daughter was the one referred to. Barby had indeed gone to sleep, as suddenly and deeply as if she'd been drugged. The WAVES hat was tilted at a drunken angle over one ear, and her feet dangled appealingly from the window seat, but she still had her flashlight in one hand.

"Let's not wake her," Georgine said, struggling to her feet. "She's really had enough to eat today. Right after supper, if you'll forgive us, Mrs. Peabody, we'll get her home."

They closed the sliding doors between dining room and sitting room, and sat down at one end of an immense old walnut table. Mrs. Peabody's cooking was quite as appetizing as her personal appearance, and under the stimulus of food and hot coffee Georgine found herself having an extremely good time. What a nice woman, she thought more than once; so gentle, but with that crisp little sense of comedy.

She and her hostess swapped anecdotes of wartime shopping, with much laughter; Mrs. Peabody praised Georgine's child with exactly the right amount of warmth, doing herself no harm in the mother's eyes. After a time, Todd, no longer preoccupied, gave a masterly description of the battle at El Alamein, illustrating with tableware and using a bread tray for the Qattara Depression. "Do you smoke?" Mrs. Peabody asked. "Oh, please do, I'd enjoy it myself but I mustn't, on account of a silly heart condition." The room swam into a pleasant haze of candlelight and drifting wreaths of smoke; Georgine could see the three of them reflected in the mirror of a massive buffet that stood at right angles to the windows.

"Now, I'm really afraid that we—" Georgine began at last; and at almost the same moment Mrs. Peabody turned to glance at the windows. "Oh! It's *dark!*" she said abruptly, in an unsteady voice.

The sweet hollows below her cheekbones seemed to deepen, and for a moment her eyes were filled with apprehension. Georgine thought, Here's another poor gal who's afraid of the dark; but I hope I never show it as obviously as that.

"Isn't it foolish of me," said Nella Peabody, and for a moment clasped her hands in a curiously appealing gesture, "but I—I have a quite unfounded dislike of being alone here. An old house seems so very large at night, don't you think? It begins to settle and creak as soon as the air cools, and I can always imagine… Oh, I really do wish the family had consented to my making this into a tourist home, I'd always thought it would be a good plan, there are those five bedrooms upstairs if you count the little sewing room—but I rather gave up the plan when the highway was cut off, and then afterward Mary Helen and Horace wanted to come and live here, so it seemed best to keep it in the family. But they're not here much. Horace is part owner of our drugstore, and his hours are very peculiar, and he's like as not to be so keyed up after work that he'll thumb a ride to Vallejo or some town that's wide open all night for the shipyard people, and not get home until after breakfast. And Mary Helen has friends—If they only stayed all the time, if I could count on them—but to be here *alone...*"

She looked down at her hands, pressing tighter and tighter together. She unloosed them, with an effort, and laughed shakily. "I'm babbling. Please forgive me, I didn't mean to inflict my foolishness on you. Will you open the folding doors for me, Mr. McKinnon?"

Todd had said nothing, but stood looking at her with his peculiar air of attention. Now, as he slid the doors apart, he glanced once more about the sitting room, whose appalling furniture seemed to start out and then retreat from the candle-light. Georgine saw him shake his head almost imperceptibly. She thought, It's almost as if he knew that Mrs. Peabody was afraid of something definite instead of just plain being scared the way I am, alone in the dark.

"Still dead to the world," he said, laying a gentle hand on Barby's cheek.

"Does she feel hot, Todd?"

"No, just normal. I suppose I'd better get the robe out of the car to wrap her in?"

Mrs. Peabody switched on a lamp, shaded with a huge globe of painted glass. "It seems almost dangerous to take her out in the night air, after she's been warm under that afghan," she said quietly. "I—I don't suppose you'd consent to stay overnight?"

Georgine felt as if she'd seen this coming, a long way back; as if something had been settled, hours ago, without reference to any of the three adults who now stood looking at each other before the dim cavern of the dining room. Even as the words of refusal shaped themselves in her mind, she could hear how futile, how petty they would sound.

"It's almost as if you were in the family," Mrs. Peabody was saying, with that attractive smile. "And I'd like to see a little more of you. I'd be so—so *grateful* if you'd stay."

Georgine thought queerly, They're all against me: Mrs. Peabody, and Barby—it was true that sudden changes in temperature sometimes brought back remnants of Barby's asthma, which she had battled for so many years—and Todd. Todd wanted to stay, she knew with a sixth sense, and his quiet face confirmed it when she glanced at him. There was nothing to set up against the three except her own selfish wishes.

She made the sounds anyway, but she was beaten before she started. There wasn't even the problem of nightgowns and toothbrushes. To get an early start on the wonderful day with Dyke, they had driven to Sacramento the night before, and stayed at a hotel.

Mrs. Peabody mustn't go to the least trouble, she heard herself saying weakly. She must be allowed to help her hostess with the dishes, and to make up the beds for the three of them. Well, no, Barby wasn't used to sleeping with anyone, but for one night—oh, if there was a cot which could be set up without too much fuss, that would be perfect.

She felt Todd's eyes, amused and loving, resting on her during this highly feminine conversation. Luckily he was one of those men who like women to be themselves. She grinned at him now, mutely apologizing for all this flutter, and asked if, after he'd put the car away in that shed at the rear, he'd stay with Barby and wake her by gentle degrees.

"Don't be surprised if you find some dust upstairs," said Nella Peabody cheerfully, climbing the soaring flight with one hand on the rail. "I don't get up more than once or twice a day, on doctor's orders. Luckily there was a maid's room downstairs with a lavatory attached, that I could take for my own after— after my husband went to war." She said the last words quickly, resolutely. It was her first mention of her own circumstances,

Georgine realized with some surprise. "Oh, by the way," Mrs. Peabody went on, stopping a few steps from the top, "are you by any chance afraid of rats?"

"*Yes*," said Georgine in a horrified whisper.

"Oh, please don't look like that, we never see them. They never leave the attic, I promise you. Nobody's ever seen them up there, as it happens, nor even caught one in a trap—though not for want of trying. I just wanted to warn you you might hear them; at least, that's what the children say makes the pattering and rustling noises upstairs. They don't mind it in the least, they tell me."

"Then I mustn't either," said Georgine grimly. They crossed a shadowy upper hall, wide with the splendid wasteful-ness of space favored by architects of the past century, and, like the one downstairs, walled with doors and doors and doors.

"I'll put you and the little girl in here," said Mrs. Peabody, opening the door of a large room on the front corner and flipping a wall switch. Georgine looked in, and felt her eyes widening in sheer amazement.

She had the third tiny, undefined shock of the last few hours. The hall was furnished with more buttoned plush chairs and hung with yet more chromos. Coming out of it into this room was like stepping from one century into another. There was a plain broadloom rug; there was a good, ordinary bedroom suite of double bed, vanity and chest and chair and bed table, certainly bought within the past few years. It was more than an anachronism; in some mysterious way it was almost an insult to the eyes.

Mrs. Peabody must have read her thoughts or her expres-sion. "It was the only one we did over. Most of the rest of the house is just dreadful, of course, and we'd meant to get at that too when we could afford it; but of course I shouldn't think of touching it until Gilbert comes home. There isn't going to be one thing different," she said fiercely, as if challenged, and gave her dark head a little shake. In the next moment she was all business. "The cot is right here, in the sewing room." She opened a door which Georgine had thought led to a closet and disclosed a small room built across the front of the hall. "Oh, no, it isn't. We must have taken it up attic the last time I made Mary Helen a dress; it's so seldom I really get around up here. I'll go up and make sure."

"Among the rats?" Georgine inquired, with an attempt at laughter.

"My dear, I keep telling you they never appear... No, certainly I won't try to get it down alone, I'd just better make sure before we call Mr. McKinnon."

"I'll come too. If it's one of those Army cots I could get it myself." She caught the relieved expression in her hostess' eyes, and they both began to laugh.

"You can't imagine, my dear," said Mrs. Peabody earnestly, "how much good it does me to find somebody who's scared of the same things I am."

"I'm determined I'm going to break myself of being a coward." Georgine followed her into the hall. "I might as well, I can't show it in front of Barby anyway. She is *not* going to grow up the way I did, afraid of thunderstorms and snakes and burglars, without any foundation. With any luck, she'll never find me out."

Mrs. Peabody opened one of the numerous doors, midway on the side of the hall opposite the guest room. It gave on a sort of entry in which mops and brooms were visible; beyond them were uncarpeted stairs, going both up and down, and protected by banisters which, Georgine saw with amusement, were as elaborate in their gingerbread trimmings as the outside of the house. A yellowish bulb partly illuminated both flights and the closetlike entry. Mrs. Peabody, beginning to climb with her usual caution, remarked that there was a better light at the top.

"And now," she added, pausing for breath, as the stairs debouched into a large attic with a skylight, "I imagine Susan Labaré will be over tomorrow, if she doesn't telephone tonight, to ask if we've had prowlers in the attic. She's thought so once or twice before, and it took all three of us to convince her that the moon on the skylight gave exactly the effect of a light in this room!" She turned on a blue-white bulb by the stairs as she spoke; her eyes darted quickly from side to side of the big, irregular space.

Georgine afterward confessed to herself that she didn't know what she had expected to find. Logic told her that there could scarcely be a mad relation kept chained up here, like Rochester's wife, but that figure by the window had stayed in her memory. Now she saw dangling from a hook in a rafter a large chintz dress bag with a zipper. Its top was curved in hanger shape, or like the slope of a shoulder, and it was beside one of the front windows.

"Forgive my laughing to myself," she said, lugging the camp cot down the stairs. "It's about something so silly I couldn't even put it into words."

Strange house or no strange house, she was so tired that once in bed she was asleep in a few minutes. In that short time a succession of talking pictures flicked through her mind: Barby, still two-thirds asleep, tottering up the front stairs—"You don't haff to carry me. It's just babies that get carried. Mamma said when I was eight I wasn't a baby any more. She said I could get up and go to the bathroom at night by myself, if had to, and I'm going to, because I've got my flashlight." Nella Peabody, scrubbing away at the dishes with delicate thoroughness, chatting with such apparent freedom and yet letting fall so little about herself —"What a charming man Mr. McKinnon is, if you don't mind my saying so. I do like the way his face—how shall I put it?—comes alive when he looks at you." Todd himself, saying good night at the top of the stairs; "comes alive" was a very good way of describing what happened to his face when he was relaxed or interested. The day at the army camp had been hard on him; it must have been; all those men, some of them older and less healthy-looking than he, in uniform. A flattened lung didn't show. It was hard on him, but wasn't she glad of it for herself! He had something new to think of, in this hospitable house—had anyone in pioneer days ever asked strangers to "'light and set'" more cordially than Nella Peabody had invited them into her home? "I'm so grateful to you for staying," she had said.

Just before she fell asleep, Georgine thought of what it was that had happened in Fall River, Massachusetts, in 1892.

She woke only once. The moon, a night or two past its full, poured light through the angled bay window; that must have been what awakened her, for the sounds in the garret were barely perceptible. Pattering, scraping, now and then a little rattling shower as if bits of plaster had fallen. Georgine, burrowing deeper into bed, hoped it was true that nobody ever saw the rats. She wondered drowsily what it was they did that sounded like tapping, very far off but regular. It was true that the old house creaked and cracked alarmingly as its atmosphere grew cooler. She was glad she knew the reason for it, because those sounds could not be laid to the rats, nor could the impression that she had heard a door closing somewhere below.

She was also glad, the next morning, that she hadn't let herself imagine anything sinister, for it was plain that at some time during the night one of the other occupants of the house had arrived. Georgine saw him, to their shared surprise, in the hall: a tall youngish man, his blond hair in a mat of dishevelment, lightly clad in the lower half of his pajamas and just emerging from the bathroom. "Great God!" the man exclaimed, peering nearsightedly at the open door of her room; and then bolted incontinently across the hall to disappear behind one of those other doors.

Georgine had clutched her dark silk robe more tightly around her at this vision, but was moved more to laughter than to horror. That must be Horace, whom Mrs. Peabody had mentioned; what was he, her nephew, cousin, or what? She spoke of him as part of "the family." Well, if Horace never let his aunt know when he was coming home, it served him right to be confronted by strange women.

Horace's door opened a crack, though he remained invisible. From behind it his voice came, an oddly soft and breathy voice that made his words all the more apologetic. "I do beg your pardon, but I just got in and I didn't know anyone was here. Should I—uh—have we met?"

"No," said Georgine, stopping halfway across the hall to laugh silently.

Horace seemed to be communing with himself. "I know I'm in the right house," he said tentatively.

"You are. Don't worry, we're just overnight guests."

"Well, as long as I didn't startle *you* too much. I thought I was having a bad dream," said the voice chattily. "Not that you look like a nightmare, God knows, but to see somebody coming out of *that* room—"

Georgine shut the bathroom door behind her without answering. Horace, she thought, might not be quite sober; or perhaps his night duty at the drugstore made him lightheaded.

When she returned Barby was up, bristling with energy after a fourteen-hour sleep. She jigged from one foot to the other as Georgine attempted to braid her hair and button her dress. "Mamma, this is fun! Just think, night before last we stayed at a hotel and last night we stayed here, I wish we didn't ever have to go back home."

"I don't," said her mother, brushing vigorously.

"Well, I guess I'd like to be back for Betty Dillman's birthday party, but I love it when we go on travels like this. Mamma, where'd Toddy sleep? Can I go and wake him up, if he's right down the hall? Listen, Mamma, when I kiss Toddy I pick out that little smooth spot right under his eye, if I try anywhere else his whiskers prickle me. Don't they ever prickle you?"

"Sometimes, but I don't seem to mind it," said Georgine. "And those aren't whiskers—stand *still*, Barby!—that's a neat military mustache."

Barby thought this was very funny. She was still giggling ecstatically as they started down for breakfast. Georgine should have noticed that she was a little above herself, but her attention was diverted by the sight of an entire pound of butter furnishing forth the breakfast table. "You mustn't!" she said reprovingly to Mrs. Peabody. "All those points! Luckily we brought our ration books, we'll—"

"No, you won't," said Mrs. Peabody briskly. "The judge sends me butter from the farm, and chickens and vegetables too. It's fun to be able to share them. I have the children's food stamps, too, and they eat so few meals here—Good morning, Mr. McKinnon, I do hope you're hungry."

Todd, coming quietly in and smiling at the three ladies, said that he was. And yes, he had slept well, and no, he had not heard any rats; it took more than that to waken him—an earthquake, say.

"Toddy," Barby squeaked happily, "did your brain come back together again?"

"That was a figure of speech, Barby," said Georgine repressively; but their hostess looked an astonished question.

"I had the feeling that I'd been here before; I had it last night, and Barby heard me mention it," Todd said with an odd gravity. He inquired if there was any news in the paper, and applied himself to his breakfast. Sunlight came through the new-leaved vines over the kitchen window, and spattered on the shining nickel of the percolator. Nella Peabody said how becoming that orchid cotton print was to Barby's fairness; had her mother ever thought of a deeper, bluer shade, almost violet? No, indeed, it wouldn't be too old for her. Mrs. Peabody had a lovely piece of challis that had been meant for a little girl's dress, but the parents had changed their minds. "I just love to sew for little girls," she added, smiling at her youngest guest. Barby looked at her mother with a slow dawn of hope, she adored new clothes, and heaven knew she didn't have many; but Georgine had to shake her head and see the radiant look die out slowly.

"There's nothing we'd like better than to have you make something for her, if we were staying here, Mrs. Peabody," she said, "but you know we must be starting home in an hour or so. No, darling, don't even ask to stay. We mustn't argue, you've talked plenty this morning already."

"I was just talkin' to myself, then," Barby said. "Toddy does that, he was doing it last night when I woke up. Was I in bed? Where was I when I heard him? You know what you said, Toddy? You said somepin' about had a lie, 'n tells it. Who had a lie?"

At this seeming irrelevance Georgine was surprised to see Todd's lips tighten. He glanced at his hostess. She had turned off the spigot of the percolator, though his cup underneath it was only half full, and was returning his look intently, her eyes wide, her breast rising and falling with uneven breaths.

"Adeline Tillsit," said Mrs. Peabody softly. "That was what you said, wasn't it? You've heard her name, then? It meant something to you?"

It was a minute before he spoke. "Yes, I've heard her name," he said in that casual voice that was so restful, so unexcited. "She was very old when she died, wasn't she? And this house was a showplace in its day. I remembered why I had thought I'd been here before; one of my newspaper friends had a full set of photographs that were taken—while she was still alive. They'd planned to run a feature story on it some time: famous belle of the eighties, that sort of thing, but I believe the war pictures rather crowded it out."

"Yes," Mrs. Peabody said, with a quiet that matched his, "she died on the same weekend that France fell. That was why there was no publicity at all; we were spared that, because nobody outside of town heard much about it. In the old days, it would have made a—a small sensation, let's say, but the reporters from the city papers were too busy just then to follow it up."

Barby asked for another muffin.

"May I ask," said Mrs. Peabody, breathing a bit more rapidly, "when you saw those photographs? Was it before or after she died?"

"After," Todd said.

"Then perhaps you heard that she was supposed to have been—m-u-r-d-e-r-e-d?" Mrs. Peabody spelled rapidly.

"I know what that spells," said Barby boastfully. "It spells murder, doesn't it? That's what Toddy's writing is about. Whenever he hears about a good one he goes and studies it, don't you, Toddy?"

There was the briefest possible pause. It fairly hummed with consternation.

Unluckily Georgine was drinking coffee at the moment, and could not flatten her child properly without a whole lungful of air. She inhaled hastily, but Todd forestalled her.

"Good for you, cricket," he said kindly. "Your spelling's getting better. It's quite true, Mrs. Peabody. I am interested in murders, though seldom from the criminological or technical aspect. That can be left to the specialists. What does interest me is, you might say, the more esoteric phenomena surrounding the barren circumstance of a homicide; the interplay of psychological manifestations, the recurrent, uh, syndromes of behaviorism displayed by the variant types of criminal. My approach—"

The interest had faded from Barby's face, and she had begun to fidget long before he got to this point. She now asked her mother, in a stage whisper, if she could go out and look around the garden.

"Yes," Georgine said, "but take care of you know what, first. And get your coat."

Todd was grinning faintly as he watched the pigtails whisk out the door. "It's a shame to take her money," he murmured.

"Mrs. Peabody, what must you think of us? But I'd be ready to swear Todd didn't know!"

"I didn't," Todd said gravely. His deep-set eyes turned toward the woman at the head of the table. "My word of honor on that. No one had told me the name of the town where those photographs were taken. I saw them more than three years ago, so when I came into the house there was only that uncanny sense of familiarity. There was no clear memory, though I was racking my brain for it all evening. And then, while I was waiting down here with Barby, the name came back to me. If I had thought she'd tell you what my special interest is, I should have left the house last night."

"We—we couldn't have outraged your hospitality so," said Georgine unhappily.

"I know, I know." Mrs. Peabody brushed her aside. Her heart-shaped face looked set, and a patch of color stained her cheekbones. "Your newspaper friend, Mr. McKinnon, must have explained to you that the place where those photographs were taken had become the setting of a crime. What did he tell you about it?"

"Very li'le that I can remember. I did watch the papers for a few weeks afterward, but I never saw any other mention of it."

"There was a reason for that. I think you're being kind to me, not telling me his suspicions." The small gentle woman actually grasped the edge of the table and shook it. "My husband did *not* do it! Gilbert is absolutely innocent, it was just those wicked rumors—and never anything you could put your finger on, nobody saying openly what he thought, so you could tell him he lied. That sort of indirectness—it's a stab in the back, you don't know you're struck until you find yourself slowly bleeding to death. Maybe those rumors sent him to his death, I haven't had a letter in two weeks. He may be dead this very minute. And he needn't ever have enlisted, he never would have gone away after we'd been married less than a year, he wouldn't have left me—like this—if he hadn't been driven. They'd give him an honorable discharge, if he applied—if he's alive. He was forty before Pearl Harbor, Gilbert was. He needn't—"

Her breath seemed to give out, and for a brief minute she put both hands over her eyes. Todd and Georgine gave each other a horrified look.

"I can't tell you how sorry we are, Mrs. Peabody," Todd said gently. "I can only assure you I hadn't heard a word of your husband, nor of the family, from anyone; that is, not in connection with a murder. Will you forgive us, and let us go as gracefully as possible?"

"I don't know what you're talking about, forgive you," said Nella Peabody fretfully. "What difference would it make if you *had* heard about it? The fact's there."

Georgine got up. "We'll never forget how good you've been to us, taking in perfect strangers like this. If you'll excuse me now, I'll put things in my suitcase and get hold of Barby—"

"Do you have to go?" Mrs. Peabody looked up, startled. "I—if Mr. McKinnon is interested in murders, at least he might want to hear what happened."

"I'm sure he would," said Georgine somewhat dryly.

"He—he might be able to help me. I've never known the truth. Sometimes I think I may die if I can't get at the truth!"

Todd chuckled quietly. "My dear Mrs. Peabody, surely you're not thinking of me as an armchair detective? I'm not any kind of detective. I'm a hanger-on of the police, and sometimes if I behave myself they give me a few details of an investigation. And then, you must know, I use what I've learned and write a half a dozen ridiculous fiction treatments of possible aspects of the crime, and sell them to the pulp-paper detective magazines. Not even books, Mrs. Peabody; trashy short stories, under different pen names." He leaned forward. "It would be tempting me a li'le too much if you were to give me details of what happened in a background like this."

"What do I care what you do with it?" said Mrs. Peabody in honest surprise. Her eyes went to Georgine, who was still standing. A charming smile, at once wistful and mischievous, came over her face. "Mrs. Wyeth, you can't rush away now, and leave me with the breakfast dishes to do alone...You see, I'll use any weapon, even when it's an unfair one!"

Georgine sat down slowly. For some reason she felt cold.

(HAPTER TWO

SHE MUST HAVE SHIVERED, for Mrs. Peabody said, "I'll make us some fresh coffee." Georgine did not meet Todd's look. For a moment there was no sound in the kitchen except the homely ones of running water and a spoon clicking against metal. Mrs. Peabody's movements were nervously quick.

Presently she sat down again, and the percolator began its first pale bubbling. "Now," she said, turning her gray eyes on Todd, "I'm going to tell you why you never heard any more about Miss Tillsit's death. And don't let me forget and let the coffee stew itself to nothing, because I'm likely"—she laughed a little—"to get passionate about this affair.

"You see, there was never an investigation. For all anyone knows, Aunt Adeline might have died a natural death, four years ago this June. She was dead and had been cremated and her will was going through probate before any of this began, and even then it was all—underground. Maybe people talk about it freely among themselves, but nobody, not one of them, has ever mentioned it to me. I've asked some of them as directly as I dared, and they look at me as if I'd invented the story myself, and they won't say a word. They think they're being kind!" Her mouth set hard for a moment. "The—the worst of it is that—after it began to dawn on me, I couldn't ask Gilbert. He'd never opened the subject himself, and I couldn't, I *couldn't* probe and nag and—have it look as if I—"

She stopped, and got up hastily to refill the cream pitcher. Todd lit his cigarette and Georgine's without expression, without a meeting of eyes. When the woman had returned to the table and switched off the percolator, he said calmly, "I gather that all you know about the case is completely objective? That may be the best way for us to get the outline." Then he composed himself to listen, with his motionless type of attention.

Georgine thought, He can talk more than anyone I know when he chooses, but he can be more silent too. And is the aerial out to its fullest extent!

"I'd better start with the family, I suppose," said Mrs. Peabody. She filled all three of the coffee cups but did not touch her own, keeping her hands in her lap, her eyes fixed on Todd's.

"The Tillsits were just about the earliest settlers around here. Those were the old ones, the pioneer couple that came from Maine in the sixties. You've seen their pictures in the dining room perhaps? They were Horace and Phoebe Tillsit, and they must have been magnificent and—formidable. Old Horace had simply square miles of land around here. He had this house, and much later in his life he built a farmhouse about five miles out in the country.

"There were three children. Adeline was the eldest, she'd be eighty-six now if she'd lived, that would make the date of her birth—let's see; 1858. Theron, her brother, was eight years younger, and Phoebe came last. The first generation is all dead, of course, and there's only Theron—we call him the Judge— left of the second.

"Adeline never married. She bought their shares of this house from her brother and sister, and made it hers. She'd done pretty well with managing her share of the inheritance, and though she didn't leave a huge estate, she could live comfortably enough for all that long life. I think it must have been in 1935 that she had her first stroke, she recovered from it partially at least, and went on living here; only she had Susan Labaré, a practical nurse, to look after her and run the house. She was—quite a wonderful old lady; she wouldn't give way to her illness any more than she could help, Susie couldn't keep her in bed anywhere near as much as she wanted. Aunt Adeline got so she could move round the second floor with a cane, though of course she couldn't go up or down stairs. That's one of the clearest associations I have with this house, coming in and listening to find out if she was up. You could hear her cane tapping, from any of these rooms."

She paused for a moment, looking down at her hands. Georgine glanced involuntarily at the ceiling. Tapping. *Tapping?* Yet that sound she had wondered about, that was supposed to be made by the rats, had come from the attic; she would swear to it.

Just the same—tapping.

"What kind of person was she?" Todd asked. "The word wonderful covers a multitude of sins in old people."

"She was nice." Mrs. Peabody returned her gaze to his face. "She was a lovely old lady, and everyone was fond of her; a bit crotchety, maybe, but they're really more interesting—don't you think?—with a few eccentricities, it seems to give them flavor. She could laugh at herself; she used to be very handsome, but in the last years of her life she'd dried and wrinkled up like old leather. She was fond of any kind of a joke, even the silly ones, we all used to save them up to tell her when we dropped in. Aunt Adeline—looked forward to having people drop in." Mrs. Peabody frowned a little, as if the story were growing more difficult. "The neighbors came morning and evening, usually, when Susie was up and about to let them in.

The—the family almost always went in the early afternoon when Susie was taking her rest."

"How much of her family was left?" Todd inquired.

"Only the Judge, in her own generation. In the next one—nobody but Gilbert, who was the son of her younger sister Phoebe. You see, that made him her next of kin after the Judge." She ran her tongue over her lips. "In the fourth generation, there's only Horace and Mary Helen, they're cousins, the Judge's grandchildren, and their parents are dead. They're grown up, and Mary Helen's been married—to Dr. Crane, and divorced—Well, anyway."

She took a deep breath, and her gaze on Todd deepened. "Then Miss Tillsit died. You couldn't call it unexpected, exactly, when she was eighty-two and had had one stroke already, but we all—missed her. Gilbert felt very badly. She was nearer to him than anyone in the family, and he'd been like a son to her, did business for her, that sort of thing. The very morning she died he'd been in to the county seat on an errand at the bank. He'd brought her something, I—he never said what, out of her safe-deposit box. I saw him for a few minutes at noon, and he—just mentioned it."

"He saw her in the morning, then?" Todd said, almost absently.

The pink flush burned again in Nella Peabody's cheeks. "Yes. He—as I remember, he said he might go in again that afternoon, for a minute. Miss Adeline had seemed preoccupied in the morning, and rather tired.

"I remember that afternoon. It was so lovely and hot, and the trees were all out in full leaf. People were worried about the situation in France, but somehow on a day like that you could tell yourself that it was far away on the other side of the world and couldn't touch *you*...

"It wasn't until about seven that I heard Miss Adeline was sinking. They'd got hold of Horace and Mary Helen, and Susie had called Dr. Crane, but he was out in the country attending to a difficult confinement, and he didn't get here until eight or so. She died just a few minutes after that."

She paused, and looked down. There was a silver chain around her neck, and she drew it up gently until a disk of silver showed in the V of her dress; it looked like an identification tag. She tilted it up on two fingers and gazed at it earnestly for a moment, and then, as if it were a talisman and the sight of it had refreshed her, dropped it inside her dress again.

"The doctor was present when she died. Well, that seems normal enough, so far," Todd said. He sounded casual as ever, but his attention had not wavered. It was almost, Georgine thought, as if he were listening more to the overtones of Mrs. Peabody's voice than to the words of her story. "What made you think there was anything wrong? Miss Tillsit hadn't—by any chance, she hadn't been threatening to change her will?"

"Oh, *no*," Mrs. Peabody said quickly, seeming relieved. "Her will had been drawn up years before, and everyone knew what was in it. Most of it they could have guessed even if she hadn't told them, because it was traditional in the Tillsit family that the orchard and farm property should stay in the oldest generation. That part of her holdings went to the Judge, of course. And we'd—Gilbert and I had known for a long time that he, Gilbert, was to have this house and all its contents. Mary Helen was to have the jewelry in the safe-deposit box, and there was some money for Horace—at least, there had been, but we all knew he'd persuaded her to invest in the drugstore for him. You might call it borrowing on his inheritance, I suppose. No, we all knew how she'd left her property. Nobody was disappointed. There wasn't any—hurry, you can see that, can't you?"

"None at all?" said Todd, as if to himself.

Mrs. Peabody laid down the napkin carefully. Her voice was not quite steady as she replied. "If anyone had wanted his inheritance badly, it would have been Gilbert. It meant that he and I could be married at last, that we'd be sure of a roof over our heads, and furniture, and all the things we'd been too poor to buy before. He was just getting out of debt for a—a family illness, and all I had was what I earned. And I can vouch for it, Mr. McKinnon, I can promise you faithfully that we'd never have been in that much of a hurry; never."

"Of course not," said Todd. His deep-set eyes were still intent on her face. "But, d'you know, I still don't see why there should have been any suspicion. How did they think the old lady had died?"

"At first, everyone simply thought it was another stroke. Afterward—poison," said Nella Peabody softly.

"H'm. What kind?"

"I don't know. How could I know? She looked as if she'd sunk into a coma, and died naturally. But a few months afterward, the—the queer feeling began. People were talking, but never to me—never to Gilbert or me. I can't tell you how I knew this, maybe you just absorb that sort of thing through your pores, but there was a story." She leaned forward, clasping her hands on the edge of the table. Above the blue china and the yellow checked tablecloth, her face showed white and pinched.

"The Judge lives on the farm, you know, with the farmhands and a house servant or two. One of the servants was within hearing, maybe on purpose, when Dr. Crane came out to see the Judge after Miss Adeline died, to see about the funeral arrangements. The servant said she'd heard them talking about an autopsy, and she got the impression that the doctor wanted to do one on Miss Tillsit. He couldn't have been *sure* that anything was wrong, don't you see, because surely in that case he'd have gone ahead without consulting the Judge? He just—thought there might be something. He might have known he would never get permission, because Uncle Theron hated the idea, and always had; and besides, it was a member of his family they were talking about, that would have been enough just by itself. The Judge was—well, you'd have to see him really wild about something to understand how he took it," said Mrs. Peabody with a rueful little smile. "The doctor must have been afraid he'd have one of his attacks, because he dropped the subject and—I suppose, made out the death certificate, and Miss Tillsit was cremated. The Judge wanted it that way."

"The Judge did; h'm," said Todd. "So that there was no proof then, and certainly is none now, that the death was anything but natural?"

"None," the slim woman said.

"And nobody was sure why he wanted the autopsy? Poison was never mentioned? Then it might have been some other physical condition besides her heart and arteries, that he wanted to check on."

"It might. But nobody thinks that, I'm sure of it, though not a soul has ever put it into words to me. They think it was—Gilbert."

"I'm damned," said Todd mildly, "if I can see why."

"Nor I!" Mrs. Peabody spoke with sudden intensity. "Nor I, and that's the very worst of it. Can't you see why? I can torture myself with trying to imagine what case they could possibly have worked out against him, but I don't *know!* Mr. McKinnon, I've never—I could go crazy trying to figure it out. I can almost hear these people whispering to each other, changing the subject in a hurry when I come near them. What do you suppose they say, in secret? That Miss Adeline didn't die soon enough, and that Gilbert—that *we* got tired of waiting, and hurried it up? What do they have as real evidence? I don't even know if he was seen going in and out of the house that afternoon, maybe his car was here for a while and someone saw it and jumped to conclusions. There's no one who'd want to pin it on him just out of wicked-ness. Everyone liked Gilbert. He was depressed, unlike himself, you could almost say jumpy, for months after Miss Tillsit died; possibly they try to make something out of that, but—great heavens, he was fond of her! Can't you see how I'd feel, Mrs. Wyeth? Supposing Mr. McKinnon were tried and condemned and sent to Coventry, without benefit of law, and you didn't know what the case against him was?"

She brushed the pointed bang off her forehead, as if even that slight weight were intolerable. "Gilbert felt it.

He must have known long before I did. We waited months before we were married, to be—to show respect. If only we hadn't, I'd have had that much more of him. We'd waited so long already, just to have a roof over our heads, to be secure—and then it was less than a year, it was only eight months, out of our whole lifetime. He was driven to enlisting, I tell you, he went into the army before Pearl Harbor, they took him in spite of his age because they needed photographers so badly. He may be dead this minute. And if he isn't, if there's a miracle and he comes back—what will he come back *to*? The ugliest suspicion you can lay on a man, and one that can't be disproved, ever, ever."

Nella Peabody got up blindly and flung the back door wide, as if the air from the open windows were not enough. She stood there with her back to them; tensely held, her slimness looked almost haggard.

"No, that's not good," Todd said soberly, again seemingly to himself. "That's a tough spot to be in. Didn't you ever think of picking up and starting somewhere else?"

She turned to give him a surprised look. "But—we *live* here," she said.

Georgine had sat looking at her with pity, with wonder and a sort of sympathetic anger. Now she too got to her feet, stretching after the long period of concentration. "I must go and check up on Barby," she remarked. "You haven't asked for my advice, Mrs. Peabody, and I don't often volunteer it, but in your place I'd be tempted to track down those rumors and *make* people give me some proof of their suspicions—or else eat their words."

"Oh, I thought of that," the older woman said wearily. "I tried it. And do you know why I didn't get anywhere?" She turned and faced them, with a semblance of composure. "Because they're fond of me; because they're kind. Tell them it would be kinder to talk the thing out, and they simply say, 'What thing? What is there to talk out?' What are you going to do then, when all you get is silence?"

For a moment that was all she got from either of her companions. Then Todd straightened from his temporary perch on the windowsill and smiled at her faintly. The brown-flecked gray of his eyes, usually hard as agate, was softened. "My dear Mrs. Peabody," he said, "I have only the coldest of comfort to offer. Georgine feels as sorry as I about this, I know; but all either of us could say to you is to point out that there's no proof, and never can be, that any murder was committed at all; and that people forget yesterday's scandals, particularly the kind with no real foundation."

"Thank you," Nella Peabody said, with an attempt to return the smile. "But people live a long time in this town, and they don't move away, and—sometimes I think secrecy feeds a scandal better than open discussion."

Georgine excused herself and went toward the front of the house. For the past half hour she had been hearing, with that extra ear bestowed on mothers, the sound of Barby's voice and footsteps. The child had been talking to someone else; but in the last few minutes both voices had died away.

It was all right, though, she saw as soon as she reached the front door. Barby and her companion had gone across the street and were surveying the site of the house that had burned. The other child, a somewhat older girl, seemed to wear a proprietary air, as if the ruin-showing concession belonged to her. Georgine went out into the morning sunlight, down the flight of front steps. Halfway down the walk she paused to look back at the fantastic pile of the old Tillsit house.

She thought, It wouldn't be the first old mansion of its kind that's housed a murder and a scandal and a tragedy. And yet it's not sinister; the gingerbread and the bay windows are so awful that they're almost endearing.

That left-hand window, as you faced the house, must be the one belonging to her room. Georgine was perfectly certain that it had once been Miss Adeline Tillsit's, and that there had been a reason for redecorating, and moving up to the attic the colossal walnut bedstead and bureau which, last night, had been dimly visible in the shadows.

And yet, why should one be at all uneasy at the thought of Miss Adeline, that indomitable old lady who liked company and laughter, stumping around the second floor with the aid of her tapping cane?

She turned and went slowly across the street. Barby saw her coming, and at once shut her eyes and screwed up her face, in her usual effort to remember about introductions.

The effort ended in triumph. "Mother," said Barby with terrific formality, "I want you to know my friend Virdette Bacon. Listen, Mamma, she used to live here! She lived right in this house that burned down, lookit, there's still some of the cellar left."

"Well, don't fall into it," said Georgine automatically. "How do you do, Virdette. Did you live here long?"

Miss Bacon took her time about answering. She was a stout child of eleven or twelve, with blond hair done up in a multitude of curlers, and a look of great competence. Her right hand constantly manipulated a yo-yo, but she did not once look at its most bewildering gyrations; it was very impressive. Her conversation was punctuated by the spat, spat of the flattened wooden sphere against her palm, and the faint whirr of the string.

"Yes'm," she said finally. "I was born here, and I lived here right along until the place burned down last year. My Dad was goin' to build again, but we couldn't get priorities on any of the stuff, so we moved down to my Gramma's on Oak."

"Here's Toddy," Barby screamed excitedly. "He and Mamma are going to get married, Virdette. Then he'll be my stepfather. He can play the mouth organ better'n anybody you ever heard."

Virdette accorded him, after this recommendation, far more interest than she had given Georgine. Barby displayed her family's and her acquaintance's talents, with scrupulous fairness. "Say 'little bottle', Toddy," she commanded.

"Li'le bo'le," said Todd obligingly.

"See? He can't say those t's at all. Now tell her why you aren't in the army."

"Barby!" said Georgine sharply.

"I mean one of the funny ones, Mamma. He's told me about twenty times, and it's never the same. Why aren't you, Toddy?"

Still amiable, Toddy complied. "You see, Miss Bacon, I have an upside-down stomach. It doesn't bother me at all, but the officers couldn't get used to seeing me stand on my head to eat. They said it upset discipline."

Virdette looked at him for a moment, and then giggled wildly.

"See?" Barby remarked proudly. "I told you he was funny. Now, Virdette, you show us where everything was in your house, just like you were telling me."

"Just *as*," Georgine corrected gently. Nobody paid any attention to this.

"This here," said Virdette, shooting the yo-yo in a graceful curve toward the north, "was our front parlor, with the dinin'-room right in back, and the kitchen back o' that. Here, where we're standing, was the parlor that we hardly ever used, except when my sister Rose got married. She's havin' a baby this week, most any time," she interpolated carelessly. "Doctor says it's twins... The piano was in here, though, and boy, did I see plenty of this ole room! Was I glad when the house burned down, it burned all my good clothes but it got the piano too, and I didn't have to practice any more."

"Did they keep you at it?" Todd asked gravely, seating himself beside Georgine on the cement of the ruined foundation.

"I'll say. They were going to make one of these child prod-gidies out of me, see, because I remember things. The music teacher at school, she got all excited when she found out I could play a piece once and then not forget it, so she told Mom I ought to have special training."

"But when your piano burned you had to give up the idea?" Georgine inquired.

"No, it was some before that. They decided I was too old, I was nine then so I couldn't ever be a real prodgidy. So I just play boogie now, I'm in the school orchestra, too. Boy, was it somep'm when they were makin' me practice three hours a day, though!"

Georgine wanted to know how she'd lived through it.

"Got so I didn't have to look at the keys," said Virdette, and indeed this seemed quite possible, judging by her masterly manipulation of the yo-yo. "I'd sit here, right in the front window, see, and do scales an' Czerny an' Hanan for a couple hours at a time, and all the time I could be watchin' the street. Only trouble was, Walnut doesn't go much of any place, and nothin' much ever happened over to old Miss Tillsit's. I used to watch who went in to see her, that helped some."

"It doesn't sound very exciting," said Todd with sympathy.

"Well, it was once. The afternoon she died, boy, do I remember that! Old Mis' Labaré poppin' in and out of doors like a—like a gopher, just about, and the whole family pilin' up the steps one after another. You could tell there was somethin' up just by lookin' at their backs."

Barby felt this to be very unprofitable. "Listen, Virdette, show me where the things were in the kitchen. Was that chimney for a fireplace, Virdette, or the kitchen stove? What was out back there?"

"Aw, just a garden. There's some hyacinths and narcissus and stuff in bloom right now."

"Let's go see," Barby said, dragging her off.

"Get ready to come in pretty soon, darling," Georgine called after her. "And if you tear your new coat, or get it dirty, something very unpleasant will happen. That clear?"

"Honest I'll be careful, Mamma," said Barby, recognizing the voice that meant business.

"Keep an eye on them, will you, Todd? I want to help Mrs. Peabody clear up, and then we really must be getting away."

"Wait a minute," Todd said lightly. "She wants to be alone for a while, she told me; and I'd like to talk something over with you."

Georgine resumed her perch. "What'll you bet I know it already?" she said, grinning at him. "You want to stay up here and scrape up some grist for the mill."

"Not far off," said Todd imperturbably.

"Well, why not? Barby and I can go home on the bus, that suitcase isn't a bit heavy."

"I don't want you to do that."

"Dear, you can't possibly drive us home and come back, you'll never save up gas enough again. Weren't you down to your last coupon when you got the car filled up at Sacramento?"

"I was; and that buggy is a gas-eater."

"Well, then. I must confess," Georgine added, "that I don't see many possibilities in Mrs. Peabody's story, but you can work them up from the slightest foundation, I know."

"Oh, there are possibilities," Todd said, looking at her.

"Honest and truly, didn't you know last night when you made—glancing references to Lizzie Borden?"

"Honest and truly," Todd repeated, faintly smiling. "I remembered this just as you would a photograph that you'd seen but not identified. You'll admit, Georgine, that this background alone would be money in my pocket."

"I will indeed. You want to go up garret, too, and look at the furniture that used to be in Miss Adeline's room. They took it all out and stored it, and refurnished the room I'm in, did you know that? Well, that's settled, you find out what time the busses run."

"No," Todd said mildly, "I don't want to stay without you."

She looked round at him quickly.

"Will you stay, Georgine, you and Barby? You know what I've been thinking? I wondered if we hadn't made a mistake, putting off our marriage even this long."

"But, Todd, we had to. There had to be a few weeks to get Barby used to the idea of a stepfather, and then you were called north to be executor for your brother's estate, and since you've been back—do I need to tell you about the housing situation?"

"That's it. Mrs. Peabody and her Gilbert waited all those years for a roof over their heads, and missed far too much of each other. Maybe we've been a li'le too particular about finding the right house. Maybe we're foolish not to be married right away, as soon as they'll issue the license; three days, isn't it? We can take a chance on finding somewhere to live, at worst we could all squeeze into my apartment or your cottage—if we wanted to badly enough."

"Oh, Todd, if you knew how much I want to," Georgine said under her breath.

He looked at her without touching her. He continued to sit, relaxed and graceful on his uncomfortable perch, hands in the pockets of his tweed trousers. His eyes warmed slowly.

"Then what's to stop us? We can drive in to the county seat this very morning, and apply for the license, and be married here on—what'll it come to, Tuesday? Wait, Georgine. You've got five or six objections, I can see 'em standing in line waiting to be expressed. First, Barby. She'd be in seventh heaven, and you know it, especially if we got Mrs. Peabody to make her that dress; she could be sole attendant at the wedding; and as for school—"

"She's already missed one day," said Georgine dubiously. "Still, I suppose her mother's wedding is as good an excuse as any, though I'd blame myself if she got behind in her work—"

"She's way ahead now, don't you remember?" Todd remarked. "Half her class has been out with German measles, which luckily she didn't get, and they won't be caught up to her for weeks. Might as well give the other li'le tikes a break!—Second objection, clothes. Hasn't Mrs. Dillman the key to your cottage? Couldn't you write her and tell her what you want sent up by the first mail?"

"I—suppose I could."

"Third, practical difficulties. Well, we have our ration books—"

"Ho," said Georgine.

"—which you wisely insisted on carrying with us. We'd pay our way, naturally, since there's a waiting list for rooms at

the Inn, and Mrs. Peabody said more than once that she'd like
to rent that extra space on the second floor. The cash might
help her out, between you and me."

Georgine shot to her feet. "You mean we'd be staying
there?"

He looked at her in honest perplexity. "Why not, Georgine?
You're not—is there something that frightens you?"

"Why, you lunk, what do you suppose?" said Georgine
furiously. "The house where a murder was committed, and me
in the very room where it happened, and the hostess herself
scared to stay there!"

"Only when she's alone," Todd said gently.

Georgine deflated suddenly, and sat down again. "It's
good of you to keep from laughing," she said, with a shame-
faced grin of her own. "Only, you know what a coward I am."

"I know you say so. In this case, though, I hadn't expected
you to feel that way, and I'm damned if I can see why. What is
it, the ghost of old Miss Tillsit?"

"Certainly not. I know ghosts don't exist."

"Then," Todd inquired with interest, "what scares you
about the dark?"

"Oh—just *things,* coming at me, and me not able to see
them."

"H'm. Does that include one-lunged men?"

"That's a question that hasn't come up yet, and I'll settle it
when it does." She felt restored by now, and added with some
defiance, "A ghost is one of the very few things I'm not afraid of."

"What are the others?"

"Let's see: horses, cows, and people who try to push me
around. Of course," Georgine added meticulously, "if the cows
turn out to be cross bulls, and the people get actively malicious,
they get switched to the other list."

Todd was quivering gently, but his face showed no change.
"Look, Georgine," he said, "we're not sure, you and I, that there
was a murder at all."

"But how does Mrs. Peabody feel?"

"Oh, she thinks someone killed Miss Tillsit, but it wasn't Gilbert," said Todd lightly.

"Lovely. That means there's a murderer still at large."

"Not necessarily. In any case, the affair was over four years ago, and there's been no sign of a repeat performance. It's not danger we'd have to contend with, it's obscurity. So, unless that tapping upstairs bothered you actively—"

"How did you know I'd heard tapping?"

"Your prayerful look, dear heart, when Mrs. Peabody mentioned the old lady's cane. Where was it, overhead? Must have been. Well, then, the ghost has moved up one flight, and is concerning itself with the furniture in the attic, and would leave your room alone."

"I thought of that this morning," said Georgine seriously. "Surely I'd have felt anything sinister—ah, my friend. Now you *are* laughing at me."

"Bless you, I am," Todd said. "What it is to look forward to a whole life of enjoyment; all kinds of it. Well, what do you say, Georgine?"

Again she waited for a moment before replying. The March sun beat down on their heads, the fragrance of new grass and flowering bulbs was all about them; a few yards away, just out of earshot of their murmuring voices, the little girls chattered happily. She looked across the street but she didn't see the old Tillsit house at which she was gazing. She was seeing Todd, woodenly inscrutable of countenance, strolling about the camp beside his redheaded nephew. Dyke had shown a great deal of tact, unobtrusively mentioning how much pleasure the boys got out of detective magazines, and how popular Todd's stories were for the relaxation they so badly needed.

All at once she knew why it was that Dyke had suggested they come here. He had known, he must have known, something about the background of the Tillsit family; and with unusual penetration for a young man of twenty-one, he had also known what would set up his uncle again, after that horrible strain on his pride and his self-esteem. Todd reacted peculiarly to strain. He got funny, and, judging by the yells of masculine laughter which had marked his progress among Dyke's friends, yesterday he had been very funny indeed.

If they stayed here, if he got the material for half a dozen stories, and if they were married...he would have his mind taken up by two projects in both of which he could feel entirely adequate.

He needs this, Georgine thought; and it's the first thing he's ever asked of me.

It had taken perhaps fifteen seconds for her mind to follow this whole train of thought. She caught her breath, looked at him and smiled.

"You probably know," she said, "that I have a strong instinct against staying, but maybe that's only because I'm such a fool about wanting to be at home. And if we were married—it'd be like coming home. I have an even stronger instinct about getting married to you."

She saw his face relax. Had he wanted it so much, then—so very much? He got to his feet, and bent over to kiss her; it was the lightest touch of lips, but it stung like a bee.

"Dear Georgine," Todd said, "what a nice woman you are. I'll go and talk to Mrs. Peabody, and find out about these licenses."

Georgine watched him crossing the street and going up the preposterous front steps into the preposterous house. The half smile stayed on her lips. Maybe these eight months of engagement hadn't been quite wasted. "What a nice woman you are"—those might once have seemed cold to her, as words of love; now she knew that, from Todd, they equaled the live-liest utterance of Romeo and Tristan and the Song of Solomon.

CHAPTER THREE

SEVERAL HOURS LATER Todd and Georgine came down the steps of the county courthouse. "One o'clock," Todd said. "We just got in under the wire, before the license bureau closed. Lunch now, Georgine, or shall we finish our business at the jeweler's?"

After that huge breakfast, she thought lunch could be postponed a while. They crossed the highway toward a row of attractive shops, Todd feeling in his vest pocket. Georgine realized that he must have been carrying her ring around with him for the last month, the half-hoop of sapphires which was to be both engagement and wedding ring, and which had been in his family for years. "It will have to be ensmalled," Barby had said gravely, watching her mother try it on for the first time; and it was this operation which was about to be arranged.

The jeweler was busy when they entered his shop; he was talking in low tones to a young woman who leaned on a counter at the rear, her back to them. The jeweler caught Todd's eye and nodded, to show that he'd be with them in a moment.

"I'll write to those other people, honey," he said to the young woman, "but with no results so far, it's not likely that *they'll* have any record. I'd say they were still around somewhere."

The girl murmured something, and turned away with a rattle of wooden bracelets. She tripped toward the front door, humming to herself, studying the showcases as she went; her face was still averted. Georgine stifled a giggle as she heard Todd begin, "I want to see about having this ring ensm—cut down in size; and we're in a bit of a hurry for it." Bless his heart, he was having a case of wedding excitement, under that impassive manner. It was easier for her to stay cool. After all, she'd been married before.

"Sorry to keep you waiting," the jeweler said, "but that was an old friend of mine I was talking to." He chuckled fatly. "Just one girl I can be sure isn't gold-digging when she keeps up her friendship with me! She don't like jewelry, never wears a bit of it except this junk stuff, wood and such. Can you beat that? Now, this lady, I can see she appreciates good stones. If you'd just let me measure your finger, Ma'am?"

Over luncheon Georgine asked thoughtfully, "Todd, just what is it you're going to do about this case, talk to Mrs. Peabody some more?"

"Not just that, though it'd be damned interesting if she'd expand a li'le more. I'm going to make some acquaintances around town."

"Oh. Just where does that leave us with our hostess?"

"In top billing," Todd said. "I think I got it into her head that I'm no kind of an investigator, in fact that it's unlikely I'd know the truth if I saw it; but I'm not so bad as a male gossip."

"Stop maligning yourself," said Georgine tartly. "You're just receptive, that's all. But do I understand that you're to— report what you find out to *her?*"

"It's what she wants," Todd said. His eyes were all at once remote. "At least, that's what she says. Attractive woman for her age, Mrs. Peabody; and interesting, far more interesting than appears on the surface."

"Really, Todd dear, you are a ghoul," Georgine said.

"But, thank goodness, if you do dissect her in a story and she ever sees it, she won't recognize herself."

"Thanks," said Todd with a penetrating glance. "Bouquets from my public are always welcome."

"What I still don't see is this: people will learn soon enough that we're staying with Mrs. Peabody. What makes you think, if they won't talk to her, that they'll open up to you?"

"I'll do it by implication," said Todd. Shamelessly chuckling, he tapped himself on the chest. "You see before you the uncle of the prospective groom."

"Who, Dyke? But—dear me, Todd, is he really going to marry into this family? I gathered that the Mary Helen creature was only one among about a hundred girlfriends."

"Quite likely."

"Then—wouldn't we be committing him to something, if we seemed to take it for granted?"

"Georgine, my dear—if there was ever a lad who could take care of himself, it's my young nephew. He won't let himself be committed until he's good and sure. Runs in the family," added Mr. McKinnon modestly.

"Can I count on that?" Georgine got up, laughing. "If we can keep him a bachelor for ten or twelve more years, he'd do nicely for Barby. Do you know, I've actually caught myself figuring on that. Where do we go now, back to the house?"

"I'd like your support while I make my first call. Mrs. Peabody suggested it herself, for a starting point; we're going to see Susan Labaré."

"Susan—oh, the practical nurse. Yes, she sounds promising. She still keeps tabs on the household, it seems; Mrs. Peabody said last night that the attic skylight is visible from Susan's house, and she's always worrying for fear somebody's up there that shouldn't be. They convinced her that all she saw was the moon on the skylight."

"Is that so?" said Todd with interest. He was silent, digesting this meager piece of information, for most of the nine-mile drive back to Valleyville.

"One of the most enchanting things about this town," said Georgine as he helped her out of the car, "is its compactness. It probably wouldn't take more than twenty minutes to walk the whole length of it."

"Probably not." Todd paused on the sidewalk to look about him. " 'M, yes, I figure it about four minutes from the Tillsit house to this one, and only three or four more to be in the center of the village. We'll put up the car, my dear, for the duration of our stay."

Mrs. Labaré's cottage was of the one-story type; it shone with aggressive cleanliness, not a picket was out of place in the white fence, and the garden was kept under control with a rigid hand. The mistress of the house opened the door to them, and it could be seen at once that no weed could flourish, no speck of dust remain under her management.

She was tall and gaunt, with long arms and powerful-looking hands; dark eyes were sharp under her shock of white hair. Georgine could imagine her hoisting invalids about, and taking no nonsense from them in the process. "Howdy do?" said Mrs. Labaré interrogatively. Her voice issued flatly from the nutcracker conformation of her nose and jaw; somehow it sounded very rural.

"My name's McKinnon," said Todd with his usual ease, "and this is Mrs. Wyeth. Have you by chance heard Mrs. Crane speak of my nephew, Dyke?"

"Oh, him," Mrs. Labaré said with interest. "Yeah, sure I have. Up to camp at Sacramento, ain't he?"

"We were passing through, and it seemed a good time to get acquainted with some of Mary Helen's friends. I understand that you've been almost a second mother to her, Mrs. Labaré."

It was as easy as that, Georgine thought. Not a word of untruth, a considerable admixture of charm, and here they were chatting with Susie; Todd was, at least; all she herself had to do was sit and look about her with a pleasant expression. She had never seen so many photographs. Possibly Susie exacted them from all her patients, as a sort of tribute. There was one on a gilded easel with a sheaf of wheat tied to its corner, perhaps depicting Mr. Labaré, for it showed a gentleman with no chin and a harried look. In another place of honor, on the center table, was a picture which must have been taken in the early years of the century: a Junoesque woman of about forty in a low-cut evening dress which offered an expanse of neck and shoulder admirably calculated for the display of jewelry. There was plenty of it, too: a pearl dog collar, earrings, brooches, rings on the hand that was poised across the ample bosom, and one or two extra necklaces and chains with pendent jewels.

Georgine found it difficult to take her eyes off this exhibit, and at a pause in the conversation she moved her chair for a better view. Mrs. Labaré viewed this with approval. "That's old lady Tillsit," she remarked. "Tooken a long time ago, of course. She wasn't so good-lookin' as that, time I come to nurse her."

"May I see?" Todd picked up the photograph. "This is the famous Miss Adeline, is it? I understand you were her mainstay for years, Mrs. Labaré."

"Only about four," Susie said.

"I see. She was very old, wasn't she?"

"Not for here. Healthy place, Valleyville is. Nothin' much to make people die, most of 'em live along to their nineties, just about." Susie's nutcracker jaw snapped shut with emphasis, and she swung energetically back and forth in her Boston rocker.

"So?" Todd said, smiling. "What carried Miss Adeline off so young, then?"

"Stroke," said Mrs. Labaré promptly. "Lawsy, when one o' them comes, there's not much you can do about it. She'd had one already, you know, an' it was to be expected."

Todd put back the photograph gently. His face, though expressionless as usual, somehow managed to convey sympathy. "You get fond of them, don't you?" he said. "Your patients, I mean. Isn't it a li'le trying, Mrs. Labaré, to see one of them

going through the, uh, the throes of death, no matter if it's
expected?"

"No throes there." Susie snapped it out readily. "Peaceful
a deathbed as you ever was at, children all round—not hers,
of course, but the fam'ly—and off she went to sleep, just like
a baby."

Todd said nothing, he only looked receptive, and Georgine
observed this technique with inner laughter; for Mrs. Labaré
was continuing as if dreamily.

"Yes, sir, no throes at all, you might say. I tooken my nap
just as usual, lyin' down on the couch in the sittin' room, round
two that afternoon. When I went upstairs later she was havin'
her nap out, or so I thought. Didn't wake her; maybe I'd ought
to 'a', but there, she was wakeful enough anyhow. Come about
five, I went to shake her, and I seen it wasn't no natural sleep;
more like coma. *She's had her second,* I thought." Susie's head
jerked up and down abruptly. "Took me ten, fifteen minutes
to get hold of the doctor, he was awful busy even then, Johnny
Crane was. Johnny, I says, you better come see old Mis' Tillsit,
she's had her second, I says. Well, he says there's not much to
be done, he'd come as soon as he got through where he was. So
I just waited, and called up the fam'ly, and along about eight he
come in, dog tired; and just a few minutes after he got there,
Mis' Tillsit she slipped away, like in her sleep. Real peaceful,
it was." The jaw snapped shut again, and Susie gave one of her
emphatic nods.

"But it must have left you feeling very lonely, after the
years you'd taken care of her and her household," Todd said.
"It's rare, if I may say so, to find a nurse so faithful."

This barefaced flattery, which certainly could not be
based on truth, nevertheless had a good effect. Susie preened
herself, tossing the shock of white hair girlishly. "I'd 'a' stayed,"
she said, "even if it hadn't been wuth my while. She was a grand
old lady, Miss Adeline was. Used to have lots of money when
she was thirty, forty years old, traveled all over the world, an'
in the winters she'd take an apartment in San Fran, live down

there an' go to the theaters an' buy clothes. She liked julery, too, had some fine pieces—or so I've heard tell. You can look at that photo. I dunno what-all she's got on there, most of the stuff I never seen, she'd sold it off before I went to work there. The depression come along, you see, an' she lost some, an' then orchard land went way down in value, so along the last few years she was livin' up her capital; but she paid me good, and promised to leave me something in her will if I'd stay along, and she did, too; cash, put aside."

"Good to her own," Todd commented. Somehow, among all these photographs, the most banal phrases seemed appropriate.

"Yeah, except that I wasn't her own," said Susie with logic. "She picked an' chose when it come to her family, some of 'em she was fond of, some not. Gilbert, he was the one she set store by; she was always kind of in love with Gilbert's pa, if you ask me, but he wasn't in her class, besides bein' younger. Frittered away all his wife's money she got from the old people, and had to go live on Mis' Tillsit, they did, Phoebe and the two kids, after Peabody died. Gilbert finished college, an' then he set up a place of his own, but she was still fond of him. She was fair to the rest, but not so fond. They're fam'ly, she says, and whatever they do I stick by 'em, but she had a right to her favorites. Well, how I do rattle on; but I can see, Mr. McWhatsit—"

"McKinnon."

"Yeah. I can see how you'd be int'rested in the fam'ly. Your nephew, now, he probably ain't so keen on hearin' about such things, he's thinkin' about people his own age. Well, I've knowed Mary Helen since the minute she was born, an' she's kep' the men thinkin' about her pretty near all those years." Susie laughed proudly.

"I hear she's charming," said Todd. "We hope to meet her sometime."

"Oh. You ain't met her. Well, I misdoubt she's home now. Works over to the county seat, Mary Helen does, and this bein' Saturday she's like as not goin' gallivantin' somewheres for the weekend. Too bad. Maybe you'll be back this way sometime."

Todd smiled, and brought the visit to a close with a glance at Georgine. "We may be around here for a few days," he said at the door. "May we hope to see *you* again, Mrs. Labaré?"

"Maybe so," said Susie. "I ain't workin' just now; don't have to unless there's somebody I know real well that needs me bad."

She was standing in the doorway of the clean white cottage, watching them, as Todd and Georgine drove away. It was true that from her front windows the skylight of the Tillsit house was visible; trees hid the rest of the mansion, and Georgine found herself rather glad that Susie Labaré could not see their destination.

"You didn't tell her we were staying with Mrs. Peabody, nor even that we knew her," she remarked tentatively.

"She didn't ask me," his casual voice said.

"Have you some deep dark purpose, Todd McKinnon?"

Todd chuckled. "Maybe."

"I wish I were a fiction writer. No doubt you got a whole bunch of material out of that conversation, but for the life of me I couldn't see what."

"It's better than appears on the surface." He swung the car into Nella Peabody's weed-grown driveway, and brought it to a stop in the rickety shed that served as a garage. "There's the family background, for instance, I like to get those li'le details filled in; but more interesting than that is her freedom in talking, to a perfect stranger, about the old lady's death. She talked a bit too much, didn't you think, Georgine? No need for all that artistic verisimilitude unless she thought something was wrong, and knew that we'd heard something might have been wrong, and meant to talk us out of the idea."

"That," said Georgine, starting up the steps that led to the dining room porch, "is far too subtle for me. But then, most of your methods are, my dear Holmes."

Todd gave one of his almost soundless chuckles. They went through the door that stood open to the mild spring air, and were forced to feel their way carefully through the tempered gloom, around the immense old pieces of furniture. Georgine thought, I don't hear Barby, I hope to heaven everything's all right; she was so willing to stay with Mrs. Peabody.

From the back yard a little voice raised in tuneless song reassured her; she went toward the kitchen and stopped short at the sound of another voice, harsh, nasal and almost breathless. They had left the owner of that voice on her own front porch, just five minutes ago.

"—didn't get much out o' *me*," it said. "But I want you to know, if them two come round here askin' *you* any innocent soundin' questions, then you can be *certain* somethin's up."

"But I—" Nella Peabody was saying as Georgine began to retreat.

"Soldiers or no soldiers, what call they got to dig up what don't concern them—nor Mary Helen neither? Now, you watch out for 'em, Nell; they're pleasant-spoken enough, I'll say that for 'em, but how's a body to tell what's behind it?"

Mrs. Peabody broke into despairing laughter, and raised her voice. "I keep trying to tell you, Susie; they're staying here with me. And they didn't ask me any questions. I told them!"

There was an instant of shocked silence. Then Susan Labaré said gruffly, "Nell Lace, have you lost your mind?"

"Not in the least. Come in here, Susie, I think I heard them at the side door. Yes, you will!" She appeared at the back of the hall, pushing the gaunt figure before her. "Hello, Mrs. Wyeth. I hoped that was you. Barby's digging in the yard, she's perfectly happy... Now, Susie, come into the sitting room and let's talk this over."

Mrs. Labaré gave Todd and Georgine a look, oddly compounded of suspicion, reluctance and a sort of ghoulish interest; as if, Georgine thought, we were suspected murderers ourselves. "I don't know what you want to talk over," the harsh voice muttered ineffectually.

"Oh, yes, you do. Mr. McKinnon," said Nella, the bright flag of pink in her cheeks, "you see? You've already helped me, you've brought something into the open. This is the first time that Susan has ever admitted there was anything to conceal! It was good of you to warn me, Susie," she added with a mischievous glint of laughter. "But haven't I been telling you for two years that it would be kinder to tell the truth?"

"Well, 'twouldn't," said Susan harshly.

Todd said, "What you told me this afternoon wasn't so bad, Mrs. Labaré. That was accurate, wasn't it?" His voice was infinitely easy and soothing. Georgine sent him a mental apology. She had thought him a bit obvious with Susie. Now she saw that his tactics had been deliberate, and had produced the desired result.

"Far 's it went," the old woman said. She glared around at Mrs. Peabody. "Look here, Nell Lace, if there *was* anything more to tell—"

"Which of course there is," Nella put in. "And you've gone too far now not to tell it!"

"Well, if there was, you wouldn't want I should come out with it in front of them?" She thrust out a big hand toward Todd and Georgine.

"Especially in front of them. I have a—an understanding with Mr. McKinnon and Mrs. Wyeth. I'd like them to hear what you really know."

"You've lost your mind for sure," Susie said despairingly. "Well, it's on your own head. I've kep' still all these years for— nothing, I guess. What is it you want to know?"

Mrs. Peabody's chin went up, proudly defiant. "Why does everyone think it's Gilbert? You're the one who was in the house, you ought to know!"

"Only know what I saw, an' heard, an' what everybody saw afterward. He was here in the house. Mean to say you wasn't sure of that?"

"When was he here, Mrs. Labaré?" Todd said calmly. "Besides the morning visit, I mean. Would you take us through that whole day?"

"Well—all right. He come in about ha' past eleven, walked right upstairs the way he always done, an' Mis' Tillsit she looks at him and says, 'You get it?' and Gilbert nods. Then she sends me out of the room. He was only there about fifteen minutes that time."

"Did anyone else come to see her that morning?" Todd asked.

"Nobody come in that whole eternal day, until after I'd went to take my nap downstairs, like I always done, about two. I laid on that sofa." She jerked her head toward a monstrous object in faded olive-green plush. "I hadn't been down here more 'n a few minutes when I heard somebody up above; they must 'a' gone up the side steps because they hadn't gone up the front or I'd 'a' seen 'em." Susie gave one of her sharp nods, and clamped her jaw shut for a moment on this incontrovertible logic. "They were walkin' soft, so's not to disturb anybody. I heard Miss Adeline's door open, an' she sort of laughed, an' said somethin'."

Todd rose, and strolled over to the green sofa; from this vantage point he peered through the half-open door, and then nodded. "What happened then?" he said.

"Nothin'. It was a while after—"

"You'd been asleep?"

"Well, maybe. If I had, I hadn't no more 'n shut my eyes."

"You don't know, uh, how long they'd been shut?"

"That clock ain't run since the war—the other war," said Mrs. Labaré, with a contemptuous glance at the mantel. (Georgine thought, and it was by *that* that I was planning to time our leaving, last night!) "...I gener'ly just guessed at my two hours, or she'd call me... The first thing I knew, here come Gilbert tiptoein' down the stairs; the front stairs."

"Again being considerate, trying not to disturb your rest?"

"Seemed so at the time," Susie agreed rather grimly. "I'd come broad awake. I says to him, 'Had a better visit this time, didn't you,' I says. An' he—he jumped like he'd been shot."

"Possibly startled to find you were awake after all," Todd remarked smoothly. Susie made no rejoinder to this; she gave him a calculating look.

"I heard his car start up, out front. Hadn't heard it when he druv up, but then he could 'a' coasted the last little bit, an' shut off the engine gentle. Way he was pussyfootin', that's maybe what he done." She looked quickly at Nella, seeming to regret this last turn of phrase.

"Didn't he say anything when you spoke to him on the stairs?"

"Yeah," Susie replied grudgingly. "Said Miss Adeline was asleep. Well, I knowed better than that, didn't I? Said he hadn't tried to wake her, hadn't been in the room at all. I thought 'twas funny, but I wasn't figurin' very clear just then, an' I laid down again. And that was all, until I went upstairs about ha' past four, like I told you."

"And found, then or a li'le bit later, that she was in a coma." Todd looked beyond her, far away into a distance of things imagined. "You did all the housekeeping, of course, Mrs. Labaré."

"Sure. All of it, an' waited on Miss Adeline."

"You were up early? Yes, you'd have to be. And you'd been working hard all morning, cooking and cleaning and waiting on an invalid. It was a hot day, wasn't it?"

"Broilin'," Susie replied simply. "I had them shutters closed, an' the ones upstairs, too; both of 'em, this room and hers, faces west."

Georgine, listening, had an instant picture of these rooms in the afternoons of summer: bathed in the greenish light that filtered through tree-branches and shutters, suspended in warm dimness.

"Maybe I see what you're gettin' at," said Susan defiantly. "You think I must 'a slep', don't you? Well, I tell you, if I did it wasn't more'n a minute. I hadn't no way of tellin', but I'd take my Bible oath on it."

McKinnon nodded thoughtfully. "But if you had, by chance, gone off into one of those sudden deep sleeps that come to people when they're very tired—"

"I'm strong as a horse."

"—on hot summer days," he went on imperturbably, "it is just possible that there could have been another visitor besides Gilbert; one who both came and went by the enclosed service stairs, and whom you never heard at all except for the moment when Miss Adeline's door opened. Gilbert may have told the truth about not going into the room. Possibly he was here only a few minutes, since you need not have heard him coming."

"He didn't tell the truth," Mrs. Labaré said sullenly. She looked at Mrs. Peabody again, with what seemed sincere compunction. "You made me say it, Nell."

Nella's head was still superbly poised. "Mr. McKinnon is quite right," she said. "I can't see anything suspicious about Gilbert's having been here that afternoon. He told me he meant to come, only—I never did know how often, nor what time."

"Well—" Susan hesitated. Her long neck tightened, so that the shock of white hair quivered a little. "You want to hear this?"

"Of course," said Mrs. Peabody impatiently.

"He did go in. There was a mark on the carpet, right by the bed, sort of white powder as if he'd stood there or knelt there. An' Gilbert had on them white an' brown shoes of his, that he wore with his flannels an' that open-throat shirt, like Hollywood. I seen him on the stairs, dressed that way; guess he was goin' back to the studio to take some pitchers, an' he'd just gone over his shoes with the buck-bag he kep' in the car."

"Oh, Susie," said Mrs. Peabody indulgently. "As if that mark couldn't have been on the carpet for—"

"Wasn't there in the morning. I swep' the carpets, didn't I? An' he had on brown shoes, the other time he come."

"Susan Labaré!" Nella smiled and shook her head, still indulgent. "And you figured out, just from that, that Gilbert did something to Miss Tillsit that—that hastened her death. Why, I'm surprised at you, spreading a story that had no more foundation—"

"I didn't spread it! Don't you never think that, Nell. I told the doctor, an' Horace when they ast me about it afterward.

You think I'd go babblin' around town about somethin' like that, when the Judge—" She stopped and primmed her mouth again. "If there was any spreadin' done, it wasn't me. Didn't need to be. You know as well as I do how Gilbert acted the next few months."

"Now, just how did he act?" Nella sat composed and charming against the window, the sunlight striking through the bay to illumine the curves and hollows of her face.

"Ants in his pants, that's how," replied Susie succinctly. "Jumpy, kinda dazed, cloth-headed. An' doin' all sorts of queer things. How 'bout your diary?"

"My—*diary?*" This time Nella looked really startled.

"Yeah. That line-a-day book you used to keep, the one 't you said you lost. Askin' all over town for it, you was, sayin' you must 'a' left it somewhere. Didn't you never know Gilbert had it?"

"Gilbert." Her voice came slowly, as if a small but teasing problem had at last been solved. "But what could he have wanted with it, what ever got into him—there wasn't anything *in* my diary; just the little things that happened every day, notes on my dressmaking orders, things like that; *dull.*" A little laugh escaped her. "I did put down all the meetings he and I had, but that wouldn't—there wasn't anything—what did he do with it? How did anyone know he had it?"

"Tried to burn it," said Mrs. Labaré, more gently than usual. "You never knowed? Maybe nobody would 'a, only Gilbert buried the cover in the backyard behind the studio. Did it like a ninny, too, in broad daylight, an' Horace seen him out the p'scription room window."

"Horace took it on himself to go over and dig up what Gilbert had buried, on his own property?" Nella inquired with ominous mildness. "Well, be that as it may—Mr. McKinnon, Mrs. Wyeth, do you see anything in all that to condemn a man? Why, it could be twice as bad, and it would still seem inconclusive to me!"

"I think," Todd said, "that inconclusive is just the word. There's one thing more I'd like to know, Mrs. Labaré. You

mentioned hearing Miss Adeline laugh, when her early afternoon visitor opened her door; laugh, and make some remark.
Did you by any chance—"

From the kitchen door came a loud cry; Barby's voice,
squealing, "Mamma, Mamma, are you in there? Come out
here, quick!"

In the short time it took her to reach the back steps,
Georgine imagined her child mangled in a dozen different
ways; she found that Barby, though filthy from head to foot,
was whole. It seemed that there were some little bitsy hoptoads
under a bridal wreath bush in the garden, and Barby would
burst if she didn't display them to someone.

"Where's Virdette? I thought you were going to play all
afternoon," said Georgine, conquering her repugnance as she
bent to inspect the toads.

"She had to go to a party, maybe she'll come back here, after."

"Did you have a nice afternoon, darling?"

"Uh-huh. Mrs. Peabody put a paper pattern up against
me, and cut it so it'd fit me, and she told me a story about when
she was a little girl, and made us cocoa for lunch—Virdette
stayed; and—listen, Mamma, are we truly going to stay here
for a few days? Because there's a nattic upstairs and she said
I could play up there, there are things to dress up in! *Are* we
going to stay?"

Georgine said yes, maybe. She added a few well-chosen
words on the subject of Not Bothering, and then devoted
herself to an hour or so of companionship with her daughter.

It was after five when Todd appeared, strolling bare-
headed around the corner of the house. He sat down beside
Georgine in a rickety little summerhouse at the rear corner of
the big lot, and looked about him appreciatively. "Picket fence,
all along the back property line," he remarked. "Would that be
Californian, do you suppose, or did they bring that idea from
New England, too?"

Georgine didn't know. Rested and warmed by his presence, as always, she only smiled at him and looked idly at the

orchards which stretched in unbroken line on the far side of the fence. There was an unpaved lane, just wide enough for one car, beyond the pickets; and then the lines and lines of trees, some of them beginning to flower whitely. Todd said, with seeming irrelevance, "You could walk down that lane, almost all the way to town, without being seen. The other houses have solid board fences... Tillsit, Peabody: good old Eastern names, those. They brought some other reminders of home with them, too. Did you notice that balcony that runs clear round the third floor?" He looked up at it, and at the crazy latticework that dripped from it like a hem torn from a bedraggled lace dress.

"You could climb right down," said Barby happily, "from that top porch to the next one."

Georgine took a deep breath and announced that the porches were absolutely forbidden territory; that Barby would not be allowed in the attic at all unless she promised not to set foot on that porch, with its uneven boards and rotting banisters; and that Barby might now go and do some more gardening before her bath, as it was impossible for her to get any dirtier.

"Yes, I noticed it," she replied to Todd when this brief flurry was over. "Is that New England?"

"Modification of what they used to call a Widow's Walk. In the old days, sea captains' wives used to pace back and forth on 'em, looking out over the Atlantic for their husbands' ships. Rather engaging, isn't it, to find it reproduced here, when there's nothing bigger than a creek in sight?"

"And nothing but hills beyond that. A widow couldn't see a thing." Georgine noted with interest that Todd had taken his mouth organ from his pocket, and was tapping it against one palm. "She's out of earshot now, Todd. Have you started to plan stories already, just from what Susie and Nella were saying? Or have you been doing more research?"

"Both," Todd said in a low voice. He continued to gaze out over the garden, his eyes slightly narrowed. "I paid a few more calls after Susie left; went to see the editor of the li'le newspaper, and introduced myself at the police station, and called on the rector of that church down on Elm Street. He asked if he mightn't meet you, too, before the wedding."

"Of course. That really begins to sound like business."

"Begins to sound! Woman, what do you call a license and a ring?"

"Corroborative detail," said Georgine. "I still can't quite believe it. But what did you find out, Todd?"

"Not much; not so very much; and yet—it all begins to shape up. Odd how freely people talk, there's no doubt of what they think even when it's not put into direct words. Gilbert Peabody cleared his slate when he enlisted and went overseas; that's the consensus. And there's no argument about Miss Adeline. If she was murdered, it was for gain, in money or property. She was not a tyrant, she brought no pressure to bear on her family to do what she wanted. Just a fine old lady, a li'le crotchety; that's what they all say. If anybody wanted his own way, it would be her brother, Judge Tillsit. They didn't get on too well, but that would be his fault, not hers. I gather he's the uncrowned king of Valleyville."

"I'd like to see the old gentleman."

"You probably will," Todd said, putting away the mouth organ. "The police—Valleyville boasts two constables, they'll have you know—the police mentioned him in admiring tones, very admiring indeed."

His tone seemed to convey more than the words. "Oh?" she said.

"I got the conversation round," said Todd dreamily, "to murder."

"You astonish me."

"If there were a major crime here, the county sheriff would be called in. The boys here aren't qualified to handle it. The sheriff hasn't been needed more than once in their memory, and that was for a li'le knifing party among some Italian ranch hands."

"Really no suspicion that Miss Adeline's death was—"

"Not then. Not enough suspicion for anyone to—go against the Judge's wishes."

"Todd, it really looks to me as if you'd be stymied."

"Oh, no." His smooth sandy head moved deliberately from side to side. "I'm challenged, Georgine. To begin with, there's no proof that a murder ever took place. There was no examination of the body, no evidence beyond Susie's bit about the shoe-white—she doesn't miss a great deal, our Susie, does she?—and worst of all, no one questioned at the time. Anything in the nature of a trail must have gone stone cold more than two years ago."

"I hope to goodness you're not trying to warm it up."

"We-ell," said Todd, chuckling silently, "not so it gets red hot. I must say, though, I miss the tips I used to get from reporters, and now and then the police. I knew I owed 'em a lot, but it takes a case like this to show me how much!"

"On the other hand, the principals seem to be opening their hearts to you. Ah, that old McKinnon charm," said Georgine maliciously.

"I'll let you handle the men," said Todd with imperturbable countenance. "As for the women, they needn't be telling the truth, you know. Nobody need be."

"That's so. Bar-bee!" Georgine suddenly raised her voice to a shriek. "Don't go out of the yard. Five minutes more, darling!"

"For instance," Todd said, his voice lowered almost to inaudibility, "Mrs. Peabody. Did it strike you as strange that she left out of her story some things that anyone might have known, and not only left 'em out but insisted that she did not know them?"

"Ye-es; not so much that, but that she—refused to see any significance in some of the things Susie told us. I wonder if it's been like that all along; that she talks about wanting the truth, but refuses to acknowledge it. Could she possibly think, subconsciously, that Gilbert—"

"She could," said Todd.

"Then, are we doing the right thing in going on with this, raking up old scandals? It may get worse and worse, and when we're staying right in the house—"

"She insists on it. I asked her, almost point-blank; she begged me to go on. Funny twist."

Georgine got up to collect her child; he rose with her, but got out the mouth organ again, as if he meant to stay a while in communion with it. "There was one thing Susie said, at the last," he remarked, "that meant nothing to me, nor seemingly to Mrs. Peabody; but Susie brought it out reluctantly, and looked as if she had expected it to be a clinching argument. I asked her if she'd heard what Miss Adeline said to the first visitor. She said yes, she did. The old lady's voice boomed out across the upstairs hall."

He waited a moment before going on, his sandy brows drawn together.

"For heaven's sake, McKinnon, drop that other shoe!"

"Miss Adeline laughed, you'll remember. Then she said, 'Oh, it's you. Well, be yourself. Come in, and for the Lord's sake take that thing off your head.'"

"That thing—off your head?" Georgine repeated.

"Um. Free association test for you; quick, what do you see on the head of the person who stood in the door?" She gave a brief and uncomfortable laugh. "An executioner's hood," she said.

CHAPTER FOUR

WITH RELIEF GEORGINE discovered a way to get from the garden to the second floor without wiping the mud from Barby's feet onto the carpet of the front stairs. You went past the line of drooping maples to a door that led into the basement; from this rose the enclosed stairs which connected with the first- and second-floor halls before opening into the attic at their very top. She got Barby into the tub, and into the clean dress which had prudently been brought along, with only absent replies to her daughter's conversation.

She was still thoughtful during dinner, from which "the children"—Horace and Mary Helen—were again absent. The conversation was gaily impersonal, and Georgine was glad of it. She was horribly uneasy about her position, and Todd's, in this household. Although he was paying their way, she still felt as if she were Nella Peabody's guest and under obligations to her; and to have a kind and likable hostess not only beg you to stab her in the back, but hand you the knife with which to do it—Georgine didn't like the prospect.

Barby went to bed at half-past seven. She was fast asleep, and the lovely spring twilight was deepening under the trees, when an imperious call sounded from the front walk. "Barby. *Bar*-by! Can you come out?"

It was Virdette Bacon, still decked in the curls and crepe-de-chine dress of the afternoon's party. The yo-yo was also present. "Mis' Wyeth, can't Barby play awhile?" she demanded as Georgine emerged on the front porch.

"She's in bed, Virdette. How about coming back tomorrow?" Georgine was beginning, when Todd appeared quietly beside her.

"Or stay and talk to us for a few minutes," he amended. "We might go downtown and have a soda later, if your mother doesn't object."

"She won't mind," said Virdette easily. As a one-time "prodgidy" she seemed well poised in her relations with adults, looking on with indulgent good nature when Todd borrowed the yo-yo and performed an evolution or two of his own. It seemed the most natural thing on earth that the three should gravitate across the street, and once more wander among the ruins of the Bacon home.

Neat work, Georgine thought with a private grin, as Todd took up his station at the exact point where the piano had stood. He gazed pensively across at the Tillsit house, and was heard to mention that in summer those maples must almost hide its northeast side. Somehow, Virdette was telling them again about the afternoon of Miss Tillsit's death. "Sure I remember," she said. "There wasn't much else to look at that afternoon, see, and I was the only one here, so the family all wanted to know about it. Lordy, seemed as if I told 'em about a million times. Sure, I saw it all, went to the funeral, too. I liked old Miss Tillsit, all us kids did. If we went in to see her she'd give us candy that she kept hid in her bureau drawers, only we had to wait till Mis' Labaré wasn't in the room because Miss Tillsit wasn't supposed to have candy and things... "

She had been sitting at the piano all afternoon, beginning at half-past one; spending a gorgeous June day in an old-fashioned parlor, doggedly playing over and over the scales of every key and the chromatic, up and down the whole keyboard, while her eyes searched the empty street outside. "Nobody went in for a long time," said Virdette dreamily. "I thought once or twice maybe old Mis' Labaré was workin' round in the basement, because that side door 'ud open and shut. I couldn't see because the door was between her 'n' me, and anyhow those trees almost hid it. Then about three Mr. Gilbert Peabody drove up. That was kind of fun, us kids always got a laugh out o' the way he dressed up for takin' pictures, as if he was kind of an artist, like; and he doesn't look like one, he's real tall and homely. So he stayed in there a while—"

"You don't remember how long, I suppose," Todd said as if idly.

"Just about, because I got up to get a drink and stretch, but I didn't dast to stop practicing for long," said Virdette with reminiscent gloom. "It was only about ten minutes, and he was just comin' down the front walk when I sat down again, walking slow with his hands in his pockets and lookin' at the ground. And so he got in his car and went off, and nothing more happened for about an age."

"Did he usually drive when he came to see his aunt?" Todd murmured.

"Him? No, he gener'ly walked, he just lived three-four blocks down the street and over one. That's where his studio was, you know, back to back with the drugstore. It's the Red Cross shop now. He had the car that afternoon, though, and he turned it round in the street and went off. An' then there wasn't a darn thing more until about ha'past four, and then— whoo!" said Virdette with enjoyment. "There was old Mis' Labaré poppin' her head in and out the hall window upstairs and shootin' down to look out the front door—she just scoots, when she's in a hurry—and in about two seconds here comes Mr. Gilbert back again, an' Horace over from the drugstore—

he'd come so fast he was still pullin' his jacket on while he went up the steps; and Mary Helen, she pretended she wasn't in a hurry, but she went in the house awful fast just the same.

"And a while after, Rose, that's my sister, came home. 'Where's Mom?' she says. 'Horace just got word Miss Tillsit's sinkin'.' I says, 'Ho, I knew that before you did,' I says, and I told her about it. And she said she'd been in the drugstore all afternoon—she and Martin was awful mushy before they got married, she'd go in there and when there wasn't any customers they'd sit and hold hands, and Horace used to go in the prescription room and leave 'em alone. Mom didn't like it much, but Rose says Horace was made for a chaperon and he was right in the back room all the time, they could hear him clinkin' around, and anyhow you couldn't be publicker, Rose said. Well, she said he was in and out a couple times that afternoon, answered the telephone once or twice, and then trade kind of fell off and he left 'em alone; and then just before she left he answered it again an' it was old Mis' Labaré. So we really knew about it before anybody in town, only I knew first," Virdette wound up with deep satisfaction.

"You certainly did," Todd remarked in a sincerely respectful tone. "You were the star witness, I'd say. And what a memory!"

"Oh, well," said Miss Bacon, shrugging a fat shoulder, "I c'n remember most anything. Besides, I told people about that lots o' times after, when they asked me if Mr. Gilbert—Oh gosh, I nearly forgot, Mom doesn't like me talkin' about that. She said never to."

"Then don't you do it," said Todd heartily. "How about that soda now? We'll see that you get home afterward, it'll be dark."

"Okay," said Virdette. She rose and wound up the yo-yo, which had not ceased to whirr gently up and down its string during her entire story. For eating, it seemed, one needed both hands.

It was indeed nearly dark. Georgine had not taken her eyes from the Tillsit house while Virdette talked, except once or twice to look briefly at Todd. His attention had flattered the child, but more than that it had warned Georgine that most of this was important. No need to ask if he'd thought of the same point that she had: from the rear lane, which could be traversed all the way from town, anyone could have come through the back gate and in that basement door and up to the second floor where Miss Adeline waited; anyone could have come unseen, behind high board fences and drooping branches of trees, and a door that opened toward the street so that the eagle-eyed child in her window could not have seen—whoever it was.

The monstrous pile of timber and wooden lace stood out in fantastic silhouette against the last of the sunset light. Georgine found herself, as they walked down the shadowy street, looking back every now and then to see from what points the skylight was visible. Queer that nobody but Susie had ever noticed how the moon gave the illusion of a light in that attic. The moon was not up yet tonight, or Georgine would have tested the illusion for herself.

A tag of poetry floated unbidden into her mind. "I'll come to you by moonlight, though hell should bar the way."

Rats do not read poetry, said Georgine Wyeth to herself with fine scorn.

❖ ❖ ❖

"Todd, not another call?" she protested half an hour later. "You are indefatigable!"

"I don't want to tire *you*, Georgine," his quiet voice came from the shadows beside her, "but this one's necessary—both ways."

"Both what ways?"

"Unromantic as it seems, dear heart," said Todd, "we have to have our Wassermanns taken before we can get married. And what more appropriate"—his voice dropped—"than to have it done by Valleyville's chief medico?"

They neared the door of another of those tiny frame bungalows; and under the porch light she could read the words on the brass plate by the door. "Dr. John Crane. H'm. McKinnon, have you no shame?"

"None. That is, I don't know what you're talking about, dear. Office hours, eight to nine in the evenings; we've just about hit the tag end of 'em."

Dr. John Crane was in; for a wonder, as he said himself, after shooing the last of his office patients out of the side door. "A miracle," he said with a long sigh, turning a harried face toward Todd and Georgine, "though God knows I'm glad to do the work, thankful to be left here to do it! Some draft boards have a little sense."

The taking of blood samples lasted only a minute, but he would not hear of his patients' departure immediately after. "I know who you are, heard all about you today," he said, his fatigue-heavy eyes lighting up with a nice smile. "I hope Nella's houseguests will accept a drink? I could use one myself."

More open-heartedness, Georgine thought, sipping the sherry she had chosen in preference to the men's highballs. Pioneer hospitality—I can't help wondering, I can't *help* it— would they be so kind if they knew what we were after?

She liked the doctor's long thin face, his dark eyes and graying hair. He'll be old before his time within a year, if this keeps up, she thought; the one doctor for a big farming community and a town of fifteen hundred people. "I want to consult you on something more, Dr. Crane," she said at a pause in the war talk which inevitably opened men's conversations. "You know, of course, that we're staying with Mrs. Peabody? She spoke of a heart condition, and—if it's not prying into your patients' affairs—won't it be too much for her to have three extra persons quartered on her? She won't let me help very much."

"No, no, Mrs. Wyeth. Good for her. The heart wouldn't be much by itself, just something that had to be watched; but it's easy to aggravate those conditions with worry and nervousness and uncertainty." The doctor swished the ice in his glass, and frowned. "Mothers and wives are taking it in this war, too," he said heavily. "Not good for Nella to be alone too much, d'you see? I'm very fond of Nella. Wish I could take better care of her. Horace Tillsit and his cousin, my—uh—ex-wife, are nominally staying there to keep her company, but they don't take the responsibility very seriously."

"Well, they're young," Georgine said kindly.

"Not so terribly," said the doctor with a wry smile. "They've lived pretty full lives, both of 'em... Well, Mr. McKinnon, so you're the uncle of the famous sergeant; seems Mary Helen thinks she brought back a scalp from the Stage Door Canteen." He smiled again, and let his eyes rove consideringly around the small bay-windowed parlor which was his waiting room: shabby, comfortable furniture, stiffly starched curtains and an odor of antiseptics seeping in from the office in the next room. "A narrow enough life, *this* was, for a girl," he said unemotionally. "It only lasted six or seven months, back in nineteen-forty-one. I don't begrudge her any kind of happiness she can find, now. I'd never make any trouble, you know. Is that what you wanted to find out?"

"My God, no," said Todd mildly.

The two men looked at each other for a moment; then Todd added, with some deliberation, "We didn't come to you, Dr. Crane, to find out anything except the state of our health. I thought I should enjoy meeting you personally. That's all."

The doctor relaxed slightly, smiling. "Good. Then—none of this need be taken too seriously, you know; perhaps you can just enjoy your visit."

Todd seemed to understand this elliptical statement, and nodded. "The background of Mrs. Crane's family history interests me, of course. I'm a writer, and this is something you don't often get to see in the flesh: a patriarchy, seemingly in good working order. No, I don't mean just the family, but the whole region. Am I right in thinking that Judge Tillsit has brought a good many benefits to this town?"

"A great number," said Dr. Crane, "both public and private. He controlled considerable wealth at one time. Some of it may have come back in the last year or so, with the rise in real estate values. The Judge's—investments were made according to his own plan; he'd help out young people who wanted a career, at least to the extent of financing their training. I'd be running a tractor this minute, and a borrowed tractor at that, if he hadn't started me in medical school. None of us got any more, or any less help than he'd give his own grandchildren: learn a profession or a trade, and then—no more money; you were on your own. That was supposed to show if you had the stuff in you. A fine old gentleman," said the doctor, looking intently at his glass.

"Everyone says the same, almost in those words, about his sister," Todd remarked. "Seems a pity when brother and sister can't agree."

"Oh, it was never so bad as that. Their relations were cordial enough, but they'd have grated on each other if they'd lived under the same roof. Each of 'em fond of his own way, you know. People been telling you they quarreled?"

"No," Todd said. "We've heard from all sides, though, about her death, with the sorrowing relations gathered round; and nobody mentions that her brother was there."

Georgine thought, now he's on dangerous ground; he just got through telling the doctor that we didn't expect him to talk, and here we are back at Miss Adeline's deathbed.

But Dr. Crane did not seem discomposed; he looked thoughtfully from her to Todd, as if deciding that they had a right to some knowledge of family affairs. "Nobody's thought to tell you, then, that when she died the Judge was damned near dead himself?"

"No," Todd said, "nobody has."

"That's not quite fair to the Judge," said Dr. Crane slowly. "Giving you the idea that he didn't care for his sister. Matter of fact, the family's what he cares about most. He'd have got up from his sickbed and gone to the funeral if the housekeeper hadn't held him down by main force—gone just for the sake of sincere respect, because no one expects a man who's just over the crisis of pneumonia to think of appearances. He was still so weak when she died that we debated whether he ought to be told; might have had a relapse and slipped off at any minute."

"It's obvious you pulled him through all right," Todd said, casually courteous.

"Oh yes, yes. By the grace of God, and luck, he's alive today. Touch and go there, for a while, though. He insisted on making some of the arrangements, but the details bothered him so that we had to drop the discussion. Excitement is, uh, bad for him...Sad thing to see these old families dying out," said the doctor vaguely, and finished his drink. "I didn't do much for the Tillsits, in the way of carrying on the line." He looked across at Todd, and seemed about to add something, when the telephone rang and he was out of his chair in one bound, to answer. "Yes?...Yes, of course...How long?...Well, I wouldn't give him anything, no. I'll be over, just to check up on it, before we decide to increase the dose." He hung up, made hasty excuses, and turned toward the rear of the house to shout, "Mother! My bag ready?"

Georgine, rising to leave, observed with astonishment the headlong passage of Dr. Crane out the door. In one hand was his black satchel, and in the other the empty glass which had held his drink. He must have forgotten to put it down. She hoped that something would remind him of this excess baggage before he arrived at his patient's bedside.

They started homeward, walking slowly under the arching trees. There were streetlights only at the corners, and those were shrouded by the high branches, so that the dim glow of lamps behind drawn shades, in the small frame houses they passed, gave the only light.

"A nine o'clock town," said Todd dreamily. "And no through traffic on these streets. Tell me, do you feel a strong sense of the past in this place?"

"Oh, *yes.*"

"Ladies in bustles, and turn-of-the-century tailored suits, trotting along genteelly on these same sidewalks past these same porches and bay windows; men in derbies and high collars and handlebar mustaches..."

"It's funny," said Georgine slowly, "but my sense of the past is concentrated in—in June 1940, and right in the Tillsit house. The setting's unchanged, and I suppose that's why, but I can't look at that staircase without seeing a man coming down in freshly whitened shoes, walking very softly, and stopping short when he's spoken to. If I sit on that green sofa, I hear voices upstairs. I've—I've got so that when I'm downstairs I find myself listening for the old lady moving around on the second floor."

Todd's head turned toward her in the dark. "A li'le more of that and I'll get you to put in the background of my yarns."

"Go on. You can do it yourself, because you've felt the same thing. But to you, it's—useful."

He was looking at her attentively. "Do you mind it very much?"

With swift compunction she thought of her good resolutions about overcoming cowardice; and of Todd's face, alive and interested over some obscure point in a conversation. "No-o," she said, laughing. "And I'd better start getting used to your professional research. I hope it stays like this!"

"Like what?"

"Oh—just talking politely to people, and then going away and writing it up. I mean, on this purely mental plane it's not so bad."

"I can never figure out what you expect," Todd replied mildly. "People chasing me with guns? Anonymous letters saying 'Keep out of this or you will die too'?"

"Something like that, I suppose. And yet there doesn't seem any harm in a conversation like the one we just had. It's especially goofy of me to get worried, when I can't see what you get out of these talks."

"Are you kidding?" said Mr. McKinnon. "What the doctor told me, aloud and between the lines, was worth five bucks a word."

"Oh dear. I must have been half asleep."

"Not necessarily. You got it when he indicated that he himself is under obligations to the Judge, like a good many others in town? And that the Judge wields a heavy scepter? I can do something with that," Todd said musingly. "Elegant old spider sitting in the middle of a web, now and then jerking..."

"Jerking with a heavy sceptre," Georgine murmured. "You slay me, darling."

"And surely you didn't miss the fact that Dr. Crane knew very well we were interested, somehow, in Miss Adeline's death? He couldn't tell us much about it, without destroying the fiction that she died naturally; but, certificate or no certificate, he still thinks something went on there. I've got a notion that he's bothered by what Nella Peabody is going through, and if he could he'd do something about it for her sake."

"I can see that it'd be difficult for him to do anything, without ruining himself professionally!"

"Very difficult," said Todd soberly. "What did you think of the man himself?"

"The doctor? He looked exhausted, all except his eyes. When he answered that call they were positively eager. I'd say he cares more for doctoring than anything else; bit of a martyr complex there, maybe?"

"Maybe. You might just call it wanting to be of use in the war emergency, that's easy to understand. You needn't feel sorry for me," he added rather curtly, for she had laid her hand on his arm.

"I wasn't. But, speaking of senses of the past," said Georgine, just above a whisper, "I have a strong feeling about the present, too. Someone's been following us."

"I heard that step," Todd said, unperturbed. "On the other side of the street, and just the same rate we're walking. Only for the last few minutes, though. Person could hardly have heard what we've been saying."

"Maybe not. But it seems to me now that it's been there all the time, like an echo of our steps. Todd, why should anyone want to—watch us? You're sure that's not a prelude to being chased with guns?"

"Quite sure. We might cross over—no, here's the house."

The footsteps died away. Maybe it had really been an echo? She glanced over her shoulder, as they went up the Tillsit walk, and tried not to imagine a shadowy figure melting away into the lilac bushes of that yard across the street.

"A sense of the present." That was a meaningless way to put it; what she meant was a sense of something wrong, this very season. It was strongest when they had entered the front door with the border of colored glass, strong even when Nella Peabody reported that Barby was happily sleeping and that she, Nella, had just been up to look at her. The house smelled old and clean, the lamplight was tranquil on the beautiful curve of stair rail; it gave the illusion of peace, and yet peace was not here.

The moon had not reached Georgine's window when she went up to prepare for bed. It rose an hour later every night; that meant it would reach the western sky about two or three in the morning.

The night before, she had been too sleepy to listen for long to the sounds of the old house. Tonight she lay awake for a while, hearing Barby's untroubled breathing in the cot across the room, and nothing else. How odd that there was nothing else.

Why did the rats perform one night and not the next? Had it something to do with the position of the moon on the skylight, and were they waiting until its light fell in a barred rectangle across that dusty bare floor above her? And then would they come out to dance up and down, making that slow regular tapping noise, shaking little showers of plaster down the spaces between walls?

There was a creak now and then, but nothing like the loud cracks and groans the old woodwork had given out the night before. She gave up the problem, presently, and went to sleep.

The moon waked her again, very late; or was it the subdued scramblings from the cot? "You all right, Barby?" Georgine said drowsily.

"I haff to go to the bathroom," Barby informed her, and proudly snapped on her new flashlight. Georgine wouldn't have put it past her to have waked up on purpose.

"Shan't I go with you?"

"No, Mamma! You said when I was eight I was grown up—"

"Shush, darling, don't wake everyone. All right, go by yourself. I suppose it does seem like a treat."

Seemingly it was such a treat that Barby didn't want to come back to bed. Georgine nearly drowsed off, waiting for her. After a long time there was the sound of a door, cautiously opening; then another—

A muffled clatter woke the night, and a loud thud followed. Georgine shot out of bed, barely stopping to put on the bedside lamp, and was out in the hall in a split second. She could see across its dimness, into the entry of the back stairs. Barby was on her hands and knees, sprawling across the handle of a fallen mop. Probably from surprise, she seemed unable to get up.

Her mother flew across the hall. "Darling, did you hurt yourself?" She turned her child into a sitting position, and found nothing worse than dust on the knees. "You are a silly," she commented in a sharp whisper. "Did you think this was the door of our room? What good's your flashlight, for heaven's sake?"

"I guess I was kind of asleep," Barby muttered. "I got turned around, Mamma. That thing fell down on me, and I sort of fell over it, an' I couldn't think where I was."

"It's all right, Todd," Georgine whispered to the figure that had materialized behind her. She moved modestly out of the shaft of light that streamed from the door of her room. "Nothing sinister at all."

"What?" Todd said softly. "No mysterious sounds from the attic? I thought for a moment you were investigating."

"Then you must have thought I was a perfect fool." She sat down on the floor and suddenly found herself shaking from head to foot.

Todd picked up Barby, took her across the hall and put her in bed, and was back with Georgine's robe within forty seconds. "What is it?" he said quietly. "Did you really hear something that frightened you?"

"No," she said after a moment. "Close the door to those stairs, will you, Todd? I've—I've outdone even myself, this time. What scared me was that I didn't hear anything."

"Say that again?" Todd requested.

"There's nothing up there tonight, nothing at all, and last night there was." She cast a cautious glance around the hall; it was cloudily dark, shot with a faint gleam of moonlight through the transom over the sewing room door and the thin sliver of light from her own room. You could just see the shadowy cornices of those other doors, and the pictures in their heavy frames slanting outward from the wall. "Last night there *was*. Tonight, subconsciously, I suppose, I waited for the moon to rise, there seemed to be some connection, but—I was awake for a moment before Barby got up, there wasn't any sound from us to disturb what—whatever might be up there, and there was nothing. And it frightened me, Todd. Now, isn't that foolishness, I ask you?"

"Not entirely," said Todd. His deep eye-sockets narrowed until his eyes were almost invisible. "We'll think about that. But at the moment—you know all you have to do is let out one call, and I'll hear you? Will you go back to sleep if you think of that?"

"Of course," Georgine said. She took a deep breath and turned toward her room. "I expected we'd wake the house, but I guess nobody was disturbed."

She could have sworn that one of those doors had opened a crack.

"Nella sleeps on the other side from these back stairs, you know; behind the dining room. And we haven't made as much noise as you think. Now, good night, Georgine." He gave her shoulder a little shake. "Take it easy."

She promised; but it was not so simple to get back to sleep. She lay for a while, looking into the quiet darkness and giving herself a stern fight talk. What, after all, was the situation? An old woman had died, peacefully enough, four years ago in this house. Everyone seemed to feel—for reasons that had not yet fully appeared—that her death had been hastened. Well, what of it? Everything had been serene enough ever since; it was serene now.

And yet—

Under that serenity there was something unfathomed; Nella Peabody's nervousness, for instance, which went deeper than the normal night fears of a timid woman. Without seeing it, you felt her driven and haunted by some kind of furies. She had talked for a while with her guests, after they returned from the doctor's. Horace and Mary Helen would never have been living in her home, she conveyed, if old Judge Tillsit hadn't wished it so strongly—commanded it, was a better phrase. She resented their presence, they resented their grandfather's orders. Then why were they here?

Was it all a question of money, or was something queer behind it? Nella's mouth had curved in a very odd smile when she said, "The Judge is—more than kind to me."

Todd hadn't been able to resist it. "A li'le less than kin, and more than kind," he had murmured.

Nella's reserve of manner had deepened. "He'd see to it, of course, that I wasn't in actual want. You've seen all the food he sends in from the farm, butter and cream and bacon and chickens—anything else I must have is just about covered by the children's board money, of course I can't take much from them. Oh, they wouldn't let me starve. It wouldn't look well. But if Gilbert and I couldn't scrape up the money to pay the taxes—I don't know just what would happen to the house."

"All its contents were willed to him, you said," Georgine had mentioned.

"Yes. I could sell something, perhaps, if I had permission from him. I wrote weeks and weeks ago, to ask him what he wanted done, but—there hasn't been a letter for some time. I wouldn't move, I wouldn't touch a thing, without my husband's permission."

"Certainly not." Todd was sympathetic. "But if you ever do want to sell, I know an antique dealer in the City who's as honest as they come, and who'd give you the best possible prices."

Nella looked at him with sudden gratitude. "Do you? Oh, that would be a help. I didn't know where to go, and the family would be horrified if I consulted them, as if I had no right—" She bit her lip. "I can't help feeling that they regard me as a—not exactly an interloper, I married into the family even if Gilbert was always the—least regarded member of it, but—as if I'm on sufferance, holding this property in trust not for him, but for—"

And there she had stopped. Georgine knew well enough who made her feel that way: the Judge. The figure of the Judge, as yet an unknown quantity, kept looming up in everyone's story. He loomed larger and larger. An elegant old spider, she thought, and smiled at Todd's turns of phrase; and all at once slept.

❊ ❊ ❊

Barby started talking of the attic, almost as soon as she got up, in tones of keen anticipation. "*She* said I could look in all the old trunks," she reported.

"Mrs. Peabody said," Georgine corrected patiently.

"Uh-huh. Well, anyway, she said there were lots of old things up there, and I could dress up. Mamma, can I do it today? Oh, no, Virdette's comin' to play. Well, if she doesn't come, you know what I'm goin' to do, Mamma? I'm goin' up there—*I promise* not to go on the little porch, honest I do."

Georgine was surprised by the violence of her own feeling. She didn't want Barby in the attic; there was no reason, she just didn't want it. She might not have time to stay up there every minute while Barby played. And yet, an attic was part of every child's birthright, she couldn't be so cruel as to forbid the visit; and Barby would prefer to be alone anyway, having been trained to solitary habits.

You could not forbid a child to go into a place that frightened you, without good reason. You couldn't say, There's something unknown up there, I feel that it's sinister, I hate the look of those old trunks and that chintz garment bag. It might be an effective argument, but it would give Barby a touch of those superstitious fears which her mother had sworn she should never know.

"Oh," said Georgine brightly, "but I think Virdette will be here, and you can go outdoors. It's a lovely day."

That morning Mary Helen Jefferson Crane came home.

Her arrival was not without fanfare. A large open touring car full of young people swept down the street, made a U-turn and came to a stop at the Tillsit sidewalk. Out of sheer exuberance the driver blasted his horn into the Sunday quiet, there were shrieks of protest which added up considerably louder than the horn, and a girl scrambled out of the crowd. More shrieks bade her farewell as the car moved away. She came up the walk with an extraordinary gait, halfway between trucking and a short-stepped walk, and she seemed to be humming a song.

Mary Helen wasn't pretty; she wasn't pretty at all, but you kept looking at her to figure out why not. Perhaps it was the contradiction of her features that was interesting. Under a smooth forehead and a sleek brown pompadour, her large eyes shone with an expression of alert candor. They were very light gray eyes with a ring of black round the iris, and lashes and brows were thin and groomed. Her chin was long and rather noticeably bony, but there was an almost babyish look about her mouth, since she had one of those very short upper lips which keep the mouth half open unless the owner makes an effort to close it. Mary Helen, who had beautiful teeth, seldom bothered.

Georgine, standing well back from the window of her room and observing this arrival, knew at once that she had seen this girl before. She could not remember the face from among Susie Labaré's array of photographs, though it must have been there somewhere. It was something about the walk—that was it; this was the young woman who had been talking to the jeweler yesterday noon.

Barby followed her gaze and rushed to the window. She stood gazing for a moment. Then, her voice almost breaking, she demanded, "Is *that* Cousin Dyke's girl?"

"Hush, Barby, she might hear you! Yes, I think it must be. She looks as if she might be lots of fun, don't you see that?"

"Oh, no. Oh, Mamma! I thought she'd be—I thought if he liked her, of course she'd—"

She could not finish. Georgine thought with an inward smile, Poor Barby expected a sort of princess, or at least another Ann Sheridan.

"Come on, darling, we'll have to go down," she said gently. "You want to meet her, you know."

They heard her voice coming up from the foot of the stairs. "Hullo, Nell. I brought some things home from Marge's to be washed, see to it, will you? And I don't believe I'll be home for dinn—Oh!"

There were sounds of introduction. "Oh, not *really!*" said Mary Helen with emphasis. "Oh, why didn't I know that? Dyke talked so much about you, Mr. McKinnon, and I was just *crazy* to meet you, and here I have to go and waste the whole weekend, what *luck* for me you stayed over! I just can't *tell* you how thrilled I am to meet you." Her eyes swept upward and met those of Georgine and Barby, who were halfway down the staircase. "Oh, that must be your fiancée, isn't it, and that darling little kiddie he told me about? You just can't imagine what a *surprise* this is! I could simply kick myself for missing so much of your visit. How do you do, Mrs. Wyeth. And—what's your name, sweetie? Barby? What a perfect darling you are, I *must* have a hug!" She swooped toward the bottom step and Barby disappeared among flying loose coat sleeves.

"Why, what's the matter?" Mary Helen demanded roguishly, sitting back on her heels. "Now don't tell me you don't *like* to be petted!"

"Thank you, not very much," said Barby with visible relief.

"Well, but that's just *silly*! Because we're practically in the same family, and anyway you are such a duck, I just can't help it! I just love kiddies."

Georgine said, "Barby dear, run get your hat and coat. You remember we were going to church?" She made proper excuses to Mary Helen, for departing so abruptly. "But you'll be here when we come back, won't you, Mrs. Crane? Do you know, I'm sure we might have met earlier, if we'd only known who you were. Didn't we see Mrs. Crane in Fairfield yesterday, Todd?"

"I think we did. Odd coincidence," said Todd smoothly.

"Did you? Well, it isn't so awfully funny, because I work there, and people do seem rather to remember me if they've seen me once." Mary Helen gave Georgine the sweetest of smiles. "Where was it, in the hotel at lunch? Because I know you weren't in the *office*!"

"At Bertram's; isn't that the jeweler's name?"

"Oh. Oh, yes. But how *funny* I didn't—well, of course I didn't see you, because I was just in there for half a minute, getting my watch ribbon fixed, and I had to hurry back to the office. I suppose you were just going out as I came in."

"That was it," said Todd.

He and Mrs. Crane exchanged a pleasant smile. No one could have told which of the two was the better liar.

CHAPTER FIVE

THE HOUSE WAS FULL of Mary Helen. You would not have believed that one young woman could have made herself so omnipresent, so constantly heard without being noisy; that any one person could have changed the tempo of the household from cool placidity to something almost feverish.

"Ah," said Todd benignly, meeting Georgine in the hall before lunch, "what it is to have a bit of life in the house. Ah, youth!"

She regarded him coldly. "Going into your grandfather act, are you?"

"Practicing up. Mary Helen has suggested a private interview after lunch. I'll confess," said Todd, looking more wooden than she had thought possible, "that I'm terrified. And I count on you to come round after a decent interval and rescue me from that infernal li'le prancing nymph." He cast a cautious glance over his shoulder, to make sure the kitchen door was shut. "I'm disappointed in my nephew," he remarked sadly.

"Dyke's all right," said Georgine. "Maybe, for once, I know him better than you do."

They exchanged a long look. Todd said in a thoughtful tone, "Perhaps there is more in him than meets the eye. I'd like to have a talk—" He broke off as Mary Helen tripped into the dining room with a soup tureen.

"I'll be writing him a bread-and-butter letter this afternoon," Georgine said, and gave Todd one more meaning glance.

In the good old country tradition, lunch was dinner on Sunday. Mary Helen spoke of this despairingly, gesturing at the immense damask tablecloth, the gravy boat and the heavy family silver. "Nell will do it," she said. "But then, it's all of a piece with our other quaint customs."

"I like them," said Mrs. Peabody gently. "And if you just wait long enough, most of them come back in style again."

"Yes, *wait*," said Mary Helen, shrugging. "There wouldn't be much else to do, if you lived here. You'd have to be ninety before you could get steamed up about thimble parties and swapping recipes. You can't even get to the City any more, at least as often as you'd like, and you could die of boredom in Valleyville for all anybody *cares*."

"The county fair is only a month off," said Nella, lowering her eyelids. She was baiting Mary Helen, Georgine realized with appreciation.

"Oh, yes. *That's* out of this world. You ought to stick around, Mrs. Wyeth; attractions for everyone, you can win a Kewpie doll on the Wheel of Fortune, or enter for the Mother's Sack Race."

"Thank you so much," said Georgine gravely, "but I'm afraid we'll have to be getting home before that."

Mary Helen shrugged again. A moment later, when Nella rose to get fresh biscuits from the oven, the younger woman spoke in a lowered tone. "You disapprove of me, don't you? Well, you don't know what it's *like*. All that keeps me from going mad is the fact that I work out of town; when I come back here, to this house, it all closes round me again. Well, you know, Nell's a dear thing, but she never realizes how it gets on my *nerves*, all this, 'Where have you been, how long are you going to be away, what are you doing upstairs there?' My God, I'm simply stifled!"

Georgine glanced at her daughter, but Barby had retired into a world of her own, and was eating absently with her eyes fixed on the window. She looked again at Mary Helen, and remarked as gently as possible, "If there was ever a time when jobs in big places were easy to get, this is it. But I suppose you feel you must stay here?"

"Jobs doing what? Welding? I haven't the physical strength. Being a stenographer in San Francisco? I wouldn't know a soul there, and it's expensive to live in a city. I couldn't save as much as I do here. You know, I wouldn't take any alimony from John Crane, not a *cent*." She widened her eyes appealingly, well aware that this was to her credit.

"What's your job now?" Todd asked. He was giving her his usual close attention. His manner had a subtle effect on most women, making them feel not only attractive but supremely important.

"Oh, I'm taking a man's place, all right; most of the agents are in the service. It's a realty office, in the county seat. I show farm lands to clients, most of the time. We can get gas for that, still; I drive 'em around morning, noon and night."

"Keeps you pretty busy, does it?"

"Oh, yes. Values have gone up sky-high around here, and lots of the ranchers are selling out to get into war work, and the ones who've tried it already want to go back to the land." She giggled, adding, "You might say we do a land-office business."

Todd chuckled appreciatively, without taking his eyes from hers. He began on his green-apple pie, seeming not to pay attention to what he was eating, but actually savoring every bite.

He was wondering, not for the first time, what there was about studying the background of a murder that sharpened all one's senses. At this moment he was acutely aware of every detail in his surroundings: the flavor of the pie, the light clink of forks against china, the rim of lipstick on Mary Helen's water glass, the scent of soap and ironing from Barby's clean dress. He could see the suppressed amusement in Georgine's eyes, as she looked with such seeming gravity from him to the other women. Once more he regarded with pleasure the lovely shape of her head, ringed with short brown curls, and the spirit and humor in her face; but there would be time later, lots of time, in which to contemplate these and other of her qualities.

At the moment he must concern himself with what he had just heard. He told himself sardonically, Who d'you think you're kidding? There's more in your mind than getting the background for a story. You'd like to know the truth, and you're not equipped to get it...What was it the nymph had said, that had rung a bell?...How long are you going to be away, what are you doing upstairs there...I drive them around, morning, noon and night...The little emphases, the affections that now and then fell away from Mary Helen's manner as if she had assumed an accent and forgotten to keep it up...Her manner, in Mrs. Peabody's own home, of barely tolerating any claims but her own...

This may be more interesting than I expected, McKinnon thought. She's changed things. She came home because she heard we were here; the surprise, this morning, was just a bit overdone. She really hates this town. Wonder how far she'd go, how much she'd do, to get out of it—and go well-heeled, so she'd be comfortable, so she could feel as important as she does here and still have wider scope for her talents?

Mary Helen took him, as befitted the serious tone of their talk, into the seldom-used parlor across the hall from the sitting room. His extra awareness took it in, too: the old square piano that looked as if it hadn't been touched for twenty years, the plush album on the marble-topped center table, and another of those bewildering incongruities in the shape of the handsomest carpet he could remember seeing outside a museum. "That's been in here since the house was built," said Mary Helen, seeing his eyes on its dim scrolls of fawn and blue. "Seems as if some of these old things *never* wear out!"

She flung open one of the windows in the bay, and pushed back the outer shutters to let the sun pour in. The alcove became a cave of brilliance that reflected through the whole room. Todd looked at Mary Helen Crane with sudden attention. Was it because he'd seen her only in comparative dimness before, and the clear light changed the angles of her face, or was it that her expression was different?

The very tone of her voice was deeper. It startled him. She said with cool directness, "You don't want to know about Dyke and me, do you? At least, not yet. I needn't tell you it hasn't gone that far, on my side anyway."

She waited; possibly she was hoping, Todd thought with some compunction, that he'd clarify Dyke's non-existent feelings for her.

"We're not talking under a misapprehension, are we?" he said levelly.

"Not at all," said Mary Helen. She closed her lips, and now her face was all shrewdness and decision.

"I should never inquire into your family's past for reasons of my own. It would be more than presumptuous," said Todd, and gave each oracular word its full weight. "You should know that your aunt—that Mrs. Peabody has been very kind and hospitable. She's helping me with some work I have in mind. As a sort of return favor, she's asked me to let her know"—he took out his cigarettes and offered them to Mary Helen, with deliberation—"just why it is that anyone should suspect her husband of murder."

Her hand paused halfway toward the package; her lips unclosed in stupefaction. "My God," said Mary Helen in a whisper. "She didn't—she told you *that*?"

"Why not?"

"Oh—nothing." The arrested motion flowed on smoothly now, and she held the cigarette to his match. Then she got up and went to the double doors, opening them a crack and looking guardedly out, then closing them tightly. "Nothing, except that it seems like, well, giving herself unnecessary pain."

"I've thought of that. I shall try to temper it—if I find out anything at all, which I doubt, since I'm no kind of investigator at all; I just like talking to people," said Todd, with the innocence of perfect truth.

"Well, you've a right to know, yourself," she said. The light eyes watched him steadily. "No, it's not presumptuous. You see, I'm being as open about it as I *can* be, considering I don't know a thing about the business at first hand. It might be a roaring scandal, it might not; I just know that—" She broke off and looked down, idly tracing the lovely design of the carpet with the point of a toeless sandal. "I *want* you to know everything there is."

"You don't know at first hand? You weren't here the day your great-aunt died?"

"Only late in the afternoon." She raised her eyes again. "You know that Grandfather wasn't out of danger yet, that they'd thought he was dying a few days before? Well, it suddenly struck me that—*in case*, you know—I hadn't a single thing in the way of a black sheer; and so," she said defiantly, "I drove into Sacramento to buy a dress to mourn in, if it so happened I'd need it!"

"And, as it happened, you did," Todd said, faintly smiling. "Did you get one?"

"You're rather sweet, you know," said Mary Helen irrelevantly, regarding him. "You don't think I'm disgusting, do you? No, I didn't get it. The stores were all sold out, even the first week in June, and I was having the only day off from being John's unpaid office girl that I'd had in *weeks*, and it was wasted! And then I drove home hoping for a rest and a long cold drink, and got the message about Aunt Adeline. But that isn't important, I know it, of course. What I want to make clear to you is, that Gilbert Peabody isn't any *very* close connection of mine. He and my mother and Horace's father were all first cousins, but by the time it gets down to this generation, that isn't so much of a relationship. And anyway, Gilbert got most of his character from his father. Aunt Adeline simply *adored* old Peabody, when they were both younger, but I never could see that he was worth anything at all."

"But just what was Gilbert's character?" Todd murmured.

The light eyes dilated. "Nobody told you about him? Oh, you should have seen him to appreciate it. Big, gawky, Lincoln type, patient as a plowhorse—up to a point. Why, didn't Nell say how long they'd been engaged? I can just see them, plodding along all those years wishing they could get married but never daring to throw their responsibilities overboard and *do* it! You know, her old father was a terrible tyrant, and all the years she was nursing him he wouldn't let her or Gilbert mention marriage, and they *accepted* that! And Gilbert went— plowhorsing along, taking care of a sister of his," said Mary Helen rather hurriedly, and turning away to stub out the cigarette. "Just like New England, really it was, did you ever read any of that Freeman woman's stories? People used to dawdle around for years, waiting to get married."

But you'd never be like that, Todd thought. You'd get your own way somehow, sister. He continued to meet her eyes, sympathetically. His expression did not change in the slightest.

"Well, you—I started to say you couldn't blame him and Nell for getting fed up, finally, but you'd hardly want them to go *that* far! They must have realized, after all the other obstacles had—been got over, that Aunt Adeline might live for years more." Mary Helen's voice dropped; she leaned forward in her chair. "They had to have this house, of course. It meant everything to them, a roof over their heads in the first place, but *position* more than anything; they couldn't be thought of as penniless nobodies while they owned the old Tillsit house. And so—" She took a long breath and shook her head. "I've tried to tell myself it was out of character for Gilbert, but it wasn't."

"That's bothered me considerably, too," Todd said as if to himself.

"Don't you know that it's just the patient people that break out, once in a long while, with something that just *horrifies* you? They don't calculate on it, they just endure for *years* and suddenly they find their endurance has snapped. I think it was the same way after he'd—after Aunt Adeline died. Enlisting! Gilbert Peabody! Why, nothing on earth was farther from his normal ideas. He simply broke under pressure and did something *drastic*."

Under the candid round brow, Mary Helen's eyes were lit with intensity. After a moment of silence, she went on, "That isn't like the rest of the family. We may not be patient, but we don't burst out impulsively, either."

"My dear child," said Todd, paternally, "surely you don't think I'm worried about that? Your having murderer's blood in your veins, to put it dramatically?"

"No," she said, giving him a sidelong look, "and it's not what I'm worried about, either. That's not why I told you all this, exactly. It's—" She paused, and bit her lip thoughtfully. "It's about—about Nella, and your staying here with her, and—" Her voice dropped until it was almost inaudible.

"Todd!" said a clear voice from the lawn, below the open window. "Todd, dear! Were we going to call on the Rector this afternoon?"

McKinnon, leaning out and looking down, was about to signal to Georgine when he found that Mary Helen was close beside him. He made a desperate effort to grimace with that side of his face which she couldn't see; damn it, he thought despairingly, why did I ever have to cultivate this deadpan? But I've got to tell Georgine somehow that this is too interesting to leave, that I'm sorry to let her down, but I can't quit at this moment!

Georgine, standing on the lawn with her face tipped up toward him, looked with amazement at the attempted message-sending. Todd desisted, grimly. Not my line, he thought. "Did we make an appointment?" he asked, as if seriously trying to recall.

"Oh, Mrs. Wyeth!" said Mary Helen, beside him. "*Don't* drag him away, we're just having the most *interesting* talk, I'm sure you won't mind letting us have just a little more time!"

Georgine looked at Todd again; he risked a wink, on the side away from his companion. "I shouldn't think of dragging him away, Mrs. Crane," she said crisply. "Of course some other time will do quite as well."

For a moment her eyes had burned vividly blue. Todd, turning away, repressed an inclination to mop his forehead. She's mad as hell, he thought, and I don't blame her. He knew Georgine too well to imagine that she was jealous, but he'd asked her to rescue him and then put her in the position of someone interfering. There'd be some squaring to do, after he got through here.

But in the meantime, here was this woman, displaying unexpected subtleties every time she spoke; being more nearly herself, now that she was alone with him and no longer had to compete for the center of the stage; and, with every regretful word she said, adding another fact to the case against Gilbert Peabody. For all I know, he thought, she may be entirely sincere at this moment. And there was no way to tell, for sure. If she were not—how should one interpret *that*?

To a policeman or a lawyer, it might have been maddening. Todd, being a fiction writer, was merely enthralled.

"I'm sorry about that," said Mary Helen, just above a whisper. "But I have to finish telling you now. I—I don't know exactly how to say it. If I'd—known you were coming here I'd have been glad to have you pay a call, but I'd never have encouraged your staying for more than one night; never. I don't care how inhospitable that sounds."

She moved close to him on the long, thinly upholstered settee, and its plush cover gave off a faint wave of mustiness, mingling oddly with Mary Helen's flower cologne. "It's all right for me," she said, barely moving her lips. "Horace doesn't mind either, he's used to it, and we're family, and Grandfather insisted on our being here. It's—oh, damn it. You like Nella, don't you?"

"Very much. And she's had a good deal to take." Todd's hands were in his pockets, and the right one fingered like a talisman the nickeled surface of his mouth organ. Something coming...

"Yes. Too much, I'm afraid—all her life. It's just wonderful"—the short upper lip curved in an anxious smile—"how she manages to seem so sweet and calm through it all. But—you see, we've known her all our lives, and we—understand what it means. We're prepared to take care of ourselves."

Todd stayed motionless. He allowed a look of slow comprehension to spread over his face. "My dear Mrs. Crane," he said softly. "You don't mean to imply—"

"Oh, nothing, nothing! Maybe I've said more than I should." Mary Helen got up hastily and moved toward the door. "That's all I wanted to tell you," she said, flashed an appealing smile over her shoulder, and with an air of great decision pulled apart the double doors and went out.

Todd McKinnon stayed on his feet, looking after her. In a moment he began to shake with soundless chuckles. I should have applauded, he told himself.

Almost automatically the mouth organ came out of his pocket and he blew a few thoughtful chords into it. Have to have a little jam session, he reflected; what should I play? "Get Out of Town"?

Georgine Wyeth had indeed been "as mad as hell" for the few minutes after she turned away from the window. Rescue him, that great galoot? Save him from the "infernal little prancing nymph?" A fat lot of rescuing Todd McKinnon would ever need!

She went briskly across the street to the Bacon lot, where Virdette, seated upon the cement wall, was plying the yo-yo with her customary nonchalance and telling Barby the story of Secret Agent X-9, with remarkable fidelity to detail. Both small girls seemed perfectly content.

They didn't need her, either. Georgine left them and turned down the street toward the center of the village. She swung along at a fast clip, her temper giving off almost palpable sparks. A gangling youth was coming toward her on the sidewalk, and Georgine swerved to the right, walking faster than ever so that the spring breeze flattened the silk jersey of her dress against her. The youth gave vent to a loud appreciative whistle, and for a minute she thought some glamorous babe must be behind her; but there was nobody. She turned into the drugstore with an abrupt flick of skirts.

Might as well patronize the family's business enterprises; the gold letters on the window read "Burnham-Tillsit." Georgine paused a moment at the door, her bad temper forgotten in a nostalgic delight. On either side was a glass globe filled with colored water, one green, one purple; in this age as rare a sight as a cigar-store Indian. The interior of the shop was "period" too; no soda fountain, no toys or flashlights or magazines; it was that almost forgotten establishment, a real pharmacy.

A dark-haired young man in a white coat was at a wall telephone in the rear, and she waited for his conversation to finish, looking about in pleasure. The store was a long narrow cavern, rather dim, lighted only from the front windows and through a frosted glass partition at the back, with a couple of clear peepholes in it. On her left, an old-fashioned slant-front case displayed dignified bottles of toilet water—yes, there was actually some White Rose!—and a few lipsticks. Too bad that they'd had to make this concession to the age. Behind it rose dark shelves full of bottles and jars. She moved closer to have a good look and, to her incredulous joy, saw (though they were pushed into an inconspicuous corner) bottles of Peruna, and Golden Tonics invented by long-dead "doctors." "Secret remedies of the Kickapoo tribe," Georgine said under her breath.

She turned slowly to look behind the old mahogany counter on her right, and met her own gaze in a mirror. It gave her a slight shock. Dear me, Georgine thought, I'm really looking very healthy this spring; I've gained a little weight; must be love.

Love, she thought, and began to spark with fury again; but this time there was laughter mixed with it.

The dark young man finished his telephoning, with a promise to bring something or other over just the minute Horace got in, yes, Ma'am; and slammed up the receiver. He kept glancing at the telephone as he waited on her, and was so distrait as to get down the wrong brand of toothpaste twice before he hit on the correct one.

In the midst of the wrapping process the telephone rang, one long burr and two short ones, and the young man was at it before the third ring was finished. "Yes!" he shouted. "Who? Mrs. Thorpe? No, Ma'am, you didn't leave any handbag here. Why, you haven't been in here for two days, Mrs. Thorpe. No, you haven't. *Oh.* No, this isn't the Red Cross Shop, this is Burnham and Tillsit's, and this is Martin Kinter talking. Sorry...Thanks, Mrs. Thorpe, but there's no news yet, they took her to the hospital at nine this morning, and I—Yeah, I *know* it's always slow the first time, everybody says so. Sure, I'll get Mom to call you."

He hung up again and came forward wiping his brow with his sleeve. "Party lines," he said, looking at Georgine without seeing her. "We've been hitched up on the same one as the building in back of us for years, and I'm always thinking it's a call for us, specially when I'm waiting for one—now is this right, or was it some other brand you wanted?"

Georgine said it was, smiling sympathetically. She could identify the young man; Virdette Bacon's brother-in-law, the one who was expecting twins any time this week.

The door from the prescription room was flung open, and Horace Tillsit came in briskly. He was buttoning a white coat of his own; though so much more fully clothed than when she'd seen him in the hall, he was at once recognizable. "Any news, Mart?" he said, grinning. "Not yet? Oh, well, it's always slow the first—don't hit me! Go on, get out of here and stay at the hospital. Go on, you don't need a hat."

As he talked, he had been pushing Martin Kinter toward the door. The prospective father wobbled blindly out. Horace turned around, met Georgine's eyes, and burst into laughter. He had Mary Helen's gray eyes behind spectacles which magnified them to a startling size, and the blond hair which had been boyishly tousled when Georgine first saw him was now sleeked back with water. There was a notable confidence about him.

His gaze took Georgine in frankly, and seemed approving nearly to the point of boldness. "Excuse the flurry," he said with another smile; this one was more accustomed, heartily professional. "We've been having a sort of crisis here." He spoke rapidly, and the breathy softness of his voice made Georgine wish, half irritably, that he'd put some tone into it.

"I know about it," she murmured, picking up her parcel.

"Expect you do," said Horace Tillsit. "That is, if you are the lady in the hall—Nell's guest?—There aren't many secrets in this town."

She turned to go, and he took a step toward her. "Do wait, Mrs. Wyeth. Did Martin manage to wait on you properly?"

"Oh, yes indeed." She turned back irresolutely.

"Well—could I say for myself that I'm sorry not to've been home for the past few days? You can see why. Here Nell has visitors—one of the most charming guests she's ever had, if I may say so—and the only introduction I get is kind of an embarrassing one in the upstairs hall. Well, is that fair?"

"We did rather wonder where our—fellow-lodger was, all this time." Georgine thought, He saw me only that once, for about two seconds. How'd he recognize me so easily? Strangers can't be as scarce as all that, in this town.

"Working," Horace said. "Keeping store, anyway. We have our business in spells, there'll be a dull spot and then a crowd—but somebody's got to be here!" He had maneuvered her toward a high-legged chair and she sat down, inwardly amused. Anything for company in one of these dull spots, she thought.

"I don't want to keep you from your work," she said demurely.

Horace laughed heartily for answer.

"The shop fascinates me, I must say. It's in perfect keeping with the rest of Valleyville, and I'm enchanted with your town."

"Nice little place, isn't it?" He leaned against the counter, looking at her with evident pleasure. "The town, I mean. I'd like to modernize the drugstore some, though; it's a bit too much in keeping!"

"Don't ever give away those colored globes."

Young Mr. Tillsit made a face of mild disgust at the colored globes. "I sure won't while old man Burnham's alive. He controls the stock, and sets the tone...Me selling Peruna, I ask you. The college would have refused me a diploma if it'd known I'd come to this, but we've got plenty of back-country customers—"

The telephone rang, and he waited for it to finish; one long, two shorts and a long. There was a prescription order coming from the other end, Georgine gathered; she sat in a sort of dreamy inertia, looking out from this dim cavern into the empty Sunday brightness of the village. Might as well be here, talking to Horace, as anywhere else...Easy, on these party lines, to mistake someone else's call for your own. The one Martin Kinter had taken was for the Red Cross Shop, that used to be Gilbert Peabody's studio.

Something rubbing along her ankle startled her, and she looked down to find a large haughty tomcat stalking from behind the counter. It crossed the floor with a majestic gait, gave a tremendous leap that carried it to the top of the cosmetic counter, and in one more sinuous movement reached the broad edge of a shelf. Georgine watched it, holding her breath. All those jars and bottles...

But the tomcat stepped along surely, its furry sides barely brushing the glass, it got to a spot mysteriously chosen by itself for resting, settled down in a compact bundle of striped fur, and fixed her with a yellow glance.

"Oh, hell. Get down, Rummy," said Horace ineffectually, turning away from the telephone. "That damn' cat's another of the old gentleman's ideas, if we ever kicked it out he'd raise the roof. Oh, well, he won't live forever," said Horace easily, once more taking up his perch against the counter, "Burnham, I mean—and I can buy out his share from the family. Meantime, I guess a few cats and bottles of patent junk won't kill me."

"You're very patient."

"Got to be around here. Nothing moves very fast. Well; so I hear you're onto our family scandals."

Georgine looked up quickly. Horace gave her his bright smile. "Sure," he said. "Old Susie Labaré doesn't buy many drugs, but she was in here last night to stock up—and accidentally on purpose mentioned it. Why, don't look like that, d'you suppose I mind? I can see how you'd want to know something about the family your nephew might be joining."

"I haven't a nephew. And that isn't really the reason. You can't think how embarrassing it is, Mr. Tillsit, to feel as if you're getting people to talk on—on false pretenses. Not that Todd's been in the least untruthful about it, they just seem to open up for him, but—"

"Well, why not?" said Horace reasonably. "No use pretending it didn't happen, you've got to face facts. It was damned interesting; and poor old Gilbert's made up for his—his slip, would you call it? Kind of the way that knights of old used to go on pious pilgrimages after they'd sinned."

"That's one way of looking at it," Georgine said, still uncomfortably.

"So why should we get mad if this brother, or cousin, or whatever he is of yours, gets the details?"

"Todd, you mean? He's my fiancé."

There was a moment's silence. Horace almost gaped at her before he said, "You mean that thin, deadpan guy—you mean you're going to marry him?"

"And why not?" said Georgine, her eyes snapping. She kept forgetting that to many people, on first sight, Todd appeared negligible.

"Well—I beg your pardon. Just kind of a surprise, that was all. I couldn't make out what you see in—oh, Lord. It's none of my business, I'm sure he's a great guy, it's only that I'd thought for *you*—oh gosh, will you forget I said it?"

Georgine took pity on his flounderings, and said she would. He looked pathetically large-eyed, peering through the spectacles.

"Don't hold it against me," Horace said. "And don't let him hold it against the family, either, that one of us shuffled off a bit faster than Nature intended."

He actually wanted to talk about his great-aunt's murder; he had brought the conversation back to it, himself. She looked at him in wonder.

"Look here, Mr. Tillsit, what I can't see is why everyone's so sure Miss Adeline didn't die naturally! And if there was a doubt, which there seemed to be, why it wasn't all hushed up and forgotten."

"Couldn't be," said Horace, sitting down again and fiddling with a jar of ointment. "Thanks to Johnny Crane and Grandfather's housemaid that heard the remarks about the autopsy, it got all over town. It's just the fact that it was never proved, couldn't be proved; don't you see? It's the mystery that gets us all."

"But it's all so vague! Nella said everyone suspected there was poison, but—what poison?"

"Easy." Horace flashed his smile, indulgently. "One of the barbiturates, I thought; something to simulate coma, until she was too far gone to be revived. Luminal, I make it. No obvious signs, so that it left a loophole for the doctor's certificate—oh, he was perfectly justified in signing that, since there was a doubt and the next of kin wouldn't allow a p.m., but—we all had our ideas."

"You certainly did," said Georgine, fascinated. "But, for heaven's sake, if someone was supposed to have given her a lethal dose, why are you all so sure it was Gilbert?"

Horace shook his head. He said reluctantly, "Of course you know he was there that morning."

"What's that got to do with it?"

"Well—there's this about a drug of that sort, it needn't be administered in, uh, the presence of the person who gave it to the vic—to the patient."

"You mean you think he left her a bottle of poison and said, take this at two-thirty sharp?" Georgine gave him an incredulous look.

"Maybe—not just like that. Susie was around most of the time, she might have seen Aunt Adeline taking something, and wondered if it had been prescribed—but Susie left her alone for two hours or so every afternoon. And," said Horace, picking up the jar of ointment and tossing it from one hand to another, his eyes carefully upon it, "her diet was watched, too, but Susie couldn't keep her eye on everything the old lady ate."

What was it Virdette had said, about things being smuggled in to Miss Adeline? "We kids used to get some of it—"

"That business with the candy never did come to anything," Horace lifted his eyes to hers again, "but it—rather put ideas in my head."

"Candy?"

"Funny thing." He laughed softly. "I've never been able to get up much of an appetite for Nella's almond paste since, and she complained once that Gilbert had lost his taste for it too. I say funny, because there wasn't a thing wrong with the piece we found. Johnny Crane asked me to analyze it for him... I've often wondered if anyone else saw me pick it up from behind the mattress, on the frame of the bed."

"Dear me," said Georgine. "Let me get this straight. Nella Peabody used to make almond paste, and you think Gilbert smuggled some of it in to Miss Tillsit in the morning?"

(" 'You get it?' she says, and he nods." That was Susie's tale.)

"Uh-huh. She used to put the stuff on sale at that restaurant up on the main highway. Damn' good it was, too, not too sweet—only, that hint of bitterness," said Horace, frowning slightly, "would have covered the taste of luminal pretty well. Aunt Adeline liked it. Anyway, there was this piece, half-eaten. The fact that there wasn't a trace of luminal in it needn't have meant that—well, there could have been other pieces in the batch."

"Great heavens, surely nobody thought Nella fixed it up for her—or for Gilbert to take to her?"

"Oh, no, no. But what's to prevent its being tampered with?" He smiled at her cheerfully. "You see I've thought this over plenty, since. If you have an analytical mind, which is what every pharmacist has to have more or less, you can't help figuring on the chances. A possible medium of poison right there, at her deathbed—even if it didn't prove much one way or the other—can't be ignored. Can it, now?"

"Inconclusive, you said. I think that's the word, and it makes me wonder why your mind, or anyone's, should have leapt to *Gilbert*. I still can't see that, or imagine him going on for years, seemingly fond of his aunt, and then suddenly acting like—well, not really like the Young Monk of Siberia, because this was more underhand, but breaking all at once and committing a crime."

"I wonder if it seemed like a crime to him," said Horace, once more juggling with the small porcelain pot. "I wonder. Times, you can convince yourself that if a thing's expedient, and you have the materials at hand...You see—there was Serena."

"*Serena?*" Georgine gazed at him bewildered.

"Yes," said Horace gently. "She's news to you? You haven't heard of—Serena?"

The dim cavern of the shop seemed to have gone very still. Georgine felt a faint, unaccountable chill. There wasn't anything in Horace's words, hardly anything in his tone, to disturb her; only that short hesitation before speaking a name.

"Who's she?" she asked after a moment. Her lower lip folded over the upper, and her brows drew together.

"Who was she, you mean. I—I guess it's not my place to say anything about that. There may not have been anything in it, and if ever a thing could have been condoned—no, you'd better ask someone else."

"Ask whom? Nella?"

"That's an idea." Horace smiled at her again. "You've been getting just bare facts from her, haven't you? That's all she'll give you on this; and that might be as well, then anything you may think would be all in your own mind. Anyone else might— color it for you, and—as I said—nobody could be sure—"

Behind the frosted glass partition a door opened and shut briskly, and someone came hurriedly across the prescription room. "That can't be the proud father already?" Horace began, swinging himself off the counter.

"Horace!" said Susan Labaré, whisking with amazing speed into the front of the shop, " 'Bout an hour ago I had a phone call from the J—*Oh*. Beg pardon. Didn't see you had a customer—it's Mis' Wyeth, ain't it?"

She stopped dead by the end of the mahogany counter. The cat Rummy rose from his perch on the shelf, and, with a faint clinking of the bottles behind him, launched himself into space across the showcase. Alighting with a slight thump, he stalked out with his tail in the air.

"Great God, Susie," said Horace with irritation, "I wish you'd come in the front door like a human being."

"Human enough," said Mrs. Labaré, snapping her mouth. "I'll come in any way I've a mind to." Her eyes shifted to Georgine, and back again. "Band-aids you sold me yesterday got that red stuff on 'em, and I wanted 'em plain."

"Okay, okay," Horace said, sighing. "Did you bring them back to exchange?"

"No. I—"

The front door opened and two little boys tumbled in. "You got any lickrish in, Mr. Tillsit?" The telephone began to ring. A middle-aged woman bustled in, asking if that prescription wasn't ready yet. Horace had been right; there were dull spots, and then all at once the store was a beehive. Georgine went away, seemingly unnoticed.

The little girls were still playing on the Bacon lot, but now they seemed to have set up housekeeping among the ruins. Georgine blessed Virdette for being so conveniently at hand, waved to her child, and climbed the front steps of the Tillsit house. She was thinking, *Serena*; ask someone about Serena— Nella would be as good as anyone, would she? She knew nothing but the barren facts about Serena? For a woman who'd lived in Valleyville all her life, it seemed there were many subjects on which Nella Lace was oddly ignorant.

"Georgine," said Todd's voice from the sitting room. She stopped in the hall and gave him a bright, incurious glance. "Yes, dear?" she said.

"Do come in a moment, won't you? Dear Georgine, I owe you an abject apology." He drew her in and closed the door. "Did you make anything of what I was trying to convey through the window? Unforgivable of me, asking for a rescue party and then discovering I couldn't afford to be—"

"Oh, Todd! Don't give it a second thought. I understood perfectly."

Todd uttered a loud groan. "When a woman says that, one is sunk," he observed.

"Why, not at all!" She beamed on him. "It's absolutely all right; and I've had a most instructive afternoon myself."

"Have you indeed?" Mr. McKinnon looked at her warily. "Won't you sit down and tell me about it?"

"Oh no, thanks, there's hardly time." She looked off into space. "And it might not be fair to tell you *all* the details. I'm afraid you have a rival, dear."

"I'll slit his throat," said Todd, still wary. "Who is it?"

"Horace Tillsit. He wants to know what I see in you."

She let it lie there. She swung her handbag gently to and fro by her side, and continued to smile at him with dreadful brightness. He had *something* coming for that moment at the window.

Todd leaned a shoulder against the golden-oak mantel, and seemed to be reflecting. The silence persisted; and after a moment he yielded visibly to temptation.

To Georgine's incredulous joy he said, "Well, I've often wondered myself. What *do* you?"

She looked down at the handbag. "I told him—and it's true, of course—that a widow with a child has a terrible time finding someone to support her, and if someone comes along who doesn't seem to mind... "

Todd straightened, and put his hands in his pockets. His eyes were almost colorless in their hardness, and there was not a trace of expression in his face. "So that's it," he said quietly, heavily. "Funny way to find out, isn't it? But I'd better know now than go on hoping—" He walked past her toward the door, so quickly that she felt a whiff of breeze as he passed.

Georgine's lips parted slowly, and her eyelids stretched. He couldn't have taken that seriously? Not Todd, who ought to know...She swung round, in actual panic, and began, "Todd! You don't—*Oh!*"

Mr. McKinnon had executed a neat flanking attack, and had taken her, by no means gently, in his arms. A moment later he said, with some grimness, "I hope that'll cure you of lying to infatuated young men."

She leaned back against his hands. When she got breath enough to speak, she sounded almost angry. "I didn't tell him that, he's not infatuated, and—if I'd told him the truth it would have burned his ears off—*No*, you wolf, that's plenty. Do you want Barby to turn up in church with a shotgun?"

"That's something I'd give quite a lot to see," said Todd equably, and tightened his grasp. "Dear Georgine. You don't think you can fool me with—oh, hell. Hell and damnation on that kitchen door, it would fly open just now."

"Let that be a lesson to you," said Georgine, hastily removing herself to safety. "No lovemaking in the public parlors. I must say this house wasn't designed for much privacy...Todd, there's something you ought to ask Nella. I don't know what it means, but I gathered from Horace's tone that it's part of the evidence against Gilbert Peabody. Maybe, if you ask her in just the right way, she'll—realize that she doesn't want to hear any more."

His eyebrows went up. "As sinister sounding as that?"

"So I gathered. Horace didn't want to give me the details, though he'd been simply pouring out the rest of the evidence. Isn't it queer—Todd, doesn't it strike you as unnatural that the family all talks so freely?"

Todd smiled at her. His voice went even lower than hers. "My dear, not at all. They love to make out the case against Gilbert. They want to pile it up until there's no doubt that Miss Tillsit's murderer is—now in the South Pacific."

Georgine cast one wild glance around her, as if seeing an alternate murderer in every corner.

"And for all I *know*," Todd finished, his eyes on hers, "that may be correct."

CHAPTER SIX

NELLA PEABODY WAS in the kitchen. Perhaps, Georgine thought, it was she who had overheard that brief passage with Todd, a moment since; but there was no way to be sure, for Nella might just have entered. She was in the very first stages of some cooking project, getting out eggs and gelatin from a cupboard. The cool north light fell through gingham curtains onto the yellow mixing bowls, and on Nella's face bending over them. She was humming an airy little tune, she seemed much as usual, yet Georgine wondered if there wasn't something closed and secret about her expression.

"Here," Georgine said, "please let me help a bit. I can at least whip egg whites! How do you want them, dry or only stiff?"

She stood there at the table, turning and turning the handle of the eggbeater, and listening while Todd's easy flow of words came from the corner where he was carefully keeping out of the way. "Yes, I've had pretty good luck so far, Mrs. Peabody, from my own point of view at least. Whether I've found out anything that you don't know already is another matter... Yes, I'll tell you about that in good time. You'd be surprised at the way a fiction writer's mind works, though; my best haul so far has nothing to do with this family at all, it's the plan for a story about Ed, your village policeman here..."

And then, dropped casually into the middle of an outline of this plot, the question: "By the way, several people have mentioned the name of Serena, as if I should recognize it. Who was she?"

Nella did not start, nor seem troubled, nor hesitate. She looked round at him, her face sweeter than ever in its absolute calm. "Oh, poor Serena! She taught us all what tragedy was, dying so young—the first one out of our generation to go. Why, she was Gilbert's sister. She was much younger than he, but when he got out of college they set up housekeeping together. He simply adored her, and so did John Crane. All of us did, but John was so—do you know, I've often thought that the old-fashioned phrase about the heart being buried with the beloved could really apply to the doctor; it broke him up so when Serena died that I don't believe anyone else could have made much of a success of marrying him. Of course," said Nella, delicately lifting her eyebrows, "Mary Helen didn't bring much—*thought* to her part of the marriage."

"And Gilbert's sister died. How long ago?" Todd asked.

"Oh—five years ago. Her illness was long and terribly painful, inflammatory rheumatism. Of course Gilbert gave her every care. He had doctors—John couldn't bear to attend her toward the last, he handed the case to the other doctor in town, the old one that's dead now; and Susie Labaré nursed her when things got too difficult." She stopped for a moment, counting the spoonfuls of lemon juice she was adding to her mixture, and then resumed. "Poor Serena, she was the most beautiful thing you ever saw, and it broke her heart to be so dependent on Gilbert, and know that he was going deeper and deeper into debt over her illness. And such pain! None of us can really bear to think of it, even yet, though she was kept under sedatives part of the time. It's no sin, I hope, to say that it was the most blessed relief when she died—to all of us.—Thanks, Mrs. Wyeth, those egg whites are just right now."

"Yes, that's dreadful pain," Todd said almost absently. "I knew a young girl in high school, who—tell me, how much suffering can they spare the patient? Do they let him have morphia, or—"

"I don't *believe* so," Nella said, as if she were trying to recall.

She heaped her mixture into a baked pie shell, carefully smoothing it toward the edges. "Seems to me that Serena, at least, got along with one of the milder drugs, luminal or something. Well, she's out of it now, poor lovely thing. She died quite unexpectedly, as if in her sleep. I suppose her heart just gave out suddenly."

Georgine went to wash her hands, and stood drying them for a long time, until the paper towel was a lump of wet pulp against her palms. She thought, Horace said I could draw my own conclusions. Well, I don't like any of them. A blessed relief—luminal—Gilbert adored her—he was going deeper and deeper into debt—he and Nella had been so patient, so patient for all those years, and he couldn't have left an invalid sister to fend for herself—if you can persuade yourself—he didn't think of it as a crime—

"It is a shock, always," she said banally, "when someone who's younger than you dies. Up to then, it's always been the old people; then you learn you're mortal too."

Nella nodded at her, and smiled. "That's true. And yet, in her case, how could anyone have wanted her to live? *Anyone* who loved her and saw how much she endured?"

She looked about her, swooped on a forgotten spoon and put it to soak with the rest of her cooking utensils. "Shan't we go into the sitting room? I'm through here for the present—Oh, no, I'm sorry! I have to take something over to Rose Kinter, she knew she was having twins but of course you're never really prepared with all the things you need—two of everything—"

They stood on the front porch and watched her go down the street, walking sedately under the towering elms, her slight graceful body dappled with their shade. Georgine said on a sort of gasp, "Todd, she seems so—*unconscious*! It almost frightens me to see her skirting all those implications, talking so freely about Serena Peabody's death, just smiling calmly when you asked your questions—it gave me a cold chill."

Todd said slowly, "Let's stroll up and down the walk for a few minutes. I'd like to make sure nobody can hear us."

She glanced at him and agreed. "We haven't been any too careful about that. I wish I could remember what we were saying the other night."

"Coming back from the doctor's?"

"Yes. Todd, who was that? Who'd be interested enough to follow us that way, and listen?"

He didn't make light of it again, as she'd half hoped he would. "Almost anyone," he said thoughtfully, "who wondered about our interest in Miss Adeline's death, and our visit to John Crane. It was easy enough to follow our movements in a town this size."

"Dear heaven! What *did* we say?"

"It was innocent enough, as I recall. I could wish, though," he said slowly, "that I'd discussed nothing but the weather. Whoever it was may have learned too much about the doctor's attitude. Well, never mind. Tell me again, will you, what Horace said?

"Lord, yes," he said when she had finished. "That puts the lid on. Means: a drug right at hand, maybe three or four tablets left over from the sedative his sister had taken, and the suggestion of a painless elimination already in his mind. Motive: love and gain, mixed. Opportunity: any one of three times, the visit in the morning—interesting suggestion that about the candy—or the two in the afternoon."

"Two, Todd?"

"Did you forget Virdette's story about the door that opened and shut, and Susie's report of the visitor who came a li'le after two?"

"Yes, but—I knew what you were thinking, about someone's coming along the back lane, unseen, and up the enclosed stairs; but I thought that would spoil the case against Gilbert, somehow."

"That," said Todd remotely, "could have been Gilbert too. He might have made the second visit an hour or so later to see if she'd been—affected by the drug as yet. I'll admit it's not likely, but then this poor guy seems to have behaved oddly all along. If that was someone else, Gilbert may have done the drugging when he went in at three o'clock. It needn't have taken the old lady very long to go under."

"Todd, I don't like it. I wish you'd never made that promise to Nella!" They were in front of the Tillsit house at the moment. She glanced up at its monstrous façade, and winced as if in physical pain. "I keep seeing him," she added piteously, "tall and homely, and dressed up in a Hollywood sports outfit that didn't suit him, to impress the bridal couples from the country. I see him paying those patient duty-visits to an old lady, and running her errands for her, and remembering jokes to tell when he called; and I can't bear to think that he—or must I?" She faced Todd with sudden hope. "Are all the returns in?"

"Just about." They reached the line of great maple trees and he swung her about to pace back in the other direction. "Just about, Georgine. There's a good hypothetical case against Gilbert Peabody, his potentialities of character, his actions after the fact, everything. And this about his sister makes me understand a li'le better why everyone thought of him as a possible murderer."

"Oh, dear!" said Georgine; nobody could make that mild phrase sound as fierce as she. "What proof is there that Serena didn't just plain die?"

"None at all. None for Miss Adeline, either. One or the other, or both, could have been natural. But," said Todd, his gaze directed far down the tunnel of spring green, "the whispers can go on from now till Doomsday. Nella was right. What is there for him to come back to, in this town?"

"And, just as there's no proof, there's nothing to refute? I see. It makes me so furious for her," said Georgine, her eyes blazing. "And yet, when she just smiles away all the implications of what she's asked or told, it gives me the most horrible feeling; like talking to a deaf person, trying to impress something serious on him, and having him simply nod and smile—there's a hint of lunacy about it. What are you going to tell her, Todd?"

"Nella? I don't quite know." He walked on soberly. "Can you see us cheerfully making out a case against her husband that seems to damn him up and down, and then saying thanks for her hospitality, and leaving?"

"Indeed I can't. There's only one thing to do: make out the case against Gilbert, and at the same time make one of your fiction cases against everyone else who could have been involved. You can, can't you?"

"I wondered if you'd think of that. I'll make some wild guesses, in good fiction form, and leave it there; but it'll take the edge off Gilbert."

Georgine's heart felt lighter than it had for hours. "Good enough," she said. "What's Gilbert's type?"

Todd had a theory that the behavior of every murderer during and after his crime placed him in one of seven categories; with these, and the four or five accepted motives for killing, he could make permutations and combinations until your head spun. In this case, she reflected, the one obvious motive was gain. In Gilbert's case it might be mingled with passion, but it remained the dominant reason for Miss Adeline's death.

"His type," said Todd musingly. "Well, you name it. If he was guilty, he went back to the scene of the crime; in any case, he lied about having been near his aunt, he had a nerve storm when he was seen coming away from her room. He abstracted a perfectly innocent diary which might have contained some ambiguous remarks about him, and destroyed the pages, and then buried the cover where he could be easily seen. Finally, he couldn't take it, and ran."

"Sounds to me just like that lad in *Crime and Punishment*, the one who jumped sky-high every time he saw a policeman. He always struck me as a perfect sap. I suppose that's Gilbert's category, the Damn Fool."

"That's what I make it," Todd said, his steps slowing as they neared the northern boundary of the lot. "Leave out Serena for the moment. If he did have anything to do with her death, seems to me he'd have been cooler the second time... Georgine, will you forgive me if I wander downtown again? Maybe I'll see some of my friends I met yesterday."

"Fine. I'll write my letter. But, Todd—are you going to use some of the queer things that actually did happen, in your plots? Because there's one of them that doesn't seem to me to fit Gilbert."

Todd's agate eyes were remote; he looked beyond her. "'Take that thing off your head,'" he murmured.

"That's it. It gives me the shivers, for no reason at all." Georgine gave his arm a little shake, to make him meet her eyes. "Listen to me, Todd McKinnon. You hurry back to that house; I don't want to be left there alone after dark!"

"And I'm ashamed of myself," she added half aloud, when a few minutes later she found herself alone in the southwest bedroom. "I promised myself to get over this cowardice!"

The house was still, with the somnolent quiet of a Sunday afternoon. She didn't know whether Nella had returned, nor where Mary Helen Crane might be. Horace might have been released from his extra trick at the drugstore, and even now be resting behind the door so blandly closed on that dim square hall upstairs. She didn't know. Seven doors; there were too many of them, old and dark and tortured with paneling.

"I hate them," Georgine muttered defiantly, and closed her own door. She opened a window in the bay, which kept her within sight and sound of her child, and settled down at the desk which stood beside the bed's head, on the opposite side from the night table.

"Dear Dyke," she wrote swiftly, "Barby hasn't yet stopped talking about her wonderful birthday, and I expect we'll be hearing a re-hash regularly, from now till your next furlough. Very empty to say thank you, you surely know the way to a mother's heart: make her child perfectly happy.

"Does the postmark on this letter surprise you? We stopped over at your suggestion, and to all appearances we're to be here for days yet. I don't suppose there's a chance that you could get another leave, within a week of the last one, and come down on Tuesday to see your uncle get married. Yes, that's part of the idea of our staying here. How about it? Just tell the Colonel you don't want to go out on maneuvers, and come along. Barby's to be bridesmaid, I've told her she gets to hold my bouquet, and she can hardly wait.

"But that's only part. The rest of it I *think* you know. Rather nice work, my boy; Todd got that unholy light in his eyes the minute he heard there was a mystery connected with the house, and he's hard at work. Nobody knows better than I how good it is for him. Thanks are due for that, too, though maybe we've got into this a little deeper than you intended.

"Look here, chum; there's something I want to know, and I want it right away. *How much did Mary Helen tell you?* Or did you gather some of the details when you were here over-night? It can't have been pure clairvoyance on your—"

She jerked to her feet as if she'd been stung. From across the street came a wild scream and a confusion of shouted words. Georgine rushed to the window in time to see Barby and Virdette facing each other like a pair of enraged cats, and Barby raising the flat of her trowel and giving her friend a brisk clip on the ear.

Georgine was out, down the stairs and across the street, before she had time to draw a full breath.

Ten minutes later she returned, leading her daughter by the hand. Barby's face, which had been so crimson with rage that her eyebrows and lashes had looked snow-white, was returning to its normal color, but she was still breathing hard.

"There," said Georgine, settling her in a chair. "I'll say again, darling, it was sweet of you to defend me, but under *no* provocation does one hit anyone else on the head, especially with something hard. You'll remember? All right. Now, just sit quietly and read your *Alice* that Cousin Dyke gave you."

"Toddy said we'd read it out loud, and I was goin' to save it."

"Barbara Wyeth, you sit there and hold that book. Hold it upside down if you want, I don't care, but don't let me hear a sound out of you for fifteen minutes."

Georgine looked round for her unfinished letter. It was not on the desk; perhaps the draft from open window and door had swept it away. Yes, there it was on the floor, face up, and very near the door to the hall. She stood frowning for a minute before she picked it up.

When Todd came up the walk, half an hour later, she ran down to meet him. "Something's going on," she said in a low tone. "Did you have any luck?"

His level gaze met hers. "None at all. One or two places I wasn't welcome. The others—people were affable enough, but they shut up like clams on the subject of the Tillsits."

"H'm," Georgine said. "Whispers do get around. Virdette's mother heard, from some source, that I was no better than I should be, traipsing round the country with a man I wasn't married to. The kid repeated it to Barby, though quite idly, so far as I can judge. She did say her mother hadn't believed it, but—I had quite a time explaining about chaperons and what not, and Barby had started a fistfight with her." She grinned faintly. "I wish you could have heard her shrieking, 'My mother is too better than she should be!' But it must have touched her, and—I don't like it much, Todd."

"Somebody doesn't like *us*," he said lightly. "The word's gone round. I wonder—Mary Helen gave me a sort of gypsy's warning—"

"I don't believe," said Georgine with deliberation, "that it was Mary Helen. Susie Labaré rushed over to the drugstore this afternoon to tell Horace she'd had a phone call from 'the J—.' I rather suspect your elegant spider."

"Interesting," Todd said. "Well, it won't take people very long to find out that I'm not really investigating."

"Maybe not, but"—Georgine laid a hand on his arm—"even if you stop short, right this minute, have we started something rolling that we *can't* stop?"

"There," said Mr. McKinnon with perfect calm, "you have me."

He sat down on the front steps, got out his harmonica, and whacked it on his hand preparatory to playing it.

There was no way to keep Barby out of the attic.

Here it was Monday morning, and a cool overcast day. Virdette Bacon, although bearing no malice for Barby's mayhem of the day before (she had returned it with interest before Georgine got to her), was in school. Barby, who had been overtired yesterday, should certainly devote herself to quiet pursuits this morning; and she had pleaded and clamored for the promised ransacking of old trunks.

"Why, of course," said Mrs. Peabody gently. "I'll go up with you for a while and show you what you can play with, though I don't believe there's a thing you could hurt. Don't you want to come too, Mrs. Wyeth?"

I hate it, Georgine told herself, standing at the top of the attic stairs. I hate every inch of it, and I don't know why.

She looked around her, at the big unfinished expanse of ceiling, at the dusty boards of the floor and the conglomeration of odds and ends that had risen to the top of the house like chips in a millpool. Beside her, leaning against the fretwork banister, was a crutch-handled stick. She was instantly sure that it had been Miss Adeline's, and that with it the old lady had gone tapping about the second floor during those years of illness. That unhandy imagination of hers saw the handle clasped by wrinkled old fingers, lifting the cane, setting it down precisely; but not upon the carpets downstairs; over these bare boards, when the moon fell upon them. A slow and aimless journey, round and round the attic…

Georgine shook her head violently.

"Should we open the skylight, do you think?" said Mrs. Peabody, reaching for a long hooked pole which leaned beside the cane. "I'm afraid these windows onto the balcony have warped shut, and I don't want to wrestle with them."

"No, don't bother. There's plenty of air." Georgine walked a few steps into the barren space in the middle, and looked about her more carefully.

The long uncurtained windows let in shafts of cool daylight, and the skylight, though dingier, left no dark spots in the attic. It wasn't the dusk, then, that she had to contend with. The headless dress bag still hung from its hook in the rafters, swaying a little as Barby rushed delightedly past, choosing which trunk she'd open first.

Rob every corner of the room of unknown terrors, and you'd be well on the way to being sensible. "That bed must have been Miss Adeline's," said Georgine, looking straight down the attic to its far end. Leaning against the wall, which was hardly high enough to accommodate it, was a tremendous headboard; the matching foot of the bedstead was turned upside down on the floor below, so that you saw a ten-foot expanse of walnut, so carved and medallioned and knobbed that the eye could scarcely take it in. An old mattress, looking hard as rock where it showed through gaps in its paper wrappings, was propped up alongside.

"That was Miss Adeline's," said Nella, seating herself on a rickety chair. "That's—one of the things I'd like to sell, if I hear from Gilbert that I'm to do so. It's solid walnut, and I'm told the carving is very good. The Tillsits had it shipped round the Horn from New England."

"It's beautiful, once you get over the first shock. And is that," said Georgine, gesturing with awe at another piece of furniture, "is that to be sold too?"

What would you call it, she wondered; a bureau? There was not much drawer space at the foot of this tower of mirror and carved shelves, and not many toilet articles could be set out on that small square of marble at the mirror's foot. A vanity? Scarcely, with all those side shelves, fretted and carved and pilastered, soaring to the skies. A whatnot? Too many cupboard doors, each a foot square, for that. It was probably a combination of all three, and the most stupendous piece of furniture she had ever seen.

"Yes; that's to be sold. I have to clean it out again before I show it to a dealer, though." Nella's sweet heart-shaped face was alight with interest. "My dear, you never saw such rubbish as Miss Adeline had put away in all those drawers and hidey-holes. Patent medicines, in the cupboards that would lock—"

"Patent medicines, really? Did the poor old lady think they'd help her paralysis?"

"Oh, she'd try anything! The doctor and Susie weren't supposed to know about those bottles, of course, and we never did know just how she got them; by mail, maybe. Gilbert and I broke about two dozen of them, to throw away. She'd taken quite a lot; some of them had nothing but dregs in them. And the drawers and shelves were—really, you never *saw* such a mess," Nella repeated, smiling ruefully. "Lovely old lace mixed with knitted underwear that's full of holes, and worthless papers fifty years old; of course we looked those over carefully before we burned them, but the rest of the things we left where they were until we knew just what was valuable and what wasn't."

"Are they still in there? Can I see?" Barby deserted the trunks momentarily.

"Why, if you like, dear." Nella stumbled a little as she crossed the floor, bent and picked up a long old-fashioned hatpin. "How on earth did that get out?" she said in wonder. "Last time I saw it, it was sticking in a cushion in one of the cupboards. Well, never mind."

Barby deserted the inspection of the bureau-whatnot, after a very few minutes. Lace meant nothing to her, she wanted something to dress up in. From the trunk she had already opened, an odor of mothballs stole out to mingle with the sweetish wood-and-dust smell of the attic, and strange musty scents were added as Nella Peabody opened each door and drawer.

The essence of the eighties and nineties might have been shut up in this room. Georgine gazed in wonder at a terrific toque, its every inch covered with feathers, beads and flowers, which was crushed flat in one of the cupboard-spaces. She said "beautiful," in rather a helpless tone, at a complete dresser-top set—bottles, jars, trays, mysterious containers—of cut crystal with blackened silver tops, all firmly stuck on. What on earth had all those jars contained? Some of them were still filmed with a sticky substance, inside. "What a pity that squat one is broken," she commented, "but I don't suppose an antique dealer would ever miss it from the set!"

"I don't suppose so," said Mrs. Peabody in a light, breathless tone. She fitted the faceted halves together, and looked at them thoughtfully. "I broke that, trying to get the top off. After that I didn't fiddle with the others! I've never told Gilbert about it, not that I suppose he'd be really angry, but all these things are his. They were left to him, everything in the house, and it's going to be intact when he comes back. *Intact*," she repeated fiercely; and then turned away, biting her lips.

"It's tiring for you, looking over these old things," said Georgine quickly, "and I know you're busy. We mustn't keep you up here."

"Oh, no, that's all right. Are you finding anything interesting, Barby?" Mrs. Peabody turned brightly to the young explorer.

Barby gravely exhibited a pile of clothing, hats and mantles and trailing skirts. "I'm going to try 'em all on, one after the other," she said, with a loving look at the jet and passementerie, and faded purple silks shirred into tight bunches and smelling of years and storage. "And there's trunks and trunks full, yet!"

She dived into the depths of the round-topped trunk with the Godey print pasted inside the lid. "Lookit the funny shoes, Mamma; they're pointed just like needles! And lookit, what's this?"

Georgine gave a loud scream. "Put it down, Barby! Oh, heavens, it's a dead rat! Don't touch it!"

"Why not?" Barby turned, looking puzzled; the horrid hairy object dangled from her upraised hand.

Georgine swallowed, repenting. "I don't know, dear; I have no idea what it is. Ask Mrs. Peabody—"

She glanced at Nella, and was startled at the fixed look in the gray eyes. Mrs. Peabody sat down again on a three-cornered chair of dull yellow plush, and grasped at its worn arms.

"I'd forgotten that was there," she said, wetting her lips. "I did put away a few—a few of Gilbert's things in the bottom of that trunk. It's—it's his toupee."

Georgine was attacked by a desire to laugh. Poor Nella needn't look so embarrassed! "Lots of the best people wear them," she said soothingly. "Look at Fred Astaire, and Boyer."

"Oh, I know! But—everyone laughed at Gilbert so, and he had to wear it to look well, a bald-headed artist seems so silly. He didn't need it in—in the army, of course...Why couldn't they have let him alone, here?" said Nella passionately. "Everyone, from Aunt Adeline down, making fun of him and—"

Georgine caught her breath audibly. She sank down on one of the trunks and sat gazing at Nella. The gray eyes, wide and piteous, returned her look.

Take that thing off your head. Be yourself—

That had seemed the one bit of evidence that was totally meaningless, that had nothing to do with Gilbert Peabody. And now...

Hadn't Nella remembered this, when for the first time she heard Susan repeat that cryptic sentence? Didn't she make the connection now? It wasn't possible that she had deliberately led Barby to open that trunk, and show the absurd bundle of gauze and hair to her mother—so that Georgine should know—

But that would mean that Nella had all along been convinced of her husband's guilt, and had wanted to gather the evidence against him for—for what? *Did she want to believe him guilty or innocent?*

And still Nella Peabody sat there, looking totally unconscious that she'd made a damaging statement; looking only troubled because, two years ago, her husband had been discomfited by laughter.

She must know, Georgine thought with horror; she must be sure—but then, why does she want us to investigate? And no matter which way it is, Todd and I have done nothing but collect stronger and stronger evidence against a man who's away fighting in the South Pacific; who refuses to come home so long as people suspect him...

Once more she gave her head a hard shake, to clear it. Warmth, imprisoned in the sun-baked old boards, seemed to be creeping round her until she was almost suffocated. She made her voice come out steadily, there was scarcely a pause between Nella's last remark and her answer. "That seems awfully petty, don't you think? Well, let's go down now; Barby's used to playing by herself, she'll be happy rummaging in all these trunks."

Nella got up, smiling. "She'll probably find more rubbish. As soon as my heart's better, I'm really going to come up here and give this furniture a thorough cleaning. Would you believe it, even down the cracks of the upholstered pieces, we found things that had been stuffed there or had slipped down; scissors, and coins, and cleaning tissues—even one of Susie's nurse caps, that she thought had been lost in the laundry. It's just incredible."

"You might even find a missing will," said Georgine idly, and could have bitten her tongue out the next minute; but Nella was not in the least discomposed.

"Oh, no," she said, "there's nothing like that. Gilbert and I were most careful to examine every paper."

She paused for a moment, and drew the silver identification tag above the V of her dress. Her other hand covered it protectively; then she dropped the chain and moved toward the stairs. "Have a good time, dear, and look at everything," she said to Barby, and descended.

Georgine looked after her, thoughtfully. She made one more tour of the attic, seemingly aimless, pausing to touch the enamel head of the hatpin on the bureau, going on to lift aside one of the papers that covered the old mattress. She glanced at Barby, who was strutting up and down trailing a blue satin dress, and then bent to the mattress for a closer look.

The ticking was colorless and old; the material had long ago lost its resilience. In every inch of its surface were tiny holes, as if it had been pierced by some pointed instrument.

Georgine's lip went up, unconsciously. She moved on and gazed up at the towering headboard. Solid walnut, was it? Medallions, and knobs, and a long panel in the middle with a beautiful burl pattern; h'm. Her hand stole out, as of itself, and tapped lightly, experimentally on the carving.

"Come in," said Barby in a high-society drawl.

Her mother pulled herself together. "Oh, good morning, Mrs. Diffendorfer. How charming you look today. Are you at home to callers?"

She went down to the second floor, presently. There was nothing in the attic that could hurt a child, and she herself would be right on the floor below, straightening her room and doing a bit of mending. Nevertheless, she paused from time to time and lifted her head, listening for the sounds that told her Barby was safe.

And there they came, noises of pattering, of plaster falling in a tiny shower, of boards gently creaking.

They were the same noises the rats had made.

After a time Barby started down the stairs, slowly, clattering on the bare boards. She must have on a pair of the pointed satin shoes; Georgine rose to deliver a caution, but Barby forestalled her by taking the shoes off—at least, that was the inference, for the clatter ceased and her socked feet came down much more quickly. Even under this light impact the stairs creaked alarmingly. She could hear them through the closed door. Each step seemed to have its separate note. You could follow a person's progress from top to bottom of the flight: ten steps.

Georgine sat down again, and sewed up the torn hem of her child's dress. Well, she thought defiantly, I said all along I didn't believe in ghosts. Now I know. Someone has business in the attic when the house is asleep.

It was none of her business, of course, and there was no reason why it should alarm her.

Someone rapped sharply on her closed door, and she jabbed the needle a quarter-inch into her thumb. "Who is it?" she cried out crossly.

The door opened a crack and Barby peered in. She was wearing on her head a frilled capelet of a dingy maroon shade, and carrying a small basket. "It's me, Grandmother," she replied in dramatic tones. "I've come to bring you a little cake my mother made. (You get in bed, Mamma, or it won't be right.)"

"I just made the bed, is it all right if I sit on the edge?—Oh, it's you, Little Red Ridinghood," Georgine added, changing her voice to suit the part. With sudden inspiration she made it gruff and loud. "Come in. Take that—" No, she couldn't say it! "Take your hood off, won't you? And come near so I can see you."

Todd was in on this. The handkerchief over the basket was one of his. "The better to see you with, my dear," she answered her new cue. "Give me your basket, Little Red Ridinghood!"

She lifted her head suddenly, her hand half outstretched. She had heard a door gently opened, and a quiet footfall on the hall carpet, and now someone was standing just beyond the door, keeping out of sight. "If that's the brave huntsman," Georgine called out, "hold everything until we've finished our scene."

There was a second's pause; then Horace's soft rapid voice replied, "It's only a member of the audience." He stepped into view, remarking affably, "You're miscast, Mrs. Wyeth." Then his head turned with a startled jerk.

Todd's voice came from the head of the stairs; it was casual, but nevertheless arresting. "Fancy yourself in the part, brother?"

Horace smiled, waiting until Todd appeared beside him. "I was thinking of the grandmother role," he said then, and strolled away as quietly as he had come.

Barby had set down her basket. Her face said plainly that grown people were always spoiling things. "Darling, I'm sorry we were interrupted," her mother said. "Come in, Todd, and close the door. Great heavens, if we can't even play a game without someone's eavesdropping—! Did you—get what you wanted?"

"Yes, thanks to the cricket. You're a good laboratory assistant, Barby." Barby looked puzzled but pleased. "You *can* hear from the sitting room," he went on. "Every word that you said, in that carrying voice. I daresay the old lady's was not unlike that."

"Hadn't you believed that Susie heard those words?"

"I'd hoped she didn't."

"I wish she hadn't, now. Barby, will you show Todd the funny thing you found in the trunks, that I thought was a rat?"

"I've got it on," said Barby happily, loosening the hood and producing the brown toupee.

"Well, take it *off!*" Georgine shrieked, covering her eyes. She added in a gentler tone, "It isn't sanitary to wear other people's hair-goods." She looked at Todd for a long moment. "That," she told him, "belonged to Gilbert."

His lips moved in a soundless whistle.

After a moment she added, "I suppose you have to make these experiments, but I rather wish you wouldn't. The people in this house watch everything we do. At the very best, it's going to make our position here difficult."

"And at the worst?" Todd inquired lightly.

"What I said about the thing—getting away from us. Todd, would you promise me not to ask direct questions, anymore?" She looked at him, troubled.

He gave one of his faint inscrutable smiles. "I can't quite promise, Georgine. I'll try not to. But when you come to think of it, we haven't had to ask many. The information has been forced on us, all along."

That afternoon the household had a caller.

Barby, who seemed to see everything, was the one to announce him. She was kneeling on a chair by the front door, peering in turn through yellow, red and purple panels of the colored glass which surrounded it; and she startled her mother by giving a loud shriek of joy. "Mamma, come quick, lookit the funny old man!"

Georgine saw him first through a square of bilious-green glass that made him look like something long drowned: a shapeless elderly man stumping deliberately up the walk, his crumpled felt hat set squarely on his head, his top chin tucked down into the folds of skin which had once been other chins. A car stood at the curb, but he hadn't been driving himself, because there was a woman behind the wheel. The old man came on with an unfaltering and somehow arrogant step.

Mrs. Peabody appeared from the rear of the house, and flung open the door. "Why, it's the Judge," she cried brightly.

"*That?* The Judge?" said Georgine in a shocked whisper.

"He looks awful funny through the purple one," Barby added, far too loudly. An ungentle hand was placed on her lips, and her mother removed her.

"Nell," said the Judge by way of greeting, reaching the top step, "who's at home?"

"Only myself and my guests, Uncle Theron."

Mr. Tillsit turned and nodded at the woman in the car. Her large face, heavy-browed and mustachioed, receded from the side window. "Won't Costanza come in?" Nella inquired sweetly.

"Brought you some butter and eggs," the Judge was saying to Nella. "They're out in the car, you can get 'em later. No, don't thank me. 'S my duty."

Georgine attempted to get upstairs, but the Judge saw her through the open door. "Who's that, Nell?" he said in a loud voice.

"My guest." Nella's chin went up a trifle.

The untidy gray head made a peremptory gesture. Nella came to the door. "Would you come in for a moment, Mrs. Wyeth?" she said in a remote tone; somehow it indicated that Georgine would be doing her a favor by complying. "And may I present Judge Tillsit?"

The old man sat heavily in the buttoned red plush chair. Georgine's eyebrows went up as she saw that he made no effort to rise. There was a curious expression in his eyes, the light gray ones of the Tillsit heritage, set in folds of loose skin. They met hers with a knowing and rather pleased glimmer.

She gave him a brisk nod and sat down beside Mrs. Peabody, thinking: He came here just to look us over. I wish Todd would get here and take his share!

"Mrs. Wyeth," the Judge said, pursing his mouth. "I hear you and your—friend are strangers in town."

"We are." She just saved herself from adding, "Your Majesty," in an acid tone.

"Here on business?"

"Not exactly."

"Staying long?"

"A day or so more, I think. Mrs. Peabody was so very kind as to take us in."

"Still got that bug about a tourist home, have you?" the Judge said to Nella, with a sort of horrid geniality. "I told you no good 'ud come of it. Never know what you're letting yourself in for."

"Uncle Theron! Really—"

"What do you do, pack 'em off upstairs together?" said the Judge, in a tone almost of relish.

So, that explained it: that look when they had met, disapproval and enjoyment mixed; the rumors that had gone so quickly round Valleyville.

"Yes," said Georgine pleasantly. "Where your grandchildren have their rooms. They are cousins, I understand."

The Judge got it, all right. He settled back, and the shrouded eyes went cold and appraising. "You known Nell very long?"

"Only a few days," Mrs. Peabody put in with a hint of defiance, "but she and Mr. McKinnon seem like old friends, and did from the first. I'm enjoying their company."

"Yes, h'm. Been going round seeing the town, I hear, making some acquaintances."

"That's quite correct, Judge Tillsit."

Nella caught a quick breath. "Uncle Theron, I don't believe you realize how you sound. Mrs. Wyeth is my guest, you know."

"Guest in m'sister's house," the Judge said. "It's all in the family. And seeing as it is, I don't know that this young woman and her friend have got any call to listen to tales *about* the family."

Georgine thought, at least he comes to the point; there's no doubt of what he means. Why, he's crude; he's so used to laying down the law that he doesn't even bother to be subtle.

"Uncle Theron," Nella was saying with considerable dignity, "you don't know how much Mrs. Wyeth and Mr. McKinnon have done for me, just by being here. They're—they're something I haven't had for a long time, friends that I made myself, independently, who hadn't grown up in this town and so weren't prejudiced about—anything." The stain of pink spread in her cheeks. "You know every thing that goes on, you must have been aware of what wicked rumors were going around, but you'd never talk to me about them; you'd never let anyone else give me the satisfaction of an honest discussion, so that I could fight—so that I could find out who started—"

"Nell, you're a damn fool woman, and always were," said the Judge loudly and with dreadful deliberation. He swung his fat body around in the red plush armchair. "You're talking nonsense; you got some bee in your bonnet a couple years ago, and if anyone's keeping scandal alive it's you. I'm sorry for you, you got yourself saddled with a worthless—don't interrupt me!—with Gilbert Peabody that's hardly worth the name of my sister's son, but I've stood by him in spite of everything because we've got the same blood. I've been sorry enough for you to keep you in food since he left you, and this is how you repay me." He ended with a fine bellowing flourish, glaring her down.

Nella put out a hand to Georgine, who was trying to rise and leave the room; she took a brief look at her as if to gain courage. "I think you're repaid, Judge Tillsit," Nella said, "or the family is. You've put your grandchildren in here to live, almost free, and treat me as if they were doing a favor to a poor relation. You keep speaking of this as your sister's house, but it's not hers any more, nor yet yours. This is my husband's house, and I'm its mistress, and if you persist in making scenes in front of my guests, I'll—I'll have to ask you to leave."

The old man drew in his breath with a rattling gasp; the flabby hands clawed at the chair arms, and then went up to tear at his collar. His eyes rolled up in his head; the shapeless body slumped in a heap.

Nella Peabody got to her feet, shaking, her words tumbling over each other. "Oh, heavens, one of his attacks...I don't care, I never dared say that much to him before, but he had it coming!...I don't know what to do—maybe Costanza would, I'll call her—get water—aromatic spirits—"

"Take it easy," said Georgine quickly. She was afraid Nella herself might faint. "I'll get the ammonia, I saw some in the upstairs cabinet."

She glanced out the window, on her way to the stairs. There was Todd, just coming up the walk; she had the impression that he had been talking to the Latin woman in the car. He was swerving toward the side of the house.

In answer to Mrs. Peabody's call, the big woman got out from behind the wheel and came up the walk. There was a flurry of medication and spilled glasses of water, and running up and down stairs; the three women hovered over the limp bag of flesh in the Victorian sitting room.

"Now he's okay," said Costanza, in a soprano voice that, coming from her bulk, fairly made one jump. "You leave 'im to me. Hey, papa, come home; you all right now. Sure, you walk down them steps easy." The Judge, with one more baleful glare around him, allowed his handmaid to support him as far as the car. He tumbled in heavily, and Costanza got in the other side and drove off with great calm.

Mrs. Peabody and Georgine fell into chairs and looked, at each other. "That was a—a nice little afternoon call," Nella quavered, almost laughing. "My dear, will you forgive me for letting you in for that? But it's so much more—you know, when I have my own friends to stand by me—" She began to gasp.

Georgine poured out some more water and gave it to her. "It wasn't me he was hard on," she observed. "When he was on the bench, did he treat people this way?"

"He never was." Nella seemed glad of the distraction. "We just got into the habit of calling him the Judge, in fun, because he was in the State Legislature for one or two terms."

"Oh. That explains a lot. I thought he was rather lacking in judicial calm. And just who, or what, is Costanza?"

"His, uh, housekeeper," said Mrs. Peabody, glancing up innocently and taking a drink of water. "She's been at the farm for years, now."

Georgine opened her mouth to reply, and then changed her mind. No comment was quite adequate. She heard a movement in the hall, and cried out, "Todd, for goodness' sake where have you been? We could have used you."

"In the back yard." Todd strolled in casually, and then seemed to gather that something was amiss.

"I saw you walking round the side of the house, but it didn't dawn on me that you wouldn't come in. I kept looking for you. The Judge had a fit, right on our hands."

Todd looked interested. "The hell he did. When?"

"Just before you came up the walk."

McKinnon looked quickly from one woman to the other. He took his hands out of his pockets and sat down. "There was a reason why I didn't know you'd need help," he said softly. "You see, I came up on the porch by the dining room. You know how that mirror in the buffet reflects both these rooms? I saw the old gentleman in the mirror. He seemed to be alone—"

"That must have been while we were rushing around for remedies," Mrs. Peabody said.

"Perhaps. He was sitting up straight," said Todd in an offhand manner, "and looking around him. Then he seemed to hear someone coming, and slumped down in his chair."

Nella Peabody got to her feet in an angry movement.

"I suppose," Todd continued musingly, "that this was the sort of attack he had, when Dr. Crane suggested an autopsy on his sister?"

"It's the kind he's been having for four or five years," Nella said in a choked voice. "But that one must have been different, it *must* have been, because Johnny Crane wouldn't be fooled as—as we've been, he'd know the Judge was just trying to get his own way!"

Todd said nothing for a moment. Then, looking out the window, he remarked soberly, "Maybe he did know."

Georgine sat up, gazing at him. "But—but that was the reason Dr. Crane didn't insist on the autopsy. He was afraid of his patient's getting another attack."

"Oh, yes." He caught her eye and looked away again. "The Judge and Dr. Crane are the only two persons who insist that Miss Adeline died a natural death."

"I won't even try to think what you mean," said Nella in a whisper. Her voice was horrified, but her eyes were shining.

CHAPTER SEVEN

"TODD," GEORGINE SAID in a low voice when Nella had gone, "she does know how strong a case there is against Gilbert. Otherwise would she—grasp so eagerly at any other suggestion?"

He shook his head thoughtfully. "May be that, may be something else. Curious lot of undercurrents in this business."

"I know." Georgine repressed a shiver. "And queer things going on in this family. I think some of 'em are happening in this very house. Do you want to see something in the attic, that seemed interesting to me?"

"Certainly. I—by the way, is that door open from the dining room into the hall?" He moved silently to the archway, and nodded. "Hello there, Mrs. Crane. Did they let you out early this afternoon?"

"They did, rather," said Mary Helen's lilting voice from the staircase. Georgine wandered out, as if idly, into the hall, and saw her descending the last few steps. "You may see us around here for the next few days, Horace and me," Mary

Helen added, with a flashing smile. "When there's something to come home *for*, you know! Well, hello, *kiddie!*" This was to Barby, who had just emerged from the door to the back stairs.

"Hello," said Barby with horrid politeness, and no answering smile.

"Darling," her mother said with sudden inspiration, "did you put away the things you were playing with this morning? All the dress-up clothes?"

Barby looked into space. "Well, maybe not quite all," she said carefully.

"How many of the dresses did you leave out—lying on the floor?" Georgine knew her child, and her voice was firm.

"Well—all of 'em, I guess."

"I was afraid of that. You go up now, before supper, and put every one back in the trunks."

Barby's agonized look couldn't have been better if Todd had coached her in it. He stood beside her now, laying his hand briefly on the towhead. "If there are a lot of 'em, I might be induced to help," he murmured.

"Gee, Toddy, *could* you be induced?" Barby said, stumbling over the words in her relief.

"All right, all right, I'll come too," said Georgine. As they went up the stairs she returned Mary Helen's flashing smile, and waited until the tripping footsteps had died away in the sitting room before she muttered, "How long had she been outside, do you think, Todd?"

"No telling. You can always start coming downstairs the minute someone sees you."

Georgine made a mental resolve that when she built her own home it would have no halls and very few doors. And no attic. But she didn't mind the attic at all when Todd was with her. She thought, maybe it'll be like this with everything I'm afraid of; a hardheaded Scot at one's side, and the terrors vanish. Her determination to reduce everything about this marriage to its least sentimental value sometimes struck her as funny.

"Take a look at the mattress when you get the chance," she said almost inaudibly. She watched him taking the look, glancing round and going with unerring instinct to the bureau-whatnot, on one of whose marble-topped shelves the hatpin lay, beside the faceted crystal of the dresser set. As she folded the last beaded cape and banged down the lid of the trunk, she saw Todd's interested study of the skylight and the blue-white bulb that illuminated the garret.

"All right, Barby," said Georgine briskly. "That's a good girl. You can run down now and wash your hands before supper. And shut the door at the foot of the stairs, will you?"

Todd came close to her. "Every inch of it punctured," he said, his agate eyes narrowed. "Probably that hatpin has been jabbed into all the upholstery, too, only the plush doesn't retain the marks. H'm. Enterprising rats, these."

"That means a systematic search, doesn't it?"

He nodded. "And in secret. Soon as you told me about Susie and her delusions about the light in the attic, I wondered. Someone began the search not long after Nella moved to the downstairs bedroom, knowing that either she couldn't hear or would scarcely come up three flights, with her heart condition, to investigate. The person was careless at first, and then, after the warning about the lights, he waited until the moon on the glass alibied him."

"Sounds as if it must be one of the cousins," Georgine said, troubled.

"H'm. Perhaps." Todd looked round him again, at the harsh sprawling shadows cast by the naked bulb, at the long shadow of the dress bag that still swung gently from the last time he had brushed against it. "But the cousins aren't home every night, remember. It'd be easy enough to check on their whereabouts. Could be anyone who's at all familiar with the house, and knew about the side stairs that are enclosed all the way up—and the unlocked lower door."

"That's right," said Georgine slowly. "Nella leaves it open so the tradesmen can get in, they leave the milk and the laundry and stuff in the basement. She locks her own room door, but—isn't that queer, when she's so nervous about being alone?"

Todd said, "I doubt that she's afraid of burglars, or of the milkman." He took another turn about the room. "Horace and Mary Helen might seriously think that rats make the noises. Maybe they've never heard 'em, and are just reassuring Nella."

"Oh, dear Lord," said Georgine despairingly, sitting down on one of the trunks. "To think that on that first night I convinced myself that it *was* rats; and I heard the stairs creak…But Todd, what are they after? Do you—do you think it's something to do with Miss Tillsit's death?"

Todd grinned. "Fiction writer's mind leaps to it. Incriminating documents, somehow concealed among the old lady's effects. Can't be looked for, after her death, until the coast is clear: Gilbert away, Nella on the first floor; and then only on moonlit nights. That's a honey."

"There can't be any documents," Georgine said, frowning, "because the Peabodys went through all the papers carefully."

"Maybe the searcher doesn't know that. Anyway, they might have missed something. I can think of twenty possible hiding places in this furniture," said Todd, his eyes taking on an unholy gleam. "Think of the tapping."

"I have."

"Secret drawers, hollow places behind the medallions in that bedstead—I'd like a try at it myself."

"Don't you dare," said Georgine fiercely. "You'd get caught and knifed in the back."

"Doubtless," said Todd with one of his soundless chuckles, "just after I'd unearthed the jools or whatever, and was standing admiring my find, or reading the full confession which the murderer had written out and then carelessly left in a hollow chair leg. My detectives often do just that, turning their backs on the shadowy end of the room."

"If I thought you were as much of a fool as your chief characters," said Georgine, getting up, "I'd tell you good-by right now, McKinnon. We'd better go down."

The dinner table seemed positively festive, set for six and graced with the presence of both the Judge's grandchildren. It was, however, the scene of a curious battle of words. She could hear the sounds of play outside, Barby and Virdette making the most of the sunset hour while the adults sat over their coffee, and it seemed to her that never before had she been so distinctly two persons: a mother placidly glad that her child was safe and happy, and a stranger unwillingly drawn into an ominous conflict.

The conversation began with someone's innocent mention of "Judge" Tillsit.

"Grandfather's *livid*, I should imagine, about our discussing the late unpleasantness," said Mary Helen with a giggle. "But he *must* know that everybody's been hashing it over for four years—everybody except him, that is."

"And me," Nella murmured.

"Oh, *you*, Nell! But you must have seen—"

"I saw very clearly."

"You amaze me," Horace said, lighting a cigarette and giving her a curious look. "You really amaze me. Nobody'd ever have thought that you'd take it this way."

"You've known my attitude all along," said Nella mildly, with a slight lift of her eyebrows.

"Yeah, but do you mean to say it hasn't changed, now that you know the facts?"

Todd had not spoken for some minutes; he sat turning a spoon over and over on the shining damask of the tablecloth. Georgine saw his deep-set eyes moving, alert and inscrutable, from one speaker to another.

"Do I know all the facts?" Nella said, looking at him in smiling appeal.

"Shall we rather say—all the circumstances?" Todd replied smoothly. "I think you know about everything *I* do. No, there's one thing nobody seems to have known until this afternoon. Costanza told me."

"Costanza?" said Mary Helen, turning her large light eyes toward him in amazement. "You mean to say you got some information out of that old Mexican hag?"

"We held a conversation," said Todd, faintly smiling. "Damned if I can tell you now how it got round to the afternoon of Miss Tillsit's death; but—did any of you know that Gilbert was out at the Judge's house that afternoon, between two and three?"

"Was he?" said Mary Helen blankly. Her unclosed lips gave her a look of peculiar innocence. "What's that got to do with—anything?"

"Nothing at all, perhaps." Todd was bland, but Georgine knew what he meant. That explained Gilbert's use of the car; and it meant he couldn't have been the person who came up the side stairs.—Or could he? Susie's ideas of time must have been faulty, that afternoon. No, Virdette was a corroborating witness; but that still left the morning visit, and the second one in the afternoon.

"It seems," Todd continued, "that the Judge was a bit delirious when he went into his relapse; he kept calling for Gilbert, something about Miss Adeline's estate. Costanza took it on herself to summon Gilbert by telephone. He came out, but by then the doctor had been there and gone again, and the Judge was asleep. Gilbert sat in his car for half an hour or more, waiting to see if the old gentleman would wake up, and when he didn't, came back into town to see his aunt and keep his appointment."

Horace and Mary Helen exchanged a glance of bewilderment. There's a good understanding between them, Georgine thought suddenly; you might almost call it complicity.

"I just offer that," Todd concluded, "for what it's worth."

Horace shrugged. "I hope it means something to you," he said kindly, to Nella.

"Only that there's a piece fitted in that I hadn't seen, nor known about, before," said Mrs. Peabody. She sat with her hands clasped on the table, her eyes downcast.

"Because otherwise," Horace went on, "it's—you'll have to admit things don't look so well. Now, don't misunderstand me, Nell. You started all this, you know. We've been trying to keep it from you, for years. But since you insisted—why not face facts?" His soft voice was almost caressing. "You'd be happier."

"I have faced them. I can't see that they add up to anything damaging to my husband!"

"Oh, come, Nell. Come, *come!* I won't say anything about, uh, the past; what happened before 1940. Just take Aunt Adeline's death, and think what's the most important thing about that mystery."

"What is it, Horace?" said Nella meekly.

"Motive."

"Yes? Go on."

"Oh, don't," said Mary Helen anxiously. "You'd be so much better off to forget the whole thing, Nell."

"Really? I'd like to hear what Horace has to say, first."

"You might as well," said Horace, sighing. "Who'd benefit; that's always the first thing they ask in cases of this kind. You can't say *my* circumstances were changed in the slightest, when Aunt Adeline died. Oh, well, yes; slightly; I'd been paying her interest on the money she advanced for the store, but that was nothing. I knew the capital was mine no matter what happened, and it was right where I wanted it, working for me. And as for Mary Helen here, all she got was a bunch of garnets and amethysts. That's all that was left in the safe-deposit box after the old lady got through selling off the good pieces. Why, hell, she doesn't even like jewelry, except that glass and wood and pottery junk. Can you see her"—Horace gave his cousin a swift automatic smile, and she smiled back—"hastening anybody's death for that brooch with a lock of old man Peabody's hair in it? But—I hate to say this, Nell, but you keep asking for it; you and Gilbert got something you wanted, had been wanting for a long time."

Nella lifted her head courageously. "That still isn't enough," she said. Horace looked from Todd to Georgine and lifted a shoulder despairingly.

"All right," he said. "All right. Then what about the diary?"

Mary Helen stirred and smiled flashingly. "You're the one who's kept *secrets*, if it comes to that, Nell. Nobody but you and Gilbert knows what was in that diary, don't forget that!"

There was a curious little silence; under those relaxed, pleasant faces something waited with a breathless eagerness. Outside, in the last of the sunset light, the children's voices sounded in an amicable squabble.

Nella Lace Peabody let them wait for a moment. Two fingers went to the V of her dress, where the silver disk was hidden. Then she raised her head with an answering smile, the pink flags flying in her cheeks.

"Why Gilbert should have wanted to burn it is as much of a mystery to me as it is to you," she said smoothly. "He was very strong for the honor of the family, of course, just as you and your grandfather are. He may have felt that I'd been indiscreet to put down even those innocent little notes in black and white, where someone else could possibly have got hold of them."

"*What* innocent little notes?" said Mary Helen, almost peevishly. She stubbed out a cigarette half-smoked, and at once lit another one.

"Oh—let me see." The sweet eyes moved composedly from Horace to his cousin, and back again. "I mentioned your movie career, Mary Helen. We were all terribly excited when you got the bit part in that picture that Vachell made, on location, up the valley. I must confess I didn't take it very seriously at first, when you told us that he'd offered you a real screen test and a chance to work up a career, if you could go to Hollywood and—wait for the breaks; but I changed my mind later."

Again there was a brief silence. Georgine felt nervously impelled to join the conversation. "How exciting, really!" she said. "What sort of parts were you to do?"

"Oh—sort of female character parts, like Gale Sondergaard, you know," said Mary Helen, turning the bright smile on her. "We all dream of it now and then, but I don't suppose more than one out of a *thousand* ever makes it."

"You could," Nella said. "We all have great faith in you. I always thought it was tragic that your Aunt Adeline couldn't spare the money to finance you. I don't blame you for crying and storming at her. Of course it wasn't the slightest use asking the Judge, and you wouldn't take anything from John Crane though he would probably have been more than glad to help you."

All this was delivered smoothly, in a tone of gentle raillery. Mary Helen merely looked at her, and then away. "I've got my pride, after all," she said with some dignity. "Johnny thought he was doing me such a great favor in marrying me—and it was Grandfather who really pushed us into it—you think, when something like that doesn't work out, I'm going to be *paid* for my time?"

"No, dear, naturally not; but John would have been relieved to see you in Hollywood—making some kind of happiness for yourself," Nella finished her sentence after a quite perceptible pause.

Georgine thought, oh, dear heaven! She's getting back at these two for months of slights, and for what they believe about Gilbert; and she'd never be doing it if Todd and I weren't here, sort of backing her up. Just the same, she's got plenty of spirit.

"And how about you, Nella?" Horace remarked softly, coming to his cousin's rescue. "Didn't you put down any of your hopes and dreams, in your little line-a-day?"

"Plenty of them." She turned to him, and now the glint of something like deep triumph was clearly visible in her eyes. "I wasn't always as patient as I should have been, I used to wish and wish that the time would come when Gilbert and I could be married and have our own home; but I usually got over it. After all, there was always your example before me."

"My—"

"Waiting so patiently for that Mrs. Hurst down in Vallejo. I do so sympathize with you, Horace. It may be years before her children are near enough grown up so that she'll feel it's right to get her divorce."

Something besides the sunset light made Horace's neck and ears glow crimson. Half laughing, he said, "Beats me how you got hold of a story like that, Nell. Mean to say you put *that* in the diary?"

"I'm afraid so. Was it horribly indiscreet of me? But then, everyone in town has known about that for at least five years, dear. Things do get around so, and naturally people would wonder why you went down there two or three times a week and didn't get home until breakfast time. We've rather admired your faithfulness; but then you always were good at waiting until things broke just right for you." Nella's voice was all loving kindness. "As long as you're sure of getting them in the end, you can wait almost forever, isn't that so? I used to remember that, and tell myself to be patient. But, you know, it's more than likely that I shouldn't have put that down in pen and ink. Gilbert may have felt that I shouldn't. He might have wanted to—protect his family."

The air in the dining room felt sultry, as if a thunderstorm were threatening; yet the evening was a fairly cool one. Georgine felt the skin of her hands tingling uncomfortably.

"Oh, I don't see that it could have done much harm," said Horace equably. The angry flush had vanished; perhaps it was more of shock than of anger. "Sure there wasn't anything more damaging—something you or Gilbert thought about Aunt Adeline, for instance? Now that the subject has come up, I'd really like to get straight what was *in* that diary, that was— really dangerous."

"What I thought of Miss Adeline?" Nella considered, and then actually gave a brief giggle. "I did get awfully put out with her once, when I wore my new hat into her room, to show how smart I looked, and she made such fun of it that I could scarcely bear to wear it around town. And yet that was rather a pretty hat—it wasn't nearly as crazy as the one you had two or three years ago, Mary Helen—do you remember, the one she said looked like a flowerpot? You were cross, too, as I remember. I thought that was a *very* good-looking hat!"

Against her will, Georgine looked at Todd. She thought inevitably, 'Take that thing off your head.' Todd did not meet her gaze; he was sitting still and somber, only the fingers of his right hand moving the spoon, turning it an inch to the right, an inch to the left.

"How far did the diary go?" said Mary Helen, her curiosity not yet sated.

"Oh—right up to the day your aunt died, I believe. Yes, it must have done," said Nella dreamily, "because I can remember writing in it while supper was cooking that night, before I knew that she was—sinking. Just a few words about the Jessup girl's trousseau, and how I'd seen Gilbert that noon—"

There was a little stir at the back door, but the cousins ignored it. Both of them looked at Nella with peculiar intensity. "You mean *after* he'd been in to see Aunt Adeline that morning?" Mary Helen said gently. "Did you happen to note— what his manner was?"

"Why, I don't believe I did, so it must have been the same as usual. He just said he'd been on an errand to the safety deposit, and brought his aunt something she wanted."

The cousins looked at each other swiftly, again with that effect of complicity. "Something she wanted," Horace said, and smiled and shook his head.

"What're you all talkin' about?" said Susie Labaré from the kitchen door. "I come over to bring you a pie, Nell, but I declare you was all talkin' so fast you didn't hear a thing out there."

"Susie, how good of you. Would anyone have a piece of pie right now?"

"No, great God, Nell; we're all stuffed to the gills. How long have you been out there, Susie?" Horace sounded more nearly irritable than he had at any former time.

"Few minutes. Talkin' about the morning Gilbert come to see old Miss Tillsit, wasn't you?" Susie joined the party with aplomb. "I must say, Nell Lace, it's a comfort to be able to talk free in front of you, many's the time I've nearly bit my tongue out tryin' not to mention something I thought 'ud hurt your feelings. Now, here's something I've wondered about, many's the time. Was Gilbert ever hangin' round your kitchen when you made any of that almond paste o' yours? Lordy, Horace, needn't jerk your head that way. I seen you pick up that piece of candy, and you and Johnny Crane puttin' your heads together over it."

Nella looked round the table in swift bewilderment. Then she seemed to grasp the implication, and a queer light grew in her eyes. "So that's it," she remarked thoughtfully. "No, Susie. Gilbert hadn't been in my kitchen for a month. Could I ask, did you find any box or paper, or anything of the kind, in which he could have brought her candy that morning? I don't believe he did."

"Didn't find a thing," said Susie with a snap of her jaws. "Except you count that little old cardboard box, hardly bigger'n a pillbox it was, in the wastebasket. Cheap cardboard, too. Had sealin' wax on it once."

From the gathering shadows Todd spoke, with an oddly startling effect. "Was there any indication of what had been in the box?"

"Wisp or two of cotton battin'. That's all."

"You looked with interest, I'm sure," Mary Helen murmured.

The last of the light played across that candid-seeming brow of hers, across the angle of Nella's cheek; it glinted on Horace's spectacles. There was nothing, nothing you could put your finger on: only four women and two men, sitting quietly around the disorder of a dinner table, speaking in low, passionless voices, smiling often; yet Georgine Wyeth felt suddenly almost suffocated.

Murmuring something about Barby's bedtime, she got up and made her escape, calling for her daughter in a firm maternal tone. "Time for bed, darling," she said as her daughter dashed in, flushed and panting. "And do you need to wash!"

Todd caught up with them on the staircase. "This is a horror," she muttered for his ears alone. "Have they always hated each other so, or have we brought it on?"

He chuckled. "We may have given Mrs. Peabody some confidence. Feeling her oats a li'le, our Nell is."

"I don't like that, either."

He waited in the upper hall until Barby had been shooed into the bathroom and the splashing had begun. When Georgine rejoined him, "It's beautiful," he said, "to see her fetching out those motives, after she's been goaded to it. You notice how she wouldn't tell us about the cousins until she could do it to their faces? They had every chance to deny those stories, but they knew it was no use." He had the mouth organ in his hand, gently hitting it. "I've got to get to work tomorrow. There's something alluring about the lady in Vallejo, marking time until—"

"Hush, Todd!" Georgine looked round swiftly at the closed doors.

"They're all downstairs."

"I never feel sure of that! People can get around so easily in this house, I'm getting so I expect to find one of them standing there every time I open the door."

"Georgine," Todd said, with his intent look, "do you want to go home, right now?"

She glanced at his still face. Tomorrow—why, tomorrow would be their wedding day. When you got this near, a postponement even of three more days seemed like an eternity. *Two things in which he can be entirely adequate*, she thought.

"Don't let me fly off into hysteria," she said, and smiled at him. "Of course we'll wait over. After all, the box with my clothes should arrive in the morning, I don't want to pass it on the way!"

Todd took hold of her arm and shook it gently in affection. "Did you hear anything that disturbed you last night?"

"Come to think of it, I didn't. I slept right through."

"Good. I'll work in my room for a while, I think."

"With that?" Georgine inquired, gesturing at the mouth organ.

"Softly," said Todd in a meek voice. "*Very* softly."

He did not play very late, and according to promise the notes were scarcely audible, but Georgine heard them. The piece he was teaching himself was the Concerto Grosso Number 5, of Handel; she knew this only from having seen the record from which he had picked it up by ear. She considered it one of the most irritating tunes she had ever heard. There was a motif in minuet time: "Toodle-oo, *tee!* Toodle-oo, *tee!*" that went up to the same high staccato note on the end of each phrase. He had that part down pat, and now he was practicing the variations, of which there were dozens.

He has to do it, Georgine thought, lying in bed and trying to keep herself from restless tossing. I'd rather he did that than bite his nails, or pace the floor, or some of the other aids to creation. I should be glad I *can* hear it, that I know where he is, only twenty feet away across the hall...Tomorrow night he won't be playing any mouth organ...

The house was quiet at last, and still she lay wakeful, her eyes roving in the darkness.

Her mind kept hard at work, stripping the bedroom of this ordinary furniture, replacing the monstrous walnut set as it must have stood three years ago. The bed here, in the same place as hers; the monumental bureau against the inner wall, there was no room for it elsewhere. Old Miss Adeline pulling herself about with her crutch-handled stick, the other hand holding something—something that had come in a small cheap cardboard box with sealing wax on it...

She had hidden it, hidden it so that no member of the family should see it until she was ready. It was something she wanted under her hand.

Georgine felt herself in imagination limping about the room, stopping beside the bureau. There were all those shelves with the brown marble tops; would any of those slabs move, and was there a crevice below them into which a small object could be slipped? How about the countless tiny pillars and knobs, any one of which might be hollow? And how about the bed itself? Did any of those knobs unscrew, did one of the medallions move? The three-cornered chair, with its upholstery of faded gold plush, might have a dozen crevices into which something small would fit. Hidden, hidden, hidden...

Miss Adeline had lain down for her afternoon rest, and had heard a familiar tap on the door, had seen a familiar face— with something strange over its head. "Come in," she had said blithely. Come in, death.

Georgine closed her eyes resolutely. In another minute, she told herself, I'll begin to imagine that the door's opening softly; and that won't do. I'll make myself sleep. Sleep well, Todd said.—The moon wouldn't rise until late tonight, almost morning. By then she would be asleep.

But she was not.

Todd met her in the hall as she was trying to slip down early to breakfast; she thought that coffee might restore her and cure her headache before anyone noted the dark circles under her eyes.

He clicked his tongue. "You didn't sleep after all; disobeying my express orders!"

"Orders, indeed. We're not married yet, my good man."

"Did you hear something after all?" His eyes were narrow.

"You might call it that. Todd—" She drew him to the landing, where she could look both up and down for a possible listener. "We may have been wrong about anybody's going up attic by night. The—the rat noises, that mean somebody's walking around up there, and the tapping—I heard those; but *I didn't hear anyone on the stairs.*"

"So," Todd said thoughtfully. "I wish I weren't such a good sleeper, or that I'd had the sense to stay awake deliberately. Why didn't you call me, my dear?"

"Todd, don't you see? I can't go on being such a coward. That doesn't mean I'd ever go up to investigate, myself, but—I thought I'd wait until whoever it was came down, and then just open my door, naturally, as if I'd been disturbed by the noise. I hadn't heard anyone go up, but I thought I might have missed that. And then—nobody came down either."

"Sure you didn't drop off?"

"Of that," said Georgine, "I couldn't be surer."

She remembered, long afterward, her vicarious pleasure at the sight of Nella's radiant face over the breakfast table. Early as it was, the mail had come, and at last there were letters from Gilbert Peabody, four of them in a bunch. "He's well," Nella whispered to herself, "or at least he doesn't say he's not. He's alive."

Horace and Mary Helen, again unexpectedly at table, smiled at her with what seemed simple pleasure. The kitchen was full of sunshine. Georgine told herself that she had been a perfect fool. A few hours more of this and the headache of sleeplessness would have worn off, and she'd see things in their right proportions.

But somehow this didn't feel like a wedding day.

"And an answer to mine about the furniture," Nella said, becoming businesslike. "He says to sell it, just as I hoped."

"What furniture is that?" Horace inquired.

"What's in the attic. Mr. McKinnon, did you say you knew a good antique dealer in the City? Oh, I wonder if you'd write to him—or better still, telephone down. I'd like to get right at that. Ask him if he could come up at once; today."

Todd said he would. "Looks like rather a full day," he observed casually to Georgine. "You'll be busy this morning? Then I'd better get some work done and—free my mind." She nodded at him, smiling.

Horace, rising to go off to the store, said casually, "I didn't know writers had to keep their noses to the grindstone. Always seems like a sort of leisure-class job."

"I go at it fairly steadily," Todd replied with an inscrutable glance. The two men seldom had much to say to each other, they maintained a remote civility.

"Who publishes your stuff?" Horace lit a cigarette, his eyes benign through thick lenses.

"Pulpwood magazines."

"Oh. Oh, I see. No wonder your name wasn't familiar. I thought at first"—he glanced at Georgine—"that you must be somebody."

"No," said Todd, "I'm nobody." There was no expression in his face, but it conveyed the effect of amusement.

Georgine looked at Nella's pile of letters. "Was that all the mail, Mrs. Peabody? I forgot, *Nella*. Of course, I like to call you that. You know, I'm expecting a parcel."

"It'll be all until this afternoon, I'm afraid. And then—is it something you must have? Because packages always come in the morning."

Georgine's brows drew together. "Either Mrs. Dillman has failed me, or this is another example of 'There's a war on, lady.'" She sat still for a few minutes, figuring.

Todd disappeared and Horace went off to work, but Mary Helen loitered leisurely. "I'm taking a few days of my vacation now," she volunteered with an agreeable smile. "Why not, after all?"

Recalled from thought, Georgine gave young Mrs. Crane a startled look. Why not, indeed? Except that late March was a curious time for an unscheduled holiday, and Mary Helen would scarcely stay home just to entertain guests who were busy with their own concerns. Not to entertain us, she thought uneasily, but to—well, to keep an eye on us, somehow.

Todd came downstairs and started outdoors with a portable typewriter which he had managed to borrow somewhere. He was headed for the old summerhouse. Georgine followed him, hesitating over how to begin her speech.

"Something's bothering you," he said, turning to face her. "What is it, the clothes?"

"You read my face like the well-known book."

"Well, I look at it plenty. Does it matter about your package?"

"It does, rather. I—I hate to think of postponing our wedding, Todd dear, but my dress is in that box. Oh, not a white tulle number with orange blossoms, but the blue one you like." She flushed a trifle, meeting his eyes. "Informal or not, I want this to be something we can both remember as being—well, dignified and lovely. If the box doesn't get here, all I've got is year-before-last's silk jersey that I've been wearing for five days straight already. It just isn't suitable. And I'd like you to be proud of me."

His agate eyes were attentive. "We'll skip the remarks about 'I should be proud no matter what you wore.' Let's figure this. If we wait for the dress, it means a one-day postponement at most. Right? And if we go home to Berkeley for yet another dress, which is one more alternative, we take out a fresh license and wait three days more."

"Yes," she said hesitantly, all at once perceiving the dilemma. Another night deliberately spent in this house, as against the disappointing wait, the formalities all to be gone through again.

"If I'm to choose," Todd said, "I'll take the lesser evil. Is it tomorrow, then, instead of today?"

"You know," said Georgine irrelevantly, "part of why I love you is the way you understand feminine reasons for things."

His eyes glinted with sudden laughter. "That'll do until something better turns up. Dear Georgine, you have every right to arrange your own wedding. I'm going to work; the disappointed bridegroom will now sublimate his passions."

She turned back toward the house. She thought, now what have I done? I didn't think far enough ahead. But I *can't* be married in this awful rag.

She would have to spend another night in the Tillsit house.

I talked myself right into this, she thought. Oh, well, the night isn't here yet, and the postman might have a change of heart.

And the morning went on. It was so ordinary: helping with the dishes, straightening her room, washing and ironing Barby's extra dress; Barby in the attic, whose resources she had barely tapped, pattering about—perfectly safe, Georgine told herself; the sound of Mr. Handel's concerto, interspersed with rattlings on the typewriter.

Yet when she came downstairs toward midmorning, there was that feeling that someone had just passed through the lower hall; someone who had whisked rapidly into one of the old rooms, there to wait unseen until the intruder had gone. Georgine went out to the summerhouse and found her intended in the midst of sheets of yellow paper. He was grinning as he beat out half a dozen lines and ripped the paper from the typewriter.

"By early afternoon," he remarked, "I'll have a collection of cases to show our Nella, that ought to convince her Gilbert's not the only pebble on the beach."

"Have you done his?" Georgine sat down and shaded her eyes.

He nodded. "I wish it weren't quite so good."

"Such modesty. Did you put in Serena?"

"Only as a kind of inspiration for Miss Adeline's death. The luminal could have been left over, you know, and Gilbert would have known how much was a safe dose—and how much would cause death."

"Wouldn't it take quite a lot?"

"I looked it up once, years ago, for another story." His voice went down cautiously. "About ten grains is supposed to be a lethal dose. You can get tablets, I believe, anywhere from a quarter-grain to a grain and a half. Seven of the big ones would do it."

Georgine looked at him intently. "I never know how much of what you're thinking is fiction."

"My fiction has to be based on fact."

"Then—you mean to say that Miss Adeline is supposed to have swallowed seven tablets of a narcotic, willingly? Seven tablets of anything, without knowing what they were?"

"That," Todd said, "is something I've worked out in various—"

From the second floor, indoors, came a dreadful wail. "Mamma! Mam-ma!" He turned to look at Georgine, his brows raised, and found that she was already gone. She had crossed the lawn like a streak. He saw her control her headlong rush at the kitchen door, and stand still for a moment.

Then her voice came, steady and cool. "Yes, Barby, what is it now?"

There were sounds of weeping as she disappeared. Todd waited, half smiling, now and then blowing a chord into the mouth organ. Ten minutes went by, and Georgine reappeared, walking across the lawn with a sort of furious humor in every line of her body.

She looked her very best, he reflected, when she was angry. Her eyes blazed blue as—as the lights on the back of a cross-country truck, and there was a simile for you.

"We'll have to go home, Todd," she said, reaching the summerhouse. "In spite of all I said, we can't stay here another night. It's bad enough when I'm comfortable, and I can't be, without—*What* do you think that Satanic child of mine chose to do? She spilled a whole bottle of nail polish on the floor of our room, and of course was overcome with guilt, and wiped it up— with my nightgown, the only one I have with me! And did you ever see a crepe gown that's been gaumed up with heavy enamel, and that somebody has then tried to wash? I could almost *beat* Barby. There's nothing to be done about it, nobody could wear it."

"Dear heart," said Todd mildly, "what in the hell do you want a nightgown for?"

"For tonight, goon, for tonight! We were supposed to stay over, you remember?"

"You couldn't—"

"No, I could not. I never can. Drafts go down my neck. I—it seems as if I can control my nerves about ghosts and murderers, to a certain extent, but something like this simply makes me want to *yell*."

"If the nightgown is all that's on your mind, I can fix that," said Todd promptly. "Wait here a few minutes. Want to read a little number for *Thrilling Stories*, while you're at it?"

He was gone before she could marshal her forces to protest. Going to buy her another gown, probably; dear heaven, as if she couldn't have thought of that for herself...

She came back to earth with a shock. Why, how could she have thought he'd accept such a flimsy excuse for leaving? She hadn't *thought* at all, that was the answer. That mishap had simply stirred up her subconscious, and up had come her dominant feeling: I want to go home. Go home, go home; it kept repeating itself like a warning.

Well, thought Georgine dryly, there's one feminine whim he didn't defer to. She treated the handful of manuscript to an angry scowl. It was too sunny out here for reading. She went into the house, finding the lower floor deserted.

This was the story about Ed, the village policeman. He had become Al, a plodding city cop who was too honest to get anywhere under a corrupt regime, and who had happened to be first on the scene when the Mayor's niece was found dead of cyanide poisoning.

The Mayor was old, he had a broken leg, he had a sort of male-nurse-cum-butler who glided about the room looking dazed... "The hooded eyes lifted. 'You're crazy,' the Mayor said. 'There's no room for crazy men on the Force.' His thin hand gestured at the leg, stiff in its cast. 'You suggest that I walked upstairs—with that!—and dropped poison into my niece's coffee, and escaped unseen? You fool, her death was suicide.'"...The valiant Al stuck to his guns; he knew that the niece was to be married the next week, and would then will to her husband the estate which the Mayor coveted. "The hooded eyes seemed to contract until they were pinpoints of burning light."

"Oh, dear me!" Georgine exclaimed, shaking with laughter. Todd had used the Judge for his central character, and made him into a sort of Svengali. She skimmed hastily through chases, gunfights and dramatic scenes to the point where the wicked Mayor died and the manservant was released from hypnosis. "Oh, come, come, Todd!" she murmured aloud.

And yet—absurd and sensational as this treatment was, he had said that his fiction was always based on the probabilities of a real case. Was this so impossible? Leave out the burning eyes, and substitute the Judge's power over everyone near him. Grant that he couldn't have moved from his sickbed. He had sent for Gilbert on the afternoon of the murder, perhaps to make sure that this most faithful visitor wouldn't be at Miss Adeline's for an hour or so. Gilbert had sat in the car, waiting. Suppose that Costanza had been sent out the back way, to carry something—she needn't have known what it was—to the Judge's sister; she could have made the round trip in less than half an hour.

And as to motive, couldn't you add, as in this story, his desire for power, his love for being the uncrowned King of Valleyville? His sister might have threatened, as the oldest living Tillsit, to usurp that position.

"I don't like it either," said Todd's voice behind her, causing her to jump violently, "but they'll take it for about thirty-five bucks. I dislike it as fiction, and even more as a real theory, but it can't be left out."

"No. I can see that."

He laid a package in her lap, with a courtly bow. "Advance wedding present, my dear. I know you like tailored things, so I bought the plainest they had."

Georgine opened the package. The nightgown thus disclosed was of a coarse voile, acridly pink, and decorated with many blobs of machine lace. "Oh, you *shouldn't* have done that," she gushed. "Todd, dearest, it's so *beautiful*—and after all, we're not married yet, I don't know if I should accept—"

"Nothing is too beautiful for you," said Mr. McKinnon. He stroked his mustache and gave her a refined leer. "Be sure you wear it tomorrow night. Your exquisite form will—ah! I can hardly wait!"

"Neither can I," said his lady, grinning.

"And I must contain myself for hours, for days!"

"It won't be days." Georgine looked at him briefly. "That I can promise you. *No*, dear, take it easy. You cannot buy my kisses with costly gifts—not this kind, anyway."

"D'you know, if the mail were to come through, it might be tonight." Todd straightened from bending over her chair. "Georgine, you wouldn't change your mind about the men coming at you out of the dark? You did intimate that wouldn't scare you."

"I said nothing about men in the plural. If it's you, that's different." She grinned at him again, and then swung hastily sideways. "And I keep forgetting, you can't have a minute's privacy in this house. Someone would be going by just then— or moving away from the door."

"Let 'em," said Todd with some asperity. "They're all supposed to know about life."

"I can't help that, I do not like these—listeners. If we're going to talk, let's go back to the summerhouse, where we can see people coming."

Walking once more across the lawn, she thought uneasily that it couldn't do any real harm if that absurd passage had been overheard. It was only the sense of surveillance that fretted at her nerves. Why should anyone want to spy on her private life?

Todd strolled along beside her, quite unperturbed. "This should be safe," he said, pausing in the summerhouse door.

"Yes, but let's stick to literature." She looked down at the manuscript. "What was I going to say? Oh, yes. Of course we both realize that this one story is absurd, but—are the others as bad? Because if they are, how are they going to—how did you put it, take the edge off Gilbert?"

"They'll be better. There's a real case or two among 'em."

"I'd rather it was the Judge; I can't stand him," said Georgine simply, sitting down on the weathered bench.

Todd's eyes went to the house, and dwelt consider-ingly on its fantastic rear. "A painless death. D'you know, I've thought a good deal about the poison that was used. It's easy to see why luminal was chosen, not only because no one hated the old lady, but because presumably the whole lot had access to it."

"The whole lot?"

"Look at 'em. Horace in the drugstore, Mary Helen acting as the doctor's secretary and renewing the supplies in his bag, the doctor himself, Susie Labaré caring for a number of patients who might have had it prescribed—if she'd wanted a stock of luminal she might easily have held out on those patients a few times, given 'em a sugar pill instead. The Judge might have had it himself, at some time. Both Gilbert and Nella had been near Serena during her illness. It was rather clever," said Todd pensively, "to pick out one that gave lots of latitude, when it would have been so easy to turn suspicion toward just one person—and that would have been so much more dangerous."

"How do you mean?"

"Look at the possible poisons, look at the choice this murderer had. Strychnine for pests and arsenic sprays in constant use on a ranch, cyanide in a photographer's studio, the whole pharmacopoeia in the drugstore and the doctor's bag. It's almost an embarrassment of poisons. You could look around and choose, slowly and carefully—rather like that charming gal in the Browning poem, how does it go?"

"Oh, I know that one," Georgine said. "'Now that I, tying thy glass mask tightly, May gaze through this something, some-thing whitely—'"

"Ah, marvelous Browning," Todd remarked.

"Recite it yourself, then. Of course, it's 'these faint smokes curling whitely, As thou pliest thy trade in this devil's-smithy—Which is the poison to poison her, prithee?'—That always gave me the shivers," Georgine added, having one on the spot at the involuntary drama of her own performance. "I could just see her looking around greedily and licking her ch—Great *heavens*, Barby, you scared me to death, where did you come from? And who said you could go barefoot?"

Barby stood in the door of the summerhouse and looked injured. "I was in the back lane, you told me I could go out there if I kept in sight of the house, Mamma. You told me I could. And there just happened to be a little bitsy puddle by the corner there, and I stepped in it by *accident*, and I knew you wouldn't want me to go around in wet shoes and socks," she finished virtuously.

"Well, go and put on your bedroom slippers this minute, and stuff paper tight into those shoes."

"Oh, Mamma, do I haff to?"

"Certainly. You'll catch cold."

"But my feet are warm, Mamma, they're *hot!* Feel!" The small feet did indeed seem to be warm enough. Barby regained her balance and leaned with melting softness against her mother's knee. "Recite some more of that poem, Mamma, you never said me that one. Please!"

"No, not that poem. It isn't suitable."

"Well, what's a glass mask? Like Hallowe'en?"

Georgine looked at Todd, passing the buck. He said, "No, cricket, just something to hold over your face so you wouldn't breathe in poison."

"Made of *glass?* Well, I think that's silly," said Barby robustly. "You could see right through it, and everybody'd know who you were."

"No, no. Not for disguise at all, only for protection."

Unconvinced, Barby muttered something about what was the use of it then? Todd had abruptly ceased to listen; and so, when she looked at his face, had Georgine.

"For protection," he repeated softly. "That's what happened here. Can't you see it, Georgine? Poor Gilbert, with his transparent honesty, *used*; as a screen, as a mask. And anyone who could look through that could see who was protecting himself or herself."

Georgine was struggling with a mental apparition, a person standing in the doorway of an upstairs bedroom, with head and face covered by something transparent and distorting. "Who could see through it?" she said unsteadily. "Not you or I."

"Anyone who'd take the trouble. The murderer's features— plain, plain as day."

CHAPTER EIGHT

Her HEADACHE DID NOT get better.

She wondered if it was brought on somehow by the thought of the household mysteries, for at sight of any member of the family it seemed to close about her mind like an insulation of pain. Through this the voices over the lunch table came with a muffled sound.

"Did you reach the antique dealer, Mr. McKinnon?"... "Yes, and he was much interested; but he couldn't make the trip up here till later in the week."..."Oh. Oh, I am disappointed, I was rather hoping—you'd be here when he came, I was counting on it."..."But if we're not, Mrs. Peabody, does it matter so much? Your family is right here, to help you in any business matters." One of those odd silences from Nella, from Horace and Mary Helen; it could not have lasted long, but to Georgine it seemed to go on for minutes, and to have a vibration of its own like a tense singing note.

A rest would help, she thought, lying on her bed in the early afternoon and listening to the far-off strains of the mouth organ and the sound of the typewriter: less of Mr. Handel and more of the writing, as the hours went by. The women's voices were audible downstairs, fading and swelling. Once there was a strange voice added, and after a time Georgine rose and quietly opened the door of her room.

Susie Labaré was crossing the hall. "How do," Susie said, ducking her head. "I come up on an errant for Nell." She went on into the sewing room, placed a chair beside a high wardrobe, and with notable agility mounted it to get something from the top shelf. Susie was a spry old girl, Georgine thought; and—she was in the house a great deal these days.

A little after three Todd tapped on the door. She looked at the sheaf of paper he held, and asked, "Have you finished them all?"

"All but one or two," Todd said. He glanced around the dim hall, speaking in a lowered voice. So, he'd caught the contagion too. "I'm stopping work for a while, going into the county seat to pick up our license. Do you want to come?"

Georgine thought not, unless she was needed. Todd gave her a careful scrutiny, and said it might be better if she rested. "The mailman passed us up," he added. "No package. So it's tomorrow?"

She nodded. The way she felt, it was just as well.

"I may stay over in town, then," he said. "A li'le research is indicated, if I can think how to go about it. Will you keep the manuscript? I'd as soon not leave it lying about my room."

The house seemed especially still after he had gone. Her ears sought for, and detected, a small chirp which was her daughter's voice downstairs. Nella Peabody had kept her promise about the violet-blue challis, and was even now giving Barby the final fitting. How good she was!

Georgine sat down by the window and glanced at the typewritten pages. The story about the judge; the one about Gilbert...She read it hastily. Yes, this one was better. It was roughly sketched, but it was clever—clever and convincing. This central character fell into the category of Damn Fool, without a doubt. He had left a trail a mile wide, both before and after he had stabbed the elderly friend of the family whose will benefited him. He tried to deny his guilt and got in deeper at every word, and his past had been so blameless that for a time the over-astute detective thought that a man who seemed so openly guilty must have been framed! Not bad, not bad at all, the character was a honey.

The next sheaf of papers was pinned together, and was thicker than the rest. It was the start of the novelette which Todd always hoped to get out of each case. She could tell that by the more leisurely tone of the introduction. She glanced at the penciled notation, the single letter N which headed the top sheet. That meant this story would treat of the Nervous Murderer. She knew these categories by heart, now: the Standpatter, the Perfect Murderer, the Nervous One, the Policeman's Little Helper, the Repeater in his two varieties— for money, or for ritualistic pleasure—the Maniac who was sane on the surface, and the Damn Fool.

She settled herself to read. The story was rapidly sketched for a dozen pages, and then a synopsis completed it. Harrington Harte's aid had been demanded by the beautiful Gladys Fenwick, whose brother-in-law had died under mysterious circumstances a few months before. Her adored sister was suspected of having murdered him, and Gladys proved a doughty champion. Harte and his secretary were to stay at the Fenwick lodge, where other suspects had been gathered for their delectation and close study. Gladys couldn't believe that any other members of the family were guilty, but just for ducks she had collected evidence against them, and now handed it over. And such goings-on at that hunting lodge! Another murder, a disappearance, the secretary's life threatened when her employer carelessly left her alone...

"Gladys" was Nella Peabody, there was small doubt of that. She was well disguised, but there were the sweetness, the candor, the championship of someone unjustly accused... Georgine flipped hastily through the synopsis to find out who was guilty.

But, great heavens. It was Nella-Gladys herself. Too nervous to let well enough alone, she had actually summoned the detective, hoping by that very act to deceive him, and had exerted vast energy in bumping off other characters, and creating mysteries, in order to frame the uncle whom she hated.

Georgine tried to laugh, as she had at the Mayor's hypnotic eyes, and found that she could not. Under the wild melodrama of the novelette was a plausible theory, based soundly on character. She sat looking at the typed words until they danced before her eyes, the back of her neck feeling chilly in spite of the spring sunlight that fell warmly through the window.

She thought, These theories, these classifications, are based on behavior after the crime; that's how the criminals make their characteristic patterns. Suppose, just suppose, Nella had been guilty. She had means, motive, opportunity. She could have been the person who slipped up to Miss Adeline's room. Perhaps she had been wearing the smart, absurd hat which the old lady had greeted with such derision. Perhaps the candy had, after all, been the medium of poison; she might have stood there for a time and watched Miss Adeline greedily eating it, and then slipped away.

And then she had found that by horrible ill luck Gilbert, the one person she cared for on earth, was tacitly accused; and the accusation had so preyed on him that he had left her, and could not or would not come back until he was exonerated by the townspeople. Of course she could not probe for details in person; but she wanted to know how much everyone else knew, she must goad all the witnesses into giving up their evidence— because the presumptive case against Gilbert was in reality the case against herself. She must know where she stood. She invited trouble, but she had to risk it.

It hung together with a dreadful logic, so far. Todd was playing the part of detective, but with a difference; he had confessed himself that he was no expert at getting at the truth. Nella had kept him and Georgine with her, by one device after another—like the "Gladys" of the story—ever since that first night. She must have known about his profession at that minute. Dyke might have described his uncle more fully than Todd knew.

It might be the truth, Georgine told herself, her lower lip pushed up in perturbation. It might all be contrived, the rat noises in the garret—why, Nella could have made them more easily than anyone! Maybe there was nothing there at all, and the supposed search was only a blind. She's using us, in some way we haven't fathomed.

No, how stupid I've been! She doesn't care for Gilbert at all; she only wants to pile up the evidence against him, much more strongly than before, so that he *can't* come back. Then she'd be safe forever, no one would suspect her, and that's what she's been afraid of. "The nervous murderer is the standpatter gone wrong," Todd had said once, long ago...Maybe those really are rats upstairs. Maybe it is someone searching, but there's no connection with the murder at all. Maybe—

Georgine stifled a shriek, and thrust the papers behind the long curtains of the bay window. There had been a tap at her door, and Nella Peabody's voice was saying, "Georgine! May I come in?"

"Of course." She was at the dresser, powdering her nose, when the door opened. "No, I wasn't asleep. Has Barby been bothering you?"

"Oh, no," Nella said sincerely. "It's been the greatest pleasure to me, having her around. I just love little girls, I'd like to keep her forever if I could!"

Would you, indeed.

"I was wondering," said Mrs. Peabody, "if a bit of fresh air wouldn't help your head. You haven't seen some of our prettiest spots; there's a ravine on the other side of town that's at its very best now, with the wildflowers blooming."

Georgine was stabbed with a thought. Had Todd meant to warn her, by leaving that manuscript in her hands? "Why, I don't know," she began.

"I'm afraid I almost promised Barby a sort of tea-picnic. She was wild with excitement at the idea, I knew I should have asked you first, but the idea just came to me—"

"It—it sounds delightful," said Georgine. Another thought kept rising to the surface: Poison is a woman's weapon. *Which is the poison to poison her, prithee?* It was far too easy to imagine those widely set gray eyes behind the distorting mask. "Faint smokes curling whitely"...they seemed to swirl about the doorway...

And yet nothing was there but a slim woman in a nicely made print dress and low-heeled shoes. That fixed look might mean only that Nella was waiting for an answer.

"Mr. McKinnon telephoned that he wouldn't be here for supper," Nella said, "so we can stay out as long as we like."

Todd had gone away, and left her alone with Mrs. Peabody, who might be a murderess. How *could* he? And yet— she wasn't quite alone.

"Is Mrs. Crane at home this afternoon?" Georgine asked. "She might like to go with us."

"Well, that's an idea. As a matter of fact, it was she who mentioned the ravine, after you'd come upstairs. Mary Helen," Nella called. "Are you in your room?"

They were in the hall now. Behind Mary Helen's door there was an indefinable sound of movement. After a moment she said, "Yes, what *is* it?"

"We wanted you to come out with us for a little while," Georgine said. "Please do. I should like it so much."

The door opened, and Mary Helen stood there pushing up the sleeves of her sweater. Her light eyes looked from one to the other, and her lips were closed.

"There wasn't anything special you wanted to do here, was there?" Nella asked. Georgine looked over her shoulder, as beseechingly as possible.

Mary Helen began inexplicably to giggle, as if it were forced from her. "No, I guess there's nothing—nothing important," she said wearily. "I'll come."

Georgine slipped back into her room for a moment. The manuscript was still behind the long curtains; she couldn't take it along because it was too bulky, but it must not be left in sight. She put it in her suitcase, finally, wishing that the key to her bag had not been lost; and, for one extra precaution, scattered face powder between some of the leaves. At least, if anyone read Todd's stories, she'd know it afterward.

The walk across town, to the ravine, was short. Barby, running ahead and returning with questions, invading strange dooryards to smell the flowers, covered the course about three times. Georgine kept a sharp eye on her and hoped this would explain her abstraction.

The Nervous Murderer. She knew that type too well for her own comfort. The main thing, she told herself desperately, is not to let it be thought that you know anything at all; I have to act just the same as usual, because if Nella were the murderer, and if she suspected that I held the evidence against her...Oh, Todd, how could you? You ought to have remembered I can't play poker; I'll have to watch every step, every word.

"There," said Mrs. Peabody proudly. "Isn't this pretty? I've always liked to be able to get right away from things—not that one could call Walnut Street crowded, of course, but—you know; just to get out of the house, and to a place where you're really alone."

Georgine thought, she can't drown me in this little creek. She can't do anything, really. There'll be no reason for it, if I'm careful. "It's lovely," she said in a faraway voice, her eyes on the clear water running over sand and pebbles, between green banks of foliage.

The three women set down their burdens of food and cushions, talking with a sort of nervous cordiality. Barby alone was at ease. She ranged about the clearing with hummingbird swiftness, and then came up flushed and entreating. "Mamma, can I explore? Look, there's a path that goes way up the brook, kind of secret in the bushes, can't I walk up there?"

"Darling, no. You remember, in strange places you must not go out of sight alone."

"I'll take her," Mary Helen said. "Really, I don't mind, I honestly do love kiddies. Wouldn't you like that, sweetheart?"

Barby's chin went in, but she muttered, "All right."

Georgine opened her mouth to say, "Let's all go," but Nella spoke first. "Your Mamma and I will stay here where it's cool," she said with decision. "Anyway, four's a crowd when you're exploring, isn't it, Barby?"

"Uh-*huh*," said Barby with a dejected look at Mary Helen. Georgine could not insist. She reminded herself that a shout would carry a long way in this ravine.

The moment the two women were alone, Nella Peabody sat down with her back against a tree trunk and closed her eyes. "The relief," she said in a half-whisper. "The blessed relief, getting away from that strain. Think of having to escape from the house—my own house—before I can breathe freely!" She was silent for a while; then her voice came, infinitely sad. "When I thought of its coming to Gilbert I always saw the two of us alone there. It's what we planned on."

Georgine sat silent, stiffly on guard. She tried to look sympathetic in case the eyes should open.

Nella spoke again, as if from a distance. "Sometimes I wonder if those few months were—worth it. Oh, well, that's past. We do what we think must be done."

What was she saying?

She turned slowly and gave Georgine a long steady look. "You're understanding. I wish I could tell you—everything. I don't believe you'd condemn me. But I don't quite dare."

Great heavens, Georgine thought, and said hastily, "Thank you, but really, I—don't ever invite confidences."

"I know. You don't pry, either. Just the same, I think you have intuition. You know more about us than you seem to know."

"No, indeed I don't," said Georgine vigorously. "You forget I'm a stranger."

"But that makes you more sensitive to impressions, can't you see? There's something I've wanted to ask you, though you may think it's a peculiar question." Nella waited for a moment. "Georgine, what is it that you're afraid of, in my house?"

"I—what?"

"No, don't look as if you didn't understand. I know there's something, I've seen it in your face."

When? When did she see it, this afternoon when she came to my door? I've given myself away already...

"Please. It's important to me to know." Nella leaned toward her. "What are you afraid of?"

Her tone would not be denied. Desperately, Georgine blurted out the safest thing she could think of: "The rats in the attic."

Mrs. Peabody's look was intent. It did not falter for a long minute, while the creek slipped by over the pebbles, and the trees rustled overhead. Then she said softly, "Yes. I thought so. You've guessed something. Please tell me how much."

"I don't know what you mean." Georgine returned her look. "You said yourself that the sounds I'd hear were rats."

Nella sat back, shaking just perceptibly. "I'm asking too much of you, I suppose. It's meant such a lot to me, having you people here, as if there is someone on my side at last. But after all, you hardly know me, do you?"

Georgine got her voice under control. "I know you've been most kind to us. Such hospitality as I never—"

"You don't trust strangers with all your thoughts, of course. But can't you see that would help me immeasurably to know what's in your mind?"

That was clear. It was all too clear. *Be careful,* Georgine thought. She began, "Todd's told you everything he—"

"I'm not talking of Gilbert now. I'm talking about something that's alive and in that house."

Georgine took a tight hold on herself, and gave Nella a creditable smile. "Nella, my dear, you've let your imagination run away with you. I'm afraid it's my influence, it's fatal to have two cowardly women in the same household. You'll see, it'll be better when Todd and Barby and I are gone."

"Don't say that! I can't *let* you leave."

"But you'll have to, and you don't want to make us sorry we came!" Georgine rushed on. "Because how would we feel if it seemed that we'd upset you, and made you lose control of your nerves? It might affect your heart, you know."

"You too?" said Nella slowly. "Now I understand." Her low voice rang with an implacable note, and she caught Georgine's arm. "My nerves, my imagination—you've been listening to Mary Helen. I know what my dear little niece would tell you, that I'm unbalanced, maybe—dangerous. *Perhaps you believed her?*"

For one moment Georgine shuddered on the edge of breaking down, of leaping to her feet and running like mad up the path. But then she'll be *sure,* her mind cried out in warning; are you going to let her bluff you into an admission?

Her temper went off with a bang. "Nella Peabody," she blazed, "will you keep quiet and stop trying to break my wrist? Mary Helen hasn't said one word to me about you, not one; but if you go on like this I'll begin to think you *are* crazy! I'm sick of being dragged into family quarrels, that's all, and I'll thank you not to accuse me of listening to scandalous nonsense!"

The hand fell away, and Nella began to laugh helplessly and then to sob and then to laugh again. Georgine leaned over to the brook, wet her handkerchief in the icy water, and swung it against her companion's face. There was a gasp and a hiccup, and she added crossly, "If you go on having hysterics I can always get up and leave you. Really, Nella, your idea of a headache cure—!"

Mrs. Peabody controlled herself after a moment, with a visibly racking effort. "Do forgive me," she said faintly, with her head down. "It was just that I was so—relieved. You see, I've come to think of you as a friend, my friend, and the idea that— no, please, Georgine! I won't say any more about it. I've—I've talked too much already. I can see that."

I've talked too much. I've talked...The words hung in the air like the dancing motes in the sunlight, that seemed to spin before Georgine's eyes. I've talked too much...

"How *is* your head?" Nella inquired solicitously, with one last sharp intake of breath. "I'm so sorry, really I am."

"It may explode at any minute," said Georgine, not too graciously. With a great thrill of relief she saw coming down the path a flash of yellow that was Mary Helen's sweater; and, a moment after, heard Barby's shrill tones in the distance.

As the explorers came up she pulled herself together and managed the proper tone of ecstasy. "Oh, violets! Were they really growing wild, darling? It's the first time you've ever picked any yourself, isn't it—Why, Barby, your hem's wet. My dear lamb, you haven't been *wading?*"

"Wasn't it all right?" Mary Helen inquired innocently. "She was *crazy* to do it."

"She was," said Georgine grimly, "in both senses." Barby, with her tendency to asthma, had to be rigorously guarded from anything that might lead to a cold. "You knew better than that, Barb."

"You let me go barefoot for a while this morning, Mamma."

"That was my mistake. And you should have known the difference yourself, darling, this water is as cold as ice. Oh dear *me*. I'm sorry, Nella, but I think we'd better not stay out for tea. This goofy infant is shivering, no matter how she tries to hide it."

She was shivering herself, partly from strain and partly from the renewed vigor of the headache, before they reached the house. Barby had kept hanging back, forcing her mother to slow down, and muttering half sentences about Mary Helen. "I don't like her, Mamma, she laughs...She kept askin' me about Cousin Dyke, and I...How could I remember all the things he said, and I wouldn't 'a' told her." Between remarks she sniffled, and not with tears.

Georgine got her upstairs and in bed, and fed her milk toast, refusing food for herself. There was no sign of Todd, who might have quieted her nerves. There was no more aspirin in her suitcase.

"That puts the lid on," she said wildly, half aloud. "And we went right by the drugstore, I could have got it in a minute."

"What, Georgine?" said Nella's voice from the doorway. She suffered one of those galvanic starts to which the afternoon had made her subject. "Nothing, Nella, only the aspirin," she said vaguely, clasping her temples.

"Is that all! Why on earth didn't you ask me? I have something better than aspirin, much better for pain of any kind," said Mrs. Peabody; and gave her a charming smile. She turned toward the stairs. "Would you mind awfully coming down to get it? This is my second trip up today, and I mustn't make too many. Now, I'll have the tablet ready for you... "

The voice died away. Georgine stood gazing after her hostess, in a sort of throbbing stupor. Something better for pain of any kind. I've talked too much...If I said *no,* I won't take your medicine, I don't dare take anything from your hands that I haven't seen you taste yourself, first—she'd know. There'd be no doubt in her mind.

She went slowly down the stairs, her heart banging against her ribs at each step as if it were hung in a balance. If the tablet were only white—if she could avoid Nella's eyes for one moment—

"And a nice hot cup of tea afterward," Nella said soothingly. "Nothing could do you more good."

"No, thank you so much. No tea." The tablet was white, not much larger than an aspirin.

"But you need something hot to dissolve it."

"That's easy. I'll just have some hot water from the tap." Georgine took the tablet from Nella's fingers, and went quickly into the kitchen. She heard the light footsteps following her. "I never can take things if they're already dissolved," she said breathlessly, "but I can swallow any size in pills." Her hand came out of her pocket, the white disk visible in its palm. She tipped her head back, swallowed, and drank quickly.

"There," Nella Peabody said with quiet satisfaction. "That'll fix you up beautifully. You'll sleep, now. I can guarantee it."

❀ ❀ ❀

What was it that had awakened her? The first instinctive listening for the sound of hoarse breaths from the cot fell away; there was no sound across the room. When had she heard a turning knob, and felt a cool draft across her neck? A moment ago, hours ago? There had been a dream, something about soft footsteps and a movement on the far side of the bed where the desk stood. She could not remember when that had happened. Was it at the same time as the faint noises by the door? All of it was receding faster than she could catch it, back and back into the hours of the night.

The door opening and closing, twice, three times?...No, it was no use.

There was some kind of a noise right now, teasing at her ears. Not overhead; she knew that sound; in the attic there was nothing but silence. Outside in the hall?

And had Barby ceased to breathe entirely?

She reached out for the bedside lamp and pressed its switch; there was no answering glow. Great heavens, Georgine thought crossly, I must have pulled the plug clear out of the wall. She slid out of bed and crouched beside the small table, feeling behind it. Her fingers encountered the cord of the lamp, which was inexplicably taut; followed along it; found it still firmly plugged in...That was queer. It ought to light, it had been all right the night before.

Her bedroom door *was* opening; there was that tiny rattle that the latch made, and a current of air along the floor. She twisted about quickly, soundlessly. She couldn't see the door; the hall outside was as dark as this room; but she heard the faint whish that meant it had been pushed to without quite closing.

"Barby dear, is that you?" Georgine said, just above her breath; and heard something like a gasp. "Turn your flashlight on, sweetheart—or did you forget it?"

Whoever was standing immobile by the door was not Barby.

"Who is it?" Georgine said in a harsh whisper. "Who's there?" She seemed to be frozen in this posture, crouching by the bed, her head on a level with the pillow.

Again there was that swift intake of breath from across the room; and a whisper answered her.

"Dear Georgine, who did you think it was?"

The scream that had been rising in her throat died abruptly. She might have let it out a minute before, but for waking her child into sudden terror. Now she thanked heaven for her silence.

"Not you, Todd?" she whispered incredulously. "Is something the matter?"

"No. Why?" It came on the merest breath from the darkness, and a staccato sound followed, as if of a subdued chuckle. Feet moved slowly, almost inaudibly, across the carpet, as if he were groping.

"But—but what do you want? You frightened me! The light won't go on—"

"Sh-h. What do you think I want?"

Georgine did not move from her kneeling position, but her reply almost sizzled. "If you mean what that sounds like, Todd McKinnon, you ought to be ashamed of yourself!"

She waited a moment. There were the infinitesimal noises again, brushing the carpet, and something added: a soft patting as if of hands against some flat surface, and a clink from the direction of the dressing table. "I don't know what gave you the idea you could come into my room!"

There was another pause. Then the whisper came again, from a point nearer the bed. "But—you gave it to me, this morning. You said I wouldn't have to wait. You're not letting me down?"

The breathy words seemed to be covering something else; again the brushing of hands across a surface. Georgine felt the roughness of the blanket against her face, where she crouched cold and sick beside the bed. She felt dismay rising in her throat as if it were a tangible thing.

Oh, no, Todd! Not from you, the kind of cheapness that one expects in the professional wolf—not after all these months of consideration, the days of control in this house. It isn't like you!

It isn't like Todd, she thought on the very heels of the first phrase. It can't *be* Todd.

And yet the possibility held her silent for a few seconds more. If it were, and she screamed mistakenly and woke the household—and he were found in her room...

"Is that how you think of it?" she whispered. There had been only the briefest of pauses since the person had spoken last. "Todd—did you bring the little bottle?"

The whisper did not come again for the space of a few breaths. She had never lived through a longer period of waiting. What if—what if he were to say "What li'le bo'le?" And if it were Todd, that should be his reply.

"Sure," the voice said at last. "I've got it right here." And on the words, the whisperer was no longer disembodied. It was beside the bed, bending over the place where she should have been lying, feeling rapidly about the bedclothes, under the pillows.

Georgine was rocked by a wave of such fright as she had never felt in her life. Not Todd, bending within a few inches of her, but someone else—someone who had thought she was asleep—someone who, if she gave away her position now, could have his hands around her throat before she could draw breath to yell for help.

Her hands were pressed flat on the carpet, chilly in the draft that sucked along the floor. It was blowing toward the open window, bellying the long curtains outward; it grew stronger and she realized that the door must be swinging inward. Her fingertip touched smooth leather: her slipper—still hidden in the black shadow of the bed, she caught up the slipper and threw it low across the carpet. She could hear it slide the last few feet, and strike against the far wall with a soft thud. She heard, too, a stirring of the air over the bed as the whisperer straightened abruptly; the hurry of feet across the room, a door swinging wider.

It worked, Georgine thought, struggling against a wave of faintness. She found herself upright, beside Barby's cot, as if to protect the small sleeper. Her hand fell to the pillow. The cot was empty.

Then she did scream; over and over, with the full power of her lungs. She was beside the door, finding the wall switch and clicking it up and down without result. There were no lights anywhere. There was, however, an answering stir from the other rooms. Startled voices were raised in response, other light switches were jiggled with the same futility. Doors opened. She saw Todd first, holding up the tiny flame of a cigarette lighter; then Mary Helen, blundering out of her room after seemingly falling over something. Mary Helen had a flashlight, and its dazzling circle swung about the upper hall. Nella Peabody was standing at the top of the stairs, and Horace came plunging into the hall just as the light reached him.

"What *is* it?" Nella cried out, a hand to her heart. The silver plaque at her bosom winked and glittered on its chain. "I heard noises—Georgine, is Barby ill? What *is* it?"

"She's—gone; she's not in her bed," Georgine said, half choking. "There aren't any lights. I got up to—I couldn't find her—"

Todd was beside her, supporting her with a steadying grip. "She was up a li'le while ago," he said calmly. "I heard her stumbling past my door half asleep, with her light."

"She's fallen downstairs," Georgine said, moving toward the opening.

"No," Nella Peabody told her. "I was coming up, slowly—but I thought I saw—or felt, rather—someone coming out of your room, just now."

"Where'd you get that torch?" Todd inquired, holding his lighter close to Mary Helen's hand. Horace had vanished into the attic entry; the hall was full of voices, all crying at once as the bedroom lights flashed on. Horace came out, remarking competently, "Main fuse was loosened," just as Mary Helen gave a bewildered inspection to the flashlight in her hand, and answered, "Why, I fell over it in my room, it was lying on the floor."

It was Barby's treasured possession. Over the babble her own small voice sounded from across the hall. "Mamma! Mamma, where are you? There was a noise—I'm cold, Mamma—"

She was on the chaise longue in Mary Helen's room, trying to sit up. "I called and called when that noise came, but I couldn't make you hear for the longest time, Mamma! I couldn't make any noise myself, at all."

"I don't wonder," Georgine said, maternal calm falling on her like a cloak. "You're hoarse as a hoot owl, my poor lamb. Come back into your own bed."

Todd put her in and tucked the blankets tightly about her; she was wheezing and flushed. "I know what happened," Georgine said in a low voice. "She got up by herself, and then couldn't find her way back to her room because she was half asleep again. It's happened before. Didn't you hear her come in, Mary Helen? She must have thought your couch was her cot, and just dropped onto it."

"Hear her? Good Lord, no," Mary Helen said. "I did think there was a kind of thud, somewhere in my dreams"—she giggled pleasantly—"but that must have been when the flashlight went down. You're certainly a tender mother, Mrs. Wyeth, *imagine* yelling like that because your kiddie wasn't in her crib!"

"I'll yell louder," said Georgine tartly, "if she's in for another bout of asthmatic croup, after getting chilled this afternoon and again tonight."

"But, my dear," said Nella, with an intent glance, "was that all that frightened you?" Horace's voice covered hers. "Damned queer about that fuse, it was okay when we went to bed. Is something—going on, or shouldn't we ask? What did you say, Nell, about seeing someone—"

He stopped and turned his eyes away. Georgine's lips had parted to cry out, "Yes! There was someone in my room; it must have been one of you, what did he want?" But the words held themselves back.

Horace and Mary Helen had both glanced at Todd, and then at each other. There was comprehension and amusement in their eyes.

It would be of no use to ask, to accuse. She'd never get an answer, for the whisperer had Todd for a scapegoat. "You must have seen me, wandering out into the hall, Nella," she said smoothly. "I'm terribly sorry I disturbed you all. There was nothing more, of course, than finding that Barby had disappeared."

Todd remained at her side, inscrutably smiling. She let her eyes travel from face to face, meeting each look, knowing or puzzled. One of these three had been, not ten minutes before, whispering from the darkness of her room. Or—was that the only possibility? Across the half-dark of the hall, lit by the shafts of light from the bedroom doors, she saw the dark rectangle of doorway that led to the attic. Had that door been open when Horace plunged through to grope around the fuse box? Had it been hastily closed only a second before she roused the household, and had the whisperer been drifting down the stair toward the basement door all the time they were chattering in the hall?

"Mamma," Barby said hoarsely, "I can't breathe right."

"She is going to be ill," said Georgine despondently, and turned into her bedroom.

There was no terror now. This was something that could be fought, coped with by direct measures and in full light. Georgine's knees, which had threatened to give way a dozen times during the scene in the hall—her invariable reaction to shock—were steady now, as she worked over Barby. Nella Peabody had been disproportionately alarmed by the inevitable choking and struggling for breath, and had called the doctor. He came, drawn and exhausted-looking as ever, and yet completely alert at this strange hour of the morning.

Georgine watched him as he bent over the cot, gentle and reassuring. There was a look in his eyes, through all his professional composure, that teased her memory; like something she had felt herself, that she recognized with her heart.

Why, she thought, he can't bear to see people suffer. How can he stand to be a doctor, when he has to fight not only with disease but with his own compassion? It must be twice as hard for him, he's never got used to it...

"Now we'll pretend I'm a beetle, with one big shiny eye," said John Crane, putting on his metal reflector for a look into Barby's nose and throat. "You ever see one of these before, little girl?"

Barby nodded and smiled faintly. She accepted all treatment with the dreadful patience of a child who has been ill a great deal, and the doctor saw that too. The shadow flickered across his eyes again.

"Well, this isn't so bad," he said after a time. "Better get her bed into the sewing room, these medications work better in a small space. Did the men get back with the inhaler?"

Todd, who without waiting to dress fully had gone out with Horace in tow, now appeared with a load of supplies from the drugstore. The croup kettle was set up beside Barby's cot, and John Crane said, "This'll fix you up in no time, young 'un. No, don't feel that way, Mrs. Wyeth. It's my job to come out at all hours, isn't it? You keep the young lady quiet, and in bed, all day tomorrow, and I'll come in once or twice to make sure she's all right." He picked up his medical bag and looked vaguely around as if to make sure he hadn't left anything.

Mary Helen was standing in the hall; the whole household had been caught up in the turmoil of night alarms and illness, and everyone was drifting about, up and down stairs, unable to settle down. She smiled at her ex-husband, not altogether pleasantly. "Up to your old tricks, are you, Johnny?"

"What?" the doctor said. "What is it now?" He looked himself up and down and finally put a hand to his head, where the reflector was still strapped. "I thought there was something missing from that bag. Thanks, Mary Helen."

He looked at her with perfect politeness, but as if he didn't really see her. Georgine wondered for a split second how those two felt about each other.

"Like old times," said Mrs. Crane, looking after him with the jeering smile still on her lips. "Nobody ever knew whether he'd forget his hat in the dead of winter, or sit through a call with it on his head, or drive right by his own house in a kind of stupor. *I* never knew what he had on his mind."

"You've got to admit he never forgot to call on a patient," Horace remarked, yawning heavily, "or made the wrong diagnosis. Well, I'm turning in."

The doors closed, the careful footsteps died away down the stairs; once more the hall was dimly lighted only by the reflection through the transom of the sewing room. It smelled now of some strongly aromatic compound, coming out in little puffs from the mouth of the steam kettle. Georgine withdrew into her own room, shivering suddenly in the chill of early morning. Todd, who had been exercising his gift for keeping out of the way when not wanted, seemed to materialize out of the shadows. "Can you talk now, Georgine?" he murmured.

"Oh, yes. Barby'll be all right, she's going to sleep now that her breathing's easier. I could have handled this myself if I'd had the proper stuff to work with."

Todd perched on the edge of the slipper chair inside her half-open door, hands in the pockets of his dark robe—how like him, Georgine thought, to be sleek and immaculate looking at three in the morning!—and looked at her with intent, concerned eyes. "Now, my dear. What really happened?" His questions were interjected so quietly as scarcely to break the flow of her murmured narrative.

"You didn't hear Barby get up? Yes, that's probably what disturbed your sleep in the beginning...It was some minutes, maybe twenty, after I heard her, when the other sounds began; and five or ten more before I heard you scream...Why the hell, my dear, didn't you yell at the very first?" The answer to that one made his brows go up comically.

"Someone who made you think he was I," he repeated thoughtfully, under his breath. "Means it was the person who slipped past the door this morning while we were talking about, uh, the nightgown. I see. I see. You're very diplomatic, Georgine; I wondered why you didn't give an alarm the minute we were all in the hall." The climax of her story came, and he got to his feet, frowning. "Good Lord! Feeling about your pillows... Damnation, I wish I had stood guard outside your door, the way my instinct told me—and yet, I couldn't see why..."

Georgine drew her hand across her eyes. "It may not have been—someone who meant to harm me. I don't know. It just felt dangerous."

"It was," Todd said softly, his jaw tightening. "I shan't leave you upstairs alone, from now until the minute we can go. I shouldn't leave you at all, if I had my way."

"A bit difficult to manage, don't you think? But it was this afternoon that I could really have mangled you, for giving me the tip about her and then going off."

"About whom?"

"Nella. How *could* you, Todd? Maybe you thought she wouldn't dare do anything openly, but I'm sure she tried to drug me tonight. She thought I was fathoms under, that's how she could dare to come into my room openly. Probably she saw

Barby go out, and wander into Mary Helen's room and stay there; and that was her chance—"

"Wait a minute!" Todd said levelly. "What made you pick on Nella? Not the case I made out against her? But, dear heart, hers was no more convincing than any of the others."

Georgine gazed at him, stupefied. "I didn't read the others. You mean to say—"

He seemed to be struggling with amusement. "I had to include her, Georgine, but—this isn't a Nervous Murderer, I give you my word. If you'd only read a bit farther, you'd have seen that Mary Helen, or Horace, or Susie, or the doctor might just as easily have been a murderer; better, judging by temperament. The case against Horace, for example—maybe I flatter myself, but I think if you'd read that one, Nella's wouldn't have seemed so likely."

"Wh-which type was he?"

"For lack of a better, I made him the Policeman's Li'le Helper. There weren't any police, of course, but we're pinch-hitting for them now; and he's rather an eager beaver, discovering the candy and having it analyzed, and talking so freely about facing facts." He was watching her narrowly, seeing her relax little by little under the subdued flow of his words. "Look; I've figured out that he must have been the one to bring in all that patent medicine the old lady liked to guzzle in secret. Who'd be in a better position to add luminal to a bo'le of Peruna and give it to her? Nobody analyzed the dregs of those bo'les in her dresser. As for opportunity, the physical possibility, he could have slipped out the back door of the drugstore and walked over here in a few minutes for that two o'clock call. You can't prove a perfect alibi by two lovers who're busy gazing into each other's eyes in another room."

Georgine gave him an incredulous glance. "Horace," she said, meditating. "But, Todd, how about motive? He had all his money from Miss Tillsit already."

"This one needn't be gain; it could be the fear of loss. Suppose Miss Tillsit had found out about the lady in Vallejo, and disapproved, and threatened to change her will so he'd be in debt to the estate?"

"But he hasn't done anything with his ill-gotten gains, if he's the murderer! And if Miss Adeline had threatened him with being cut out of her will, can you see her accepting medicine from his very hands within the next few days?"

Todd shrugged. "Maybe it wasn't that. It's the motive I gave him in the story, it needn't be the real one. But can you really, dispassionately, see Nella Peabody being so afraid that you knew her secret that she'd try to poison you—knowing all the time that I'd be on hand and she couldn't possibly escape this time?"

Georgine said, "I kept the tablet she gave me. We could find out for sure."

"You managed not to take it?"

"I made a little pill out of a piece of Kleenex I had in my pocket, and took that instead, where she could see me." She began to chuckle quietly. "I darned near choked myself on it, too. Be a good joke on me if she weren't—But look here, Todd, we still don't know what that—that voice was doing in my room. I thought of course it was to do me harm, finish me off somehow! That's what you did for me, making your fiction so convincing. What else could it be, though?"

Todd gave a leisurely glance at the ceiling. "The voice might be our friend the rat. Had you thought that, under the urgency that seems to've infected our searcher, it may be necessary to look for that mysterious object in this room as well as the attic? And someone might have thought you were unconscious for the night. Nella could have told the others she'd given you a sleeping pill; she might even have told the ever-present Susie."

"No!" Georgine got to her feet. "That needn't be it. How about the manuscript you gave me? The prowler could have known it was somewhere in this room. He might have meant to steal it for the night, to find out how much we know or have guessed, and then return it while I was still drugged." She stopped, narrowing her eyes. "Horace," she said deliberately.

"That soft breathy voice of his—I wonder if it wouldn't be very like the whisper I heard?"

"You didn't recognize that?"

"N-no. I never realized how sexless a whisper can be. But, *Horace*. Why didn't he come to look at the manuscript this afternoon, while we were out? Oh; he didn't know we'd be going on the picnic; of course. And Nella could have mentioned the narcotic, whatever it was—"

She broke off and went swiftly to the closet. The sheets of yellow paper were still in the suitcase; she snatched them out, and they slipped from her grasp and cascaded across the floor.

"Oh, dear!" Georgine said softly. "My lovely trap! Now the powder is all scattered, anyway—But, Todd, if anyone had read these stories—could he have found out that we knew enough to make us dangerous?"

"I doubt it." He was still watching her, and now he spoke quickly. "Don't forget, Georgine, that this search, and the one in the attic, may have nothing to do with the murder of Miss Adeline. It may be an independent hunt for something that's not in the least incriminating."

She thought it over for a minute, carefully putting together the pages of the manuscript. She handed him the sheaf. "An interesting idea," Georgine said. "Just the same—did you mean what you said about keeping a watch on my door?"

"Oh, yes," said Todd. "I meant that."

CHAPTER NINE

THEY WERE SO KIND, so solicitous. They kept coming to the bedroom door, the next morning, with questions and sympathy.

"How's the kiddie this morning?"

"Oh, much better, thank you."

"Everything all right, Mrs. Wyeth? Anything more I can bring you?"

"Thank you so much, Mr. Tillsit, but there's nothing."

Nella was resting downstairs after the night's alarms, but called out from her room when Georgine went down on an errand for the invalid. "Oh, Barby's better? I'm so glad! And how is your head this morning?"

"I'd forgotten all about it!"

"Oh, good. That tablet really did fix you up, didn't it?"

"Something did," Georgine called back to her, rather dryly.

Late in the morning, on an impulse, she closed her door against the solicitude and began some curious operations in the bedroom. Barby, propped up bright-eyed with a book, at once demanded to know what Mamma was doing, crawling around the floor by the wall.

"What I'm doing is a secret," Georgine told her impressively. "Will you promise not to tell a soul? Cross your heart? All right. I'm looking for a place where something could have been hidden."

"I want to get up and help!" Barby shouted, and was with difficulty restrained.

At the end of an hour Georgine, warm and disheveled, sat down on the slipper chair. She was discouraged, too. There were a number of places which Miss Adeline Tillsit could presumably have reached, in her own bedroom, but every one of them was a blank. The knobs on the ends of the old-fashioned thick curtain rods had nothing in them: there were no loose floorboards, the baseboards gave out no hollow sounds when gently tapped. The old-fashioned light fixtures in the walls did not come apart.

The smell of ancient woodwork and of Barby's inhalations seemed to mingle with the feeling of soreness in her knees, and with the sounds from Todd's room. "Toodle-oo, *tee!* Toodle-oo, *tee!*" and a number of assorted tweedles from the most hateful of Mr. Handel's variations, interspersed with the clack of the typewriter, combined to make this a nightmare sort of morning. She thought, why do I bother, for heaven's sake? The minute Barby can be moved we'll go.

It was nearly noon when she heard Horace's voice in the upstairs hall. It made her start so uncontrollably that she thought, here, this won't do! I'll get to the place where I can't face him, either, without a horrible strain. Todd said the other cases were just as convincing.

She found Todd in his room. The typewriter was covered and the harmonica returned to his pocket. He was just sitting there looking out the window, with a cigarette burning unregarded in his fingers. His eyes were troubled and faraway.

"Todd," she said in a low voice, when he had given her the remaining sheaf of papers, "What are you going to do with these?"

He grinned. "Give them to Nella at the very last minute, and then get in the car and run like hell. I don't want to be caught having to justify my wild guesses. They're all possible, but Lord knows which are probable."

"But you wanted me to see them, didn't you?"

"Yes, I did. Always helps to talk 'em over with someone... The cricket going to be all right?"

"She's fine. We caught that attack just in time. Come into my room while I look these over, I don't want to leave her too long."

"You're sure they won't scare you again?" Todd inquired solicitously, once more settling himself in her slipper chair.

"I'd rather be scared of everyone at once than one or two of 'em—and those maybe the wrong ones." She looked at the uppermost story, which was titled *The Aunt with the Reticule*.

"Oh," she added with interest, halfway down the second page, "one of those handy relations with a bag full of herbs and simples, who used to appear and take over every time there was sickness in the family. How often I've wished for one of those! This is Susie, I suppose?"

"That is Susie," Todd said. He looked into space, frowning.

Georgine read on. "This is very simple, isn't it?" she said rather breathlessly. "The Repeater, who wasn't suspected because she didn't invariably kill her patients; she was smart enough to let some of 'em get well. Todd, what *kind* of a Repeater would she be? The sort who killed over and over for pleasure, or the kind who always inherited a chunk of money?"

"I don't know," he said slowly. "Others besides Nella have said that Susie has a passion for money, piling it up, hoarding it. She still has every cent of her husband's insurance stowed in the bank. She'd like enough so she could live on the income. We know she gained from Miss Adeline's death, and the Judge gave her something for nursing Serena; but as to the rest of her patients—she must have had hundreds, and it'd be tough to check up on 'em."

"Can you be both kinds at once?" She felt a slight chill, remembering Mrs. Labaré's gaunt figure appearing silently in the halls, "on an errand for Nell," "to bring you a pie." Susie knew this house like the back of her hand. It might so easily have been she who had slipped quietly past the open doors when Georgine and Todd were talking! But could she have been the whisperer? "Maybe she knows how to talk correctly, but usually doesn't bother," Georgine murmured uneasily. "Todd, you've done this awfully well: the hints the Aunt always dropped about some mysterious person visiting her patients before they died. I—I hope we don't have to see Susie again."

"Chances are against it, aren't they?"

"There's no telling just when we can get away, till the doctor's seen Barby again. And I keep feeling Susie may be right out there in the hall now!"

Todd smiled, and squeezed her shoulder. "I doubt it. And somehow I don't think Susie would leave a written confession in a chair leg."

"There may be something else, in the attic or this room, that she had to get when she could."

"There was a week or two when she could have searched," he reminded her, "just after Miss Tillsit died."

"Yes, but—oh, never mind. There's Nella calling us to lunch. What do we do with the manuscript?"

"I think," said Todd slowly, "that we leave it face down on your desk, with a weight on it. I think, also, that we close the connecting doors but leave Barby's door into the hall open. It might be interesting to see if anyone comes in."

"You should be flattered," said Nella at the luncheon table, "that the children are home for all their meals while you're here."

"We are flattered indeed," said Todd expansively. Everyone smiled at everyone else, and Georgine fought down a wild impulse to laugh. It wasn't funny; she was sure of that; there was a purpose in the continued presence of Mary Helen and Horace.

"And how's the kiddie?" Mary Helen inquired. "Horace and I were in to see her this morning, and she looked so *much* brighter."

"I thought so too," Mrs. Peabody said.

"When did you two find time to pay a call?" Georgine asked casually.

"Oh, while you were down getting her breakfast. Seemed as if she might be lonely."

As if I'd been gone for hours, Georgine thought indignantly. "She's quite happy alone," she remarked in a sweet tone. "Right now she's sitting up reading the *Alice* that Dyke gave her."

"Oh, and that reminds me—if you don't mind my asking," said Nella diffidently, "was there any interesting news from the sergeant?"

"News? I haven't heard from him."

Nella gave her a look of bewilderment. "Didn't you find your letter?"

"*Letter?*"

"It came by special delivery last night about nine. I didn't want to wake you, so I just tiptoed in and laid it on the desk."

"Why, no, Nella," said Georgine slowly. "I didn't happen to find it." She could not afford to meet Todd's eyes, nor anyone's.

"Oh, dear, do you suppose that in the dark I laid it down under something, or missed the desk entirely?"

"You might have done. I'll look." She gazed at her plate and ate steadily. The letter could not have fallen to the floor, for she had been all round those baseboards this morning, tapping them. A letter from Dyke: in her mind's eye she saw a page in her own handwriting, lying face upward on the carpet near the door. It had borne the words, "How much did Mary Helen tell you?"

"Barby's going to get tired, spelling out that story," Todd remarked. "I wish we had something to give her for a change.

You haven't any illustrated books, Nella? Or some old pictures that might have a story connected with them?"

"No, I'm afraid not," said Mrs. Peabody, "unless you count those photograph albums. There's one in the drawing room."

"That ought to do." He was beautifully casual. "Finished, Georgine? We might have a look to see if it would interest her."

Georgine went with him obediently. There was method in this irrelevance, she thought. For one thing, the folding doors cut off one's view of the stairs, and any of the family could slip up to the second floor within the next few minutes. He wanted them to have the opportunity.

"These are fine specimens," Todd said, turning the pages of the plush album on the marble-topped table. He swung toward the door as if to make sure his voice would be audible. "Will you look at the gentleman in the hand-painted tie! And here's a family group, on the front porch of this house—Lord, kind of uncanny, seeing the old place when it was new and those trees were small; doesn't look real. This must be Miss Tillsit. Seems to me Mrs. Labaré had a larger copy of this same picture."

There was no answer to these comments, and Todd glanced at Georgine. Then he strolled over to a corner whatnot and picked up a small reading glass from one of its shelves. "See if you can figure out what those pieces of jewelry were," he murmured.

She looked through the glass while he stood at the door. "I can't tell what the stones were," she said very softly, "except that those must have been pearls in the dog collar. The bracelet might be garnets. Maybe pearls around the watch, too, and in that bowknot pin."

"Must have been a handsome piece of jewelry. Like as not the pearls got sold early. Nobody's ever mentioned them."

"Why, Todd? I mean, why do you want to know?" But she was beginning to grasp his meaning.

"I went in to get your ring yesterday," he said in a barely audible voice. "I wanted to ask some questions of our chatty friend in the jeweler's, but I didn't quite know how to begin. He didn't volunteer anything when I led the conversation around. I do miss the police," said Todd plaintively.

"Oh, dear me," Georgine said, gazing at him. She bent once more over the photograph. "Here's a cameo pin; and those earrings were enamel, with fringe. All beautiful pieces, but—I don't believe terribly valuable. Of course one couldn't tell—" She saw the jerk of his head and slipped hastily over to the whatnot to replace the reading glass.

"I say, Mary Helen," said Todd into the hall, "Barby's going to drive us crazy asking what all these rings and pendants and what not were, that your great-aunt had in her heyday. Was that ring an amethyst?"

Mary Helen, on her way into the sitting room, turned and came across the hall. "No, topaz," she said interestedly, bending over the album. "A great big one; she must have paid fifty dollars for it."

"And the six stones on that thin chain? It's a li'le incongruous to see that one plain piece among all the baroque."

"Those *were* amethysts," Mary Helen said. "I never cared for them at *all*, myself, unless they were deep-colored, and these were pale. I hate this kind of jewelry anyway. It wasn't worth a *thing*, but they seemed to like it in the nineties."

Todd and Georgine leaned beside her, models of attention. Only one lightning exchange of glances said that they had heard the same thing; a faint gasp, outside the drawing-room doors.

"Well," Todd said, gathering up the album, "let's take this up to Barby."

"Did anyone come up to see you, darling, while you were finishing your lunch?"

"Nobody a-*tall*, Mamma."

"Nor—go into my room?"

"I heard a coupla people go into the bathroom," said Barby with frankness, "but I didn't see who. Nobody's been even to this end of the hall, Mamma, and I'm kind of tired of reading."

Georgine closed the doors to the hall and opened the connecting one from her room to the sewing room. She heard Todd beginning a story about the gentleman in the frock-coat, as she hurried over to the desk. The manuscript, as she had expected, was untouched.

It was just possible that the letter had fallen down behind the bed, to be caught on a ledge of the headboard; but it had not. She felt perfectly sure what the midnight intruder had wanted: the letter, in answer to hers in which she had asked that innocent question—which might have been interpreted, by any one of three or four persons, as an ominous one. And when the intruder had failed to find it—had he attempted to do her bodily harm before she could read it?

And here it was. How very simple, and how natural it looked; the top drawer of the desk was open half an inch, and the letter stood upright against its front panel as if it had been brushed off the top of the desk. She took it in and showed it, unopened, to Todd; he paused in his story a minute, examined the flap closely, and raised his eyebrows; then he slit the top open, carefully, with his pocketknife and handed it back without a word.

The envelope bore Dyke's name and army address. Georgine looked in her turn at the edge of the flap, and thought that there was a thin line of gum showing beside it which, perhaps, ought not to have been there. She took out the three or four pages it contained, written with Dyke's lavish carelessness on one side of unnumbered sheets and in a large sprawling hand. She found her heart thudding as she leafed them hastily through; and then an unreasoning sense of disappointment struck her.

This couldn't have been it. There was nothing in this letter to interest the persons in the Tillsit house. There was scarcely an answer to her question.

THE GLASS MASK 193

She took it in to Todd. "Excuse me, Barby," he said punctiliously, and in turn ran his eyes hastily over the scrawled words. "I say, there are all sorts of messages for you, cricket. The whole letter's about you, nearly."

"From Cousin Dyke?" said Barby, in holy awe. Her face shone.

Todd read it aloud. "'Dear Georgine, It's good news that my girlfriend enjoyed herself on her visit. Haven't had such a good time myself in dog's years. You tell her I'll take her out again any day; popcorn and milkshakes don't run half so high as a spell of night-clubbing.'" He shifted a page. "'So you and the old man—' Don't know how much I like that title," Todd interpolated—"'the old man decided to make the break without delay. Cheers, auntie dear; all kinds of happiness and what have you. You know I think you're tops and he doesn't deserve his luck. Wish I could'"—another page was finished—"'be there to see the deed done, but the Army needs good sergeants this week.'"

"The maneuvers," Georgine said.

"'Don't suppose you could wait about eight years until Barby's caught up with me, so we could make it double?'"

"*Couldn't* you wait, Mamma?" Barby said, radiantly serious.

"No, cricket," Todd replied firmly, "we could not. We'll wait till you're well enough to be bridesmaid, and that's all. Listen to the rest of this. 'You picked a nice place for the wedding, seemed as if that old town and the old house were clean out of this world and no war on. Mary Helen was full of legends; she talks up a breeze, Mary Helen does. Seems the old lady, her great-aunt, had plenty.'" Todd flipped over another page. "'I'm with you in spirit whenever the wedding comes off, wish I could see Barby holding your flowers. Best of luck, Dyke.'"

"Did you ever read anything so useless?" Georgine inquired bitterly. "Mary Helen talks a lot, and that's *all* he had to say about her or what she told him."

Todd looked up at her, his agate eyes intent. "He had more," he said, and held out the third sheet of Dyke's letter. "Get the light across it, Georgine, and look at the period after the word 'plenty.'"

"Blotted," she whispered after a moment's scrutiny, "and the rest of the page isn't."

"Ink rather a different color, too."

"Then—someone found the letter, and steamed it open, and destroyed a page or two with something important on it?"

"I'd imagine so."

Georgine met his eyes, breathing fast. "It was taken last night, because the person in my room was feeling around on every surface where it might have been laid; and it was returned this morning sometime. Great heavens, Todd. There must have been something here worth the risk! Could we get hold of Dyke?"

Todd shrugged. "Not if the Army's deployed over half the Sacramento Valley. I can try, but I doubt we'll get him."

"The old lady had plenty. Plenty of what? There must have been more to that sentence. Enemies? Money?" She recollected herself and glanced at Barby.

"Pick out another picture and I'll tell you a story about it, cricket," Todd said, laying down the album. "I'm going to talk to your Mamma a minute." He followed Georgine into her room and shut the door behind him, leaning against it. His eyes burned coldly. "Plenty of valuable property, or something like that, I'd guess. It must have meant something to the person who read the letter, or what came after wouldn't have been destroyed. Lucky for him Dyke broke off at a place that might have been the end of a sentence."

"Him?"

"Anyone. 'Mary Helen talks up a breeze.' She might have let out, to interest Dyke, something important; maybe she didn't know, herself, how important it was; or she may have been indiscreet about her own affairs. Curious," he said, musing, "how nearly that fits with the plot I used her in."

"Which kind was she?"

"The Perfect Murderer. You needn't bother to read it; it's one of the kind with a fancy timetable, all worked out beforehand to give an unbreakable alibi in case of need. In reality, if you remember, this gal says she was in Sacramento all day, looking for mourning. Nice touch, that."

"Very." Georgine shuddered.

"It would have been possible for her to drive back to Valleyville, by some of those country roads, and leave her car behind the house, or even some distance away. Nobody need ever realize she'd been here. Those cottages farther along the street weren't built until 1941. Walnut used to run right into orchard land, and this was the last house on it. Mary Helen's got the mind to be a Perfect Murderer. She's shrewd, she thinks things out and prepares for eventualities."

"I thought the Perfect kind always made one mistake at least."

"That's the theory."

"What would hers be?"

"Talking too much," said Todd soberly. "I've made the woman in my yarn somewhat older than the man. She's trying desperately to get his attention, and drops a hint that makes him investigate, at first idly and then—Well, that's beside the point. Dyke hasn't investigated, but he's damned attractive and I think La Crane worked hard on him. She wants to be the center of attention, to be supreme. I can hear her: 'There are all *sorts* of mysteries about this house, my great-aunt was supposed to have had beautiful jewelry and *some* of it must have been valuable. If she didn't sell the best pieces they've *got* to be here somewhere.'" Todd's imitation was not too kind.

"Oh, dear. That would fit. Do you think, though, that she would let that out to Dyke?"

"I don't know, Georgine. Suppose her motive hadn't been gain at all; she might think the matter had blown over enough so that it was safe to hint at something queer about Miss Tillsit's death."

"What would her motive be?"

"I keep remembering Serena." Todd frowned slightly, and looked past her as he did when something lay heavily on his mind. "The beautiful, suffering Serena whose death was such a blessed release. It's possible that she died quite naturally. It's possible, too, that—someone hoped her death would release John Crane from his obsession."

"And," said Georgine slowly, "when she talked to Dyke she couldn't have known that he'd have an uncle who'd stir the whole thing up again."

"Probably not...Yes, cricket, I'll be there in a minute... Later this afternoon, Georgine, I'm going to take the car out by myself. I wish you'd help me with something."

"I don't much like experiments," said Georgine uneasily. "What are you going to do?"

"Something very mild. I want to drive around these back roads and then come up as quietly as the bus will run, behind the house. I'll tip you the wink when I start. Will you stay in the sitting room and listen hard?"

"Must it be the sitting room? Oh, yes, because of Susie's having been there. What is it you want, to find out if you can come up unheard?"

"That's it. See you later, if you don't want to come in now."

She didn't. She wanted to think, to correlate somehow the stories that Todd had invented about everyone's guilt. Not one of them need be true, but there was a grain of truth, or at least of probability, in each one. This was another of those hateful cases in which anyone could be the criminal; not a really airtight alibi in the lot except for Theron Tillsit's, an equal chance for everybody to get hold of the poison, and no one motive stronger than the rest—at least, so far as anyone knew. Her mind returned to that one bizarre sentence from Susie Labaré's story. What sort of headgear was it that old Miss Tillsit had seen when her bedroom door swung open? An absurd, pretty hat on Mary Helen or Nella? The pathetic vanity of Gilbert Peabody's toupee? Something that Horace had put on to make her laugh, so that her defenses would go down, or—John Crane's reflector, absently worn during the short trip from his office?

The doctor. Dr. John Crane, who could so easily have paid a brief secret call here before he went out to see the Judge, and from there to his confinement case. Perhaps Miss Tillsit would have taken from his hands the seven tablets of luminal that made up a fatal dose. If your doctor told you that it was necessary—No! If your doctor were giving you a huge dose of a narcotic, he'd give it hypodermically. Had anyone ever thought of that?

She turned to the desk and seized the manuscript. Surely Todd hadn't left the doctor out of his calculations; no, here it was, the one remaining story.

"I never thought when I killed her that some day I might need to prove I had done it. Five years ago, and no proof that I was the murderer; and another man accused in my stead, because his motive has just now come to light.

"Will they believe me? Because, you see, I had no motive that anyone could discover, I gained nothing and might have lost much from her death. And who would believe that she blackmailed me into giving her the lethal dose?

"I can see her now, gaunt and glassy-eyed with pain which all my skill could not relieve. We were alone in the dusk. She lay there unable to move, and yet her fever-bright eyes held mine. 'You see, I know what you did for your mother,' she whispered. 'I was there outside the door, and I heard her begging, and I knew you couldn't refuse. You'll do the same for me or I'll have to tell what I know.'

"I was suspected, of course. All I had to do was to deny my guilt, to remain calm and seem innocent."

Yes, of course. The Standpatter, Georgine thought, her eyes fixed on the yellow sheets that quivered in her suddenly unsteady hand. *Serena.* Serena, whom he had loved, who had died so peacefully that someone who knew or guessed at the cause of her death might long for the same ending to life. That compassion, that sensitive hatred of pain that shone from John Crane's eyes...

I can't see him actually giving the dose himself, Georgine thought stubbornly, putting down the papers and running her hands through her hair. I simply cannot see it in either case. It would be just possible that he might have said to Serena, or to Miss Adeline, "Here's something to relieve that pain. Only one tablet at a time, mind you; the nurse is asleep but I'll tell her when she wakes." And then the box left temptingly near.

And would you call that murder or suicide?

She looked vaguely at the long chintz curtains stirring in the spring breeze, at the rhomboid of sunlight that was beginning to creep across the gray broadloom of the carpet. Why hadn't anyone thought of suicide?

A shrill voice was raised from the front walk, and Georgine started out of her abstraction. "Hello, Virdette! Do you want to come up and call on Barby? She's in bed resting, maybe you could play games."

Miss Bacon appeared in the upper hall, her yo-yo rising and falling in perfect rhythm with her footsteps. "Sure I'll stay with her," she said. Barby called from the sewing room to say that she was all alone, Toddy had gone out to do something or other. Georgine thought with a small shock that she hadn't heard him go.

He appeared almost on the heels of her thought. "I got to an outside 'phone," he murmured. "Dyke's not in camp, can't be reached."

"I was expecting that, weren't you?"

"Yes; and, I think, so was the person who read your letter. He may have said in the letter that he wouldn't be available for a while." Todd kept his voice low, although he had stepped into her room and closed the door. "What was the use of stealing those pages, when it was fairly sure that in a few days we'd be able to hear what was on 'em from Dyke himself, unless those few days will see the matter cleared up?"

"Repeat that, for dumb listeners?" Georgine requested.

Todd grinned. Excitement was working in him. "I mean that things will automatically come to a head within a week, say; the game has to be won or lost in that time. And what's due to happen at any minute?"

"Our leaving—I hope."

He shook his head. "That's a movable feast. No; the telephone made me think of it. The antique dealer, Georgine, who may be here at any time, and who'll presumably take away all that fine old furniture from the attic. Nobody knows when he's coming, except that it'll be soon, but the secret will go away with him."

"Here we go again," Georgine said despairingly. "I get my mind geared to a death four years ago, and then I have to start thinking about something that's going on right now." She stopped and looked at him, her lower lip folded over the upper. Then she said slowly, "Are they the same thing, Todd? Are the past and the present closing in on us like—like pincers?"

"The attic mystery and the murder mystery," Todd said from remote thought. "They may be the same and they may not. Perhaps they touch only at one small point. But there's an interesting parallel there, Georgine: the sense of urgency, of something that has to be finished before something else happens. There must have been a reason why Miss Tillsit died at the very moment she did."

Georgine remained by the door, smoldering. "And I suppose we brought this on ourselves, just by trying to be helpful to Nella! You would have to think of the antique dealer, and offer to get him up here, and *make* it urgent for the rats-in-the-attic person to find what he's after and maybe mow us all down in the process! I hope—"

"You hope what?" He glanced round at her, his eyes alight with laughter.

"Oh, well—not that anything happens to you. I can't afford to lose you at this stage. But I certainly hope that the searcher gets cheated somehow, that maybe what he was looking for got thrown out years ago, unbeknownst, with the rest of the rubbish from the drawers and the crevices of the chairs. Handkerchiefs and scissors," said Georgine with irrelevant bitterness, "and a nurse's cap that was supposed to've been lost from the wash, and buttons—"

"Is that what Nella found and threw away as rubbish?" Todd inquired. She looked at him, startled. The aerial seemed to have shot up.

"It's nothing much," he added. "I only remembered that the clean laundry is left in the entry at the foot of the enclosed stairs."

"Well, what of it?" Georgine said crossly. "If someone's been going through all this rigamarole to find something that was lost from the wash, I'll *know* we're visiting in a loony bin!"

"Toddy!" Barby shrieked from the next room. "I told Virdette you'd play the mouth organ for us, and you never did yet, and you promised—"

"I'll be right with you, Barby," Todd said. "Finished with these, Georgine? Then I'll take 'em." He bundled his papers together.

"Yes, I've finished, and there was something I wanted to suggest; but it'll keep. Go on and perform, Barby will yell her head off if you don't."

She walked up and down her room, frowning, her thoughts going round like a roulette wheel that might deposit the ball of logic in any one of a dozen places. Gilbert—they had typed him as the Damn Fool—Wasn't it possible that he might fit in yet another category? What if Gilbert were the Noble Sacrifice? He might have seen the candy, or remembered that Nella had recently given him some to take to the old lady; and suspected, rightly or wrongly, that there was something queer about it. Supposing—just supposing that he had looked in at his aunt as she lay in the beginning of coma, had sensed that this was no natural sleep, but not being sure had yielded to temptation just enough so that he kept still instead of calling her nurse. He might have hoped, humanly enough, that she was slipping quietly away to her death. Would it be murder if he had detected this and had not given the alarm? It might have made him feel guilty enough so that he would be perturbed, then and later; and, when he found that the town was talking, he might have offered himself as a scapegoat. Going away to the war would have looked as if he were taking the easy way out.

But, she thought with a sudden leap of the heart, the same argument would hold if Miss Adeline had taken the luminal of her own free will!

Maybe nobody'd ever thought of that; maybe with the ingrown love of sensation you find in a small town, with the natural suspicion brought on by the doctor's request for an autopsy—and how beautifully that fitted with the idea of suicide, too!—it had simply suited people better to think the worst; but the theory covered everything, it should make Nella happy and relieve everyone's mind.

She had to suggest it to someone. Todd was thoroughly engrossed, in the next room, teaching the two little girls to sing "Father, dear father, come home with me now." They seemed to be almost paralyzed with giggles, but were making a brave stab at the tune. What was the time? Almost half-past three; the doctor had said he would call some time this afternoon, but there was no telling when he'd arrive. She *had* to talk over her theory.

Footsteps sounded on the walk below. Georgine looked from her window, and saw the grandchildren of Judge Tillsit strolling along side by side. They looked very much alike, all at once; Horace's receding hairline and Mary Helen's pompadour, the difference in curves and height, seemed to fade into nothing.

Georgine went down the stairs on a sudden resolve. "Hello," she said brightly. "Mr. Tillsit, you seem to be getting plenty of time off from your store, these days!"

"Sure." Horace smiled at her professionally. "The twins are here at last, d'you see? All Mart wants to do now is to stay in public where he can brag about 'em, and hand out cigars."

"Well, that makes it nice for me, because there's something I'd like to talk over with you—with Mrs. Crane, too."

"What?" Mary Helen inquired. "Isn't your pal Nella in on this, too?"

"Not yet." No use, Georgine thought, in getting her hopes up until the idea had been tested.

The cousins looked at each other swiftly. "Well, then," said Mary Helen, "we'd better go into the drawing room. There's only one door."

Georgine could not resist lifting an eyebrow. "Have you noticed that, too, the lack of privacy here?"

"Yes, indeed. Have *you?*" said Mary Helen sweetly.

It was cool in this southeast room. Georgine found herself shivering a trifle, perhaps with the chill, perhaps with hope. She was wondering just how to begin; she was wishing, all at once, that she had not embarked on this project.

She glanced up at the cousins; they sat side by side on the plush sofa, looking at her with patient pleasantness. The Tillsit eyes, shrewd and direct...

Now she found herself thinking not so much that her theory was true; but that if the family had any sense they would jump at this chance.

CHAPTER TEN

THE PAUSE WAS A BIT too long. "You're scaring us," Horace said, smiling; and leaned forward to pass her a cigarette.

"I certainly didn't mean to. On the contrary. You know, I should never bring this up again if you both hadn't seemed so willing to talk about it. Todd couldn't help being interested, and of course I—"

No. No good. Why should she feel embarrassed—except that it was the first time she'd interfered? Georgine took a deep breath. "Why," she said bluntly, "did neither of you suggest that Miss Tillsit might have taken her own life?"

The cousins sat and looked at her. Their silence was not quite that of persons dumbfounded by a new idea, but there seemed to be calculation in it. She thought she must begin to fidget before Horace finally spoke.

"How d'you figure that?" His eyes were large behind the spectacles, giving him a benign look. "With Gilbert acting the way he did—"

"I think Gilbert felt guilty; but not because he'd done anything—because he *hadn't* done anything." She began to sketch her idea, watching their faces intently. Not a muscle moved in either, but something grew in Mary Helen's eyes— was it relief? When she had finished they were silent again, for a moment.

Horace again took it up. "You want an academic discussion, h'm? Okay. Where'd she get the luminal? Because if somebody brought it to her—"

"That would be almost the same as murder. I agree. But need it be exactly like that? Look—didn't Dr. Crane carry luminal in his visiting bag, or whatever you call it?"

The two exchanged a swift glance. "I used to provide it for him, all right," Horace said. "And I guess you stocked the bag, Mary Helen. Ampules and tablets, isn't that right?"

Mary Helen's voice was weighted with reluctance. "Ye-es."

"Then," Georgine said, "why couldn't Miss Adeline have stolen it? I've had the impression that Susie wasn't always in the room during the doctor's visits. What if he left the bag on a chair and went to wash his hands, and Miss Tillsit simply reached over and got herself a tube of the stuff?"

Mary Helen's forehead wrinkled, though her eyes remained wide and candid. "But that would mean—" she said slowly, "that would mean such terrible carelessness."

"On whose part?" her cousin inquired.

"Johnny's, of course. *I* didn't have anything to do with it."

"Didn't you check the supplies?"

"Well, yes, to the extent that I renewed them when he needed them. But I'd *never* have thought to ask how come there was an ampule missing, or a tablet or two. I took it for granted, always, that—"

"He'd used 'em himself. Sure you would. But, look here, Mary Helen; you're not married to the guy any more."

"What's that got to do with it?"

"You don't owe him a thing, loyalty or anything else; certainly not keeping still about his carelessness. You might as well face facts," said Horace earnestly. Mary Helen gave a sharp giggle. He went on, "It's the truth, Mrs. Wyeth, John's absent-minded as the devil. We all know that."

"Well, we've got to be fair," said his cousin, her voice rising. "He never made a mistake on dosages, you said so yourself; he never forgot to call on a patient, or got symptoms mixed up, or—"

"But look!" Horace was visibly excited now. "He checked the supplies himself, let's say, once or twice a week—or even every day when he came in from his house calls. He might just have failed to miss *one tablet at a time.* And when Aunt Adeline died, if there was the least suspicion in his mind that his negligence had helped her to kill herself—he did his best by suggesting the autopsy. Any blaming of himself he did after that would have to be in private. If the man insisted on investigating, he'd be a fool."

Mary Helen turned her head. Her look at him had the quality of applause, and Georgine had a sudden horrifying thought.

Was that a good way of escape for Mary Helen herself? Had *she* taken the tablets from the doctor's store, and did Horace know it?

"I didn't quite mean to—" she began; and at the same moment the folding doors slid back with a dramatic squeal.

"Have you all quite finished with my reputation?" said Dr. John Crane, in a towering rage.

"Great God," Horace said under his breath. "He would hear that. Look here, John, we—"

The doctor closed the doors behind him and moved into the center of the room, his eyes fixed on the cousins. His long face seemed pinched. Mary Helen stirred uneasily, settling the collar of her smart plaid dress.

"Don't you glare at me, Johnny," she said. "I was standing up for you, though God knows why I *should.*"

"Thanks. I know the way you stand up for people. So-and-so is so fine and charming, isn't it a pity he's never been quite right in the head!" He laughed harshly, and Mary Helen closed her lips and looked at the carpet.

She's afraid of him, Georgine thought. Does *he* know something about *her,* that he's been too loyal to tell? They were still married when Miss Adeline died, perhaps that's why he dropped the matter of the autopsy...Oh dear me, what have I got into?

"Come on, Johnny," Horace said. "Be fair to her. She didn't say—"

"All right. You did. That's what I heard as I came in, and not by putting my ear against the door. You were broadcasting to anyone who stepped into the hall."

"Oh God, John, I'm sorry," Horace muttered. "But you've got to admit it's not beyond the bounds of possibility. And I'd never have said it outside the house."

"No?" The dark eyes were red-rimmed with anger. "Just insinuated it, that's all. What makes you think I couldn't hand out a few insinuations of my own? That scratch on your arm might have healed up before anyone else noticed it, but it caught my eye—while you were bending over your great-aunt's bed, five minutes before she died!"

Horace Tillsit gazed up at him, literally open-mouthed. "That scratch on my arm?"

"A fresh one," said John Crane grimly. "Painted with merthiolate. Your sleeve hid it."

"Insinuations," said Horace blankly. Then, suddenly, he began to shout with laughter. "Great God, Johnny, what are you driving at? You think I came around and had a regular fight with Aunt Adeline and poisoned her by force, all in silence, and *she* scratched my arm? Man, man!" His laughter subsided into chuckles; it had miraculously cleared the air, and Dr. Crane gave a brief tired laugh of his own.

"All right, forget it, Horace," he said. "Skip the whole thing. I don't get enough sleep."

"Dr. Crane," Georgine said, "I'm afraid this was all my fault. I didn't think ahead far enough, when I wondered if Miss

Tillsit couldn't have committed suicide. It seemed so logical at first, and so—so convenient."

The doctor's look at her was courteous, but none too warm. "I see. Well, Mrs. Wyeth, you're right; it would be convenient to believe that, *if* you want to think that there was something unnatural about her death. That is an opinion," he added bitingly, "in which you seem to share. I can't blame you for the suicide theory, in a way, since nobody seems to have told you that Miss Tillsit suffered no pain, was greatly interested in life, and had no reason for wishing to die."

"Oh," Georgine said feebly.

"Moreover," said Dr. Crane, impaling her with a look, "she had made up her mind to outlive her brother if she could. He was still very weak himself, after that bout of pneumonia, and was by no means out of danger. He'd had a sinking spell that afternoon. Can you imagine that grand old woman deciding *at that moment* that it was time for her to fade out of the picture?"

Horace and Mary Helen gave each other a swift glance, quite unreadable.

"If she'd ever thought of it," the doctor concluded, as if he were biting off every word, "she'd certainly have waited, with the idea that the Judge might die first, and that the ranch property and the position of head of the family would revert to *her.* Once in her hands, it would have passed to Gilbert, as she had always planned. You think she'd deliberately throw all that away?"

"I suppose not," said Georgine weakly.

"Then that's all." He turned away; turned back at the door to say, without meeting her eyes, "Keep that little ol girl of yours in bed and quiet for at least another day. You'd be taking a grave risk if you moved her now. Good-by."

Horace and Mary Helen rose and followed him out; you might almost say they slunk, but their attitude was as nothing to the way Georgine felt. She was still sitting there, clasping her head in both hands, when Todd appeared in the doorway a few minutes later.

"Never again," she said on a long groan. "I'll never raise another question about anyone's death, no matter how good my intentions are. Oh, Todd, what I've done!"

"Tell me," Todd said placidly, drawing up a chair.

She took a deep breath. "At least it won't make *you* fly off the handle," she said, and told him what had just happened. It was not hard to remember every word; the conversation seemed to be etched on her brain.

When she had finished, Todd rose and came over to her. "Bless you," he said, and planted a chaste kiss on her brow. "Never you worry about your good intentions. The results aren't so bad, either. I'll go out with the car now, and be back in a few minutes. Will you stay in the sitting room and listen?"

She watched him go out; he seemed to exude a brisk confidence that was near to triumph.

She had made a flying trip upstairs, to find Barby and Virdette happily planning what the bridesmaids would wear at their weddings, and was back in the sitting room gazing with distaste at the jar of pampas grass, when the car drew up in front.

Not Todd, back already? Georgine thought, glancing out. He had meant to come through the rear lane anyway, hadn't he?

"The Judge!" she exclaimed aloud, in horror, and for a minute contemplated hiding behind the sofa. The old man's footsteps were very audible on the front walk and stairs, he must be stamping hard. "Mary Helen!" he bellowed from the hall. "Mary Hel-*en!*"

"Well, don't shout the *house* down, Grandfather," came from above.

"You come down here. Want to talk to you."

"All right, all right. Only do pipe down, the little girl's been sick." Mary Helen's voice and her descent of the stairs were alike deliberate. "What is it?"

"Come in here." Georgine moved to the dining room arch, poised for flight, but the judge meant the room across the hall. A chamber of horrors for poor Mary Helen this afternoon, she thought.

The loud voice boomed through the hall. "I want to know what's the meaning of this preposterous letter you wrote me?"

"Really, Grandfather, the meaning ought to be plain enough! And why couldn't you write an answer, if you were going to say 'No?' Because that's what I see in your eye."

She wasn't afraid of him, in any case, Georgine reflected. In a moment they would close the drawing room doors—she hoped.

"More money, for *that!*" the Judge said angrily. "You haven't got it coming anyway, my girl, but for a damn-fool gamble—"

And then the doors did close. Georgine tiptoed to a seat, much relieved. She had promised Todd to stay right here, his experiment would have no value if she moved to another room. Now, if the Judge and his granddaughter would only keep their voices to that indistinguishable murmur...

She gave a violent start and swung round toward the bay window. Someone had just peered through it, someone who was standing on the front porch.

Georgine pulled herself together and marched over to the alcove. The massive figure was no longer there; it had moved to the other side of the front door and was leaning against the house wall. Costanza, the Judge's housekeeper; standing there with her arms folded, seemingly making no effort to hear what went on inside; just standing.

Why, Georgine thought, she looked like a—a bodyguard. Their eyes did not meet.

The sight of Costanza in her broad open-toed shoes, her magenta satin blouse, and the black skirt that was so badly rump-sprung should have been rather funny, but somehow was not. It was almost sinister. And how silently she got her great bulk about! Georgine had not heard her moving along the porch.

She turned away after a moment, uncomfortably conscious that the voices across the hall were rising again. The Judge spoke harshly, like one who holds a material whip hand but not a moral one. "Not out of me. No, young lady...Place not good enough for you...where you belong...wild-goose chase... "

"All right, all right. It's what I might have expected, but I thought I'd give you a chance."

The drawing room doors slid apart. "That's your last word, is it?" said Mary Helen. There was a finality about the sentence, as if it were moving her to some decision. Without waiting for an answer she flung open the front door and crossed the porch, the heels of her sling pumps clacking hard on the boards. "So you're here?" Georgine heard her remark, presumably to Costanza. "Well, you weren't needed. He wasn't in any danger." A jeering giggle died away as she ran down the steps and cut across the lawn.

The Judge, deprived of an audience, wasn't having a fit. He must have lacked the time while he fought with his granddaughter; now he simply stood alone for a moment, and then came out into the hall with ponderous haste.

At that moment Georgine heard a car drive up behind the house. There was no mistaking the sound; it was Todd returning. She moved cautiously toward the dining room, planning to head him off if the Judge were staying; but he was not. He was on the porch, saying audibly to Costanza, "Let's get out of here. Ought to know better'n to come."

"Why, Uncle Theron, you're not going?" said Nella Peabody's voice. Once more, behind its sweetness there was light mockery. "It's getting along toward suppertime; can't you stay?"

"No!" the Judge shouted back, his words also diminishing as he went. "You know there's no use your asking me!"

"But you never do stay, I wish you would some time!" Nella was calling after him now, all hospitality. She couldn't have been heard, for the Judge was now climbing into his car with every appearance of hurry.

"Yes," said Georgine softly to Todd, who had just come in the kitchen door, "I heard you."

"Thought you would. There's a rise and dip in the lane there, you can't get over it without using the gas."

"And what does that prove?"

"Nothing much, except that whoever came in that back way came on foot." He didn't look discouraged, though.

It was not until the company had gathered at dinner—Mary Helen coming in breathless, her lips firmly shut with an air of something decided on and accomplished—that Nella spoke.

She served green beans and tiny new potatoes with a deft and lavish hand. "Have lots of the beef," she said. "Six ration books to work with! We're rich this week.—Well, dear children, did you enjoy your peaceful afternoon at home?" she added. The soft shine in her gray eyes told them that she had heard everything that went on, and that she was quietly pleased.

"You hate us, don't you, Nella?" said Horace softly, looking down at his plate and stirring the vegetables with an idle fork.

"Hate you? Why, what a way to talk. Whatever makes you think that?"

"The way you act," said Horace with simplicity. "You've been feeling this way a long time. I guess it's just coming out now."

"Horace, really. I don't know what you're referring to, but in any case must we discuss it now? Georgine and Mr. McKinnon say they must leave tomorrow," she told him brightly. "I'll be so sorry to have them go! I did hope for just a few days more."

Well, you can't have 'em, Georgine told herself fiercely. It's been far too long as things are. She ate with concentration, wishing only for the end of the meal, for night to be over and morning to come. I want to go home, she thought with longing.

"You have made a difference to Nell's spirits," Mary Helen said, looking at her. The light struck gleams from her wide-open eyes. "I've noticed it so *very* definitely, Mrs. Wyeth."

"Just the stimulus of company," Nella said, "and such pleasant company—no indeed, Georgine, you haven't been the least bit of trouble. Keeping Barby in bed for a day—why, that was nothing!"

Georgine surprised herself. "Do you know," she said thoughtfully, "I think it would work out very well if we went tonight, right after dinner."

"Oh, *no!*" said Mrs. Peabody on a long gasp. "No, you can't! I mean—didn't John Crane tell you that Barby mustn't be moved?"

"He said it would be a risk, but perhaps it's one we ought to take."

"No, *please.* Horace, do you want to feel as if you've driven our guests away early?"

"Last thing on earth I want to feel," said Horace smoothly.

Perhaps it was meaningless, perhaps the words held no more than their surface value; but Georgine felt an intolerable sense of emotions rising, swelling to a climax. And there they all sat—eating! That absurd series of acts, pushing something into a hole in the face, and chewing solemnly, and exercising the muscles of the throat...

Todd had said nothing at all. He likes this, Georgine thought bitterly. He hasn't missed a thing, and he sees implications that I miss, or don't understand. He raised his head and their eyes met. She was instantly sure that all the happenings of the past few days had come together in his mind to form a whole, a comprehensible shape.

"Well, if it's your last night," said Mary Helen brightly, "let's have a game of bridge. Horace, you don't have to go right back to the store, do you? Now, Nell, you can leave the dishes for a while."

"A fine idea," said Mr. McKinnon unexpectedly. He wants this too, Georgine thought, and I'll have to follow his lead; but—bridge, of all things! A bubble of wild, helpless laughter was swelling within her.

And when he cut out for the first rubber he looked like the proverbial cat with feathers on its whiskers! He melted from the room so unobtrusively that she doubted if the other three noted his absence. He was gone now, into the dusk of the hall, and a door opened and closed softly.

She didn't know whether those faint hollow-sounding footsteps, increasing and then diminishing, were his or those of Nella who had just left the room while Horace examined the dummy she had laid down. Georgine felt her lips curving in a nervous sort of grin as she looked at the intent faces of the cousins, at the rose-painted china globe of the lamp that shed its light on the shiny surfaces of the cards...

The cards shot helter-skelter over the table, and the lamp rocked as Mary Helen leaped to her feet. They were all standing, glaring insanely at each other for a moment. "Upstairs!" Mary Helen gasped. "Second floor, somewhere—" The three of them were out of the room before the echoes of that sliding crash and the wild yelp that had preceded it had died from their ears.

Barby, Georgine thought, and found herself snatching open the door of the sewing room. No; her child was in bed and placidly asleep; she stirred and murmured something about her flashlight and subsided again. And the sound hadn't come from here, it had reverberated in some hollow space.

Horace and Mary Helen were in the enclosed side stairway, bending over someone who lay there. "Todd," Georgine said on a breath of agony, as she reached them, pushing them aside. Nella was coming slowly up from the first floor, a hand over her heart. *"Todd,"* said Georgine urgently, kneeling beside him where he lay sprawled on the stairs.

Horace was lighting match after match from a paper folder. Why didn't someone turn on the light in the entry? This well was as dark as pitch... Her hands moved over Todd frantically; he was breathing, there was no blood that she could feel, but he lay relaxed as if he would never wake.

She said in a voice whose calmness surprised her, "Get me some water, Mary Helen. I'll take those matches, Horace. Move away, can't you? If he's hurt he's got to have air."

Nella had already slipped away as silently as she had come. From the lower floor her voice rose. "Ring him again, please, keep on ringing. It's urgent."

The last match flared. Todd's eyes were open; he was looking at Georgine, his whisper just reached her ears.

"I'm okay, but don't let 'em know it." As the match went out one eye closed in a meaningful wink.

She fell back to a sitting position, her knees shaking. A number of tart comments formed themselves in her mind, but Mary Helen was on hand with the water. Nella's voice sounded again on the telephone. "John, for heaven's sake what kept you so long? Come, please, right away. Mr. McKinnon's been hurt."

Fooling everyone indeed, thought Georgine with asperity—including scaring me nearly to death. Another of his experiments, if I'm not much mistaken. This time it backfired on him.

"But what happened? What's he doing here?" Horace demanded, returning with an immense first-aid kit. He also had a student lamp on a long extension cord, and now shone this into the supposedly unconscious face.

"I don't know, I'm sure," said Georgine feverishly. "But he's hurt, he must be, isn't the doctor ever coming? It's no distance at all from his house... Oh dear, oh dear—Todd, speak to me!"

She was overdoing it a bit, judging by the suppressed quiver that ran through his body. A little water down his neck wouldn't hurt him at all, she told herself vengefully, and gave the cloth an extra squeeze. There were more voices in the lower hall; the doctor's, and another, flat and nasal. "I declare, I was just comin' up the side walk when I seen Johnny shoot up to the front and come tearin' up these stairs. Thought you was all dead, for a fact. Now, don't go to pieces, Nell Lace—"

Todd stirred and murmured with artistic faintness, "Dark. Too dark. Flying down—down from the attic—"

"No bones broken," said Dr. Crane in a puzzled tone. "Shift that light this way, can't you? He doesn't seem to be hurt; maybe a mild concussion, or bruises—shock—"

Here Todd sat up, wavering, and was at once supported by willing hands. "I'm—all right," he said unsteadily. "Damned if I know what—what made me—"

"Get him to his room," Dr. Crane said curtly. "I guess he can walk, but he'd better lie flat for a few minutes." He stood beside the massive cherrywood bed, gazing down at his patient's impassive face. Susie Labaré, in her element, bustled about the room on errands devised by herself. She seemed to feel it necessary that the shaving kit on the bureau should be closed and the typewriter covered. Through the door peered the faces of Nella, Horace and Mary Helen.

There were a few gentle questions from the doctor. "You can't have just fallen down those stairs, man, if you were going up. Your foot slipped? But how did that knock you down half a flight?"

Todd's gaze traveled slowly from face to face. After what seemed a long wait he shook his head cautiously. "I can't seem to remember much," he said, "except that the lights wouldn't work. I'd started up the stairs anyway, so I went on."

"Somebody took the bulbs out," Horace began in his hushed voice.

"But what were you *doing?*" said Mary Helen shrilly. "Why were you on those stairs at *all?*"

"Why not?" Todd murmured feebly. His eyelids flickered. "I was in the garden—shortest way from there to my bedroom—"

The others exchanged swift glances. "But what then, McKinnon?" the doctor insisted. "How did you fall?"

"Then—" Todd said, and gazed vaguely into space. "Then—no. It's black. All black." His voice trailed away.

Dr. Crane turned away, biting his lip and looking puzzled. His eyes fell on Nella. "Sit down, Nell," he said quickly, and pushed his way to her. "You look a little green. You didn't run up any stairs, did you, after all I've told you?"

Nella shook her head and sank down on the settee in the hall. "Just reaction," she said with difficulty. "I—I must have been—"

"Don't talk." The doctor bent over her. In Todd's room, Georgine came to with a start to realize that Mrs. Labaré was speaking.

"You look kind of all in yourself, Mis' Wyeth. You was up with the little girl last night, wasn't you? Now, you let me sit with the patient here. You go lie down and get some rest."

In the brief moment before Georgine answered, all the terror and distrust of the last few days struck inward. She thought incoherently of the hard Tillsit eyes and the Tillsit secrets, of accusations implied and spoken, and the aunt with the reticule in Todd's story, and a door opening when an old woman invited death to enter her room.

We've got in too deep, she thought in panic. We've started something that's going on inexorably to finish itself, and if we get in its way—

Every person here is an enemy. We can't let down our guard for a minute.

Her throat was very dry, but her voice sounded all right. "Why, thank you, Mrs. Labaré, but I don't believe it's necessary. I'll be right here, you know. Todd, dear," she bent over him and spoke gently, "do you want anyone to sit with you?"

"No," he murmured. "Just rest." Reluctantly, Susie went away.

"I'll be in my room, Todd," said Georgine clearly. "The door will be open, so you've only to call."

The group in the hall had melted away, the doctor and Susie had gone home and Horace to his night trick at the drugstore, before she let herself go to his door. She laid her ear against the panel for a moment before she tapped; the faint sound inside was reassuring enough. Todd was playing his mouth organ, pianissimo.

While he was mulling over some problem he usually practiced whatever unsuitable classic he might be trying to learn at the moment; but when the problem was solved he relaxed. It was no theme from Handel that he breathed into the reeds now, it was a simple rendition of *Three Blind Mice*.

Georgine opened the door and looked in. Todd, sitting on the edge of the bed, met her glance and got up swiftly. "Yes, I'm really all right," he murmured in answer to her gesture. "There wasn't any concussion, hardly a bruise if the truth were told."

"I gathered something of the sort," said Georgine in a low tone, shutting the door behind her. "A fine performance, chum. 'Black, all black!' Heaven give me strength."

"Dear Georgine, I beg you not to snap your eyes at me." He grinned unrepentantly. "That was the most innocent li'le experiment a man ever made, and I got a fine surprise from it. No, I was not going up to the attic in the dark, sticking out my head for someone to bop me. There shouldn't have been anyone there."

"Well, what were you doing, for heaven's sake?" Her eyes went nervously to the window, open on one of the rickety balconies, and she lowered sash and shade as quietly as is possible for one who longs to slam doors.

"Yes, I'm scared again," she added defiantly. "Good and scared, and I'm in no state to consider logic. Todd, they're trying to keep us here, by one means or another, just so they can *get* us—as they very nearly got you on the stairs."

"Take it easy," he said tranquilly. "That wasn't as bad as it looked. Sit down, my dear, and have a cigarette for your nerves' sake. In the first place, what I was doing wasn't foolhardy. I simply wanted to go up those enclosed stairs without trying to be quiet, to see if the others would hear me and come to investigate. I meant to step out on the second floor, without going near the attic."

He paused, and Georgine looked at him, frowning. His deep-set eyes held some emotion, but she couldn't decide if he were laughing or not.

"And," he went on levelly, "someone did hear me; someone who was already up there, and knew that I was coming nearer and nearer, and for all he or she knew, that I might come up through that well at any moment. The stair lights were out— has anyone bothered to replace the bulbs, by the way? I thought not. Well, as I started up from the basement there was a sort of a flicker, reflected from the stair walls; I'd guess a flashlight, being very cautiously used in the attic. The moon won't be up till early morning, you see, and someone couldn't wait."

"But—who? It must have been an outsider, Todd. Horace and Mary Helen were with me every minute, and Nella had just left the room a minute before you yelled. She—she couldn't have got up there ahead of you, could she? Run up the stairs and whisked into the attic at the very moment you chose to start up to the second floor?"

"I don't know for sure." There was a cold gleam in Todd's agate-gray eyes. "All I know is that as I came up I heard a stir at the top of the house, and then something came at me with an almighty great whoosh—shot down those stairs like a bat and knocked me halfway down the flight I was on."

"Knocked you—"

"No, I didn't really fall. You might say I slid down the banisters on my hands," said Todd, silently chuckling. "Knocked my wind out for a minute, and by then I heard the light cavalry charging up the front stairs and it occurred to me to play dead dog. Worked fine, too."

"Did it, indeed. It took a year off my life."

"I shall try to restore it, my dear," said Todd gravely. "But consider Nella's solicitude, calling for the doctor at once; it took him a fairish time to get to the 'phone, too. Consider how opportune Susie's visit was, and the fact that Horace came down from the second floor to find me, and Mary Helen came up the enclosed stairs from the first floor—almost as if I were being hemmed in so that if I'd wanted to chase my giant bat toward the basement, I'd have bumped into Mrs. Crane and been headed off. All very rewarding."

"I see. Couldn't have been better if you'd planned it. Todd McKinnon, if you'd lay off these experiments—"

"I give you my word, this wasn't planned."

"All right. But if you got to thinking of yourself as a great detective, after all you've said—"

"No." He frowned a little. "I'm no detective, except that—well, you remember what we said about the transparent mask."

"You mean you know what this is all about, this attic business?"

"I think so."

"And you know—who killed Miss Tillsit?"

"I think so."

"Well, don't tell me!" said Georgine in a vigorous whisper. "At least not until we're far away." She got up. "I've had enough of this, I want to go home and forget it."

"You're quite right. Why don't you go to bed now, and before you know it it'll be morning and we can—"

"Go to bed? You mean to sleep? Are you crazy? After all these goings-on I'm not even planning to take my clothes off, let alone lie there in the dark."

"I'll be up, if that would help any."

"What for, Todd?"

"If our impulsive friend goes up attic again," said Todd deliberately, "he's going to get caught in the act."

"You're going up there to wait?" said Georgine in icy tones.

"Not necessary. I'll let the household get settled for the night, and then I'll open the door to the staircase and sit in the hall—and watch. It'd give me some pleasure to spike that character's guns."

"You won't spike 'em alone," said Georgine. "I'll be right at your side on that settee, brother."

Barby slept in peace. Her mother stood looking down at her, giving thanks that the threatened asthma attack had not materialized. She bent over to kiss the towhead. Barby spoke distinctly in her sleep: "Virdette put it on the table in the hall, and I got up to look and it was gone."

The flashlight again: that tangible symbol of Cousin Dyke. Perhaps it had been wise to keep her in bed today, though she had seemed perfectly well when she awoke in the morning. The doctor had given orders. Georgine had obeyed them unhesitatingly, as always; but now she wondered. No better way could have been devised to keep her and Todd staying right here than to say that Barby must not be moved; to keep them in this house until the crisis—whatever it might be—of the mystery was past.

I want to go home, Georgine thought, clasping her hands hard. I wish we were home now, or that we'd never come.

The sounds of people going to bed had diminished and died to silence. It was nearly one o'clock. Georgine peered cautiously into the hall and saw that Todd was already there, on the plush settee by her bedroom door.

"Leave your door open," he said on the barest thread of breath. "Leaves us in shadow and lights up the stairs."

She lowered herself carefully to a seat beside him. When they were together there didn't seem any great danger about this vigil; it felt ridiculous and hollow.

"Are you sure everyone is in?" she said on a whisper as soft as his own.

"Yes; and asleep, I hope."

"Horace too?"

"Horace too. The lady in Vallejo must have been lonely for the past two or three days."

"Todd, dear; you made a mistake in letting so much time elapse between our last talk and this one."

"So?"

"Yes. I've had time to think. Will you take me away now?"

"Now?" His smooth head turned slowly.

"Can't you see we're foolish to stay here when we don't have to? Barby's perfectly normal, as I ought to know. You've done what you set out to do, all your stories are blocked out and you can simply leave the carbons for Nella if you still think it's your duty. I wish you'd get the car out and take us away. We can bundle up Barby just as she is. I wouldn't mind a bit stealing a couple of Nella's blankets."

Todd did not answer, but his head was still turned toward her and his eyes were on her face. "If you're thinking about the wedding," she said, breathless in her desire to convince him, "I'll sit in the car with you for the rest of the night, and the minute the courthouse opens we'll go in and get a justice of the peace—anybody—any way you want it. But let's go!"

"A moonlight flitting?" Todd's whisper sounded at last; he seemed remotely amused.

"Yes. If we let *them* know we're going they'll find some way to keep us. I know you want to stay, to—to see things out to a finish. You think something's due to happen tonight. But couldn't we—skip the last act and get out before the crowds? Look, Todd. You said you'd guessed all the answers; but you're not a detective, you're not a policeman, you're not even a private citizen who's seen a crime committed. This is all in the past, the criminal part at least, isn't it? Well, then; *what do you have to do about it?*"

The answer did not come for a full minute. Once more the details of the hall imprinted themselves on her memory: the heavy pictures leaning out from the walls, the three-cornered chair and the case of discarded books in their dreary bindings, and the bamboo table by the door to the enclosed stairs. That door stood open now, a rectangle of deep solid black in the chiaroscuro of the opposite wall. No sound, no movement came from it.

"What do I have to do?" Todd's whisper came at last. "Nothing. I don't know of any way to see justice done. Miss Tillsit's body has been ashes for all of four years, and there is no other proof that a murder was committed."

"And still you want to stay and see this out?"

"No. Not if you want to go this badly. How long will it take you to pack?"

"It's all done," Georgine whispered on a half-sob of relief.

"Then I'll put my coat on," Todd began to ease himself to his feet, "and get the car out of the shed. It'll roll down without my starting the engine." He bent to her ear. "You won't be afraid to stay alone for five minutes? If anything went wrong you could scream, you know."

"No. I'll go into my room. I—I suppose you still want me to listen for your attic friend?" She could afford to laugh now.

"If you wouldn't mind." He laid a light kiss on her temple. "It'd seem a pity to waste the chance, if it came right away. Just turn the light on the door, you needn't do anything."

She heard the front door open and close softly as he passed through, but she doubted that anyone else would have sensed it. Todd could move very quietly when he chose, and it may have been only the cool draft from the staircase that made her sure he had gone. She slipped quietly back into her own room, leaving that door open the merest crack, and stood looking round carefully to make sure that everything was packed. She could carry her own bag and Todd's light one, and he could take Barby. With care, Barby would not wake at all. If she should, and they were caught—

She lifted her head and stood gazing incredulously at the wall. The lowest attic stair had creaked.

Georgine wheeled round, her heart thudding, and moved silently toward the door. She needn't expose herself, she could open it and look through the crack. The second step creaked, as if with the stealthy, careful pressure of a foot. She knew those sounds, the note of each step. They were imprinted on her inner ear. There was the third one.

She reached the door and pulled it wide. Now the shaft of light streamed across the hall, full upon the cavern of the enclosed staircase. The fourth step creaked.

Georgine Wyeth stood paralyzed, her eye at the crack of the hinge, the doorknob slipping from a hand grown suddenly cold and wet. The fifth step of the attic stairs gave out its own peculiar cracking sound; you could almost imagine the walker wincing, trying to step as lightly as possible...

She could see perfectly. The light illuminated the full lower half of the flight, and there was nobody at all on the stairs.

CHAPTER ELEVEN

SHE WAS SITTING ON THE FLOOR when Todd came back a few minutes later. Her palms were pressed to her eyes and she was saying to herself in a low voice, "I've gone mad. I must have gone mad."

"Georgine, what is it?" He knelt beside her.

"I couldn't scream when I saw nothing at all, could I?" She took down her hands and looked at him dull-eyed. "G-get everyone up just to tell them there wasn't anyone on the stairs but f-footsteps?"

"Wait a minute. What is this?"

"The treads creaked, one after another, and no one was there!"

"You're sure you could see clearly?"

"Yes. And no one—not a thing—"

He was halfway to his feet when she caught at him. "No, Todd! Don't go into that stairwell! Please, if I've ever asked you for anything—"

"You needn't dislocate my arm." He grinned, disengaged her grip and lifted her upright. "This is the time to look around."

"No, listen to me." She took a deep breath and shuddered once, strongly. "I know that wasn't a ghost, of course. It can't have been. But—it's some kind of a trap."

"I'm not so sure." He was still unruffled. "If someone did engineer that special effect, maybe we were meant to think that we had been mistaken all along, that there had never been a living person in the attic. Or, if we didn't believe in ghosts we might convince ourselves that the house made those noises all by itself; you see?"

"Maybe," Georgine murmured, her eyes fixed on his. "But I don't like this human agency any better than the supernatural. Thank heaven we're all packed, we needn't waste a minute."

"I'm afraid we must." His arm was steady about her shoulders. "Just before I started to roll the car out I looked at the gas gauge. Somebody's let all the gas out of the tank. And the new coupons aren't good for two more days."

Georgine tore herself out of his grasp. "What did I tell you? We're being kept here, they don't mean to let us go. Todd, let's walk out to the highway, we could thumb a ride and leave the bags and the car here—"

He turned his head and glanced toward the sewing room door. "Oh, dear me," she said despairingly, and sat down on the edge of the bed. He was right, of course. It would be one thing to bundle Barby in covers and whisk her into a closed car; quite another to carry her or make her walk two miles to the main road and stand waiting in the chill of a spring night for someone to give them a lift.

"Can you take it for a few hours more?" he said levelly. "In the morning I'll see what I can do with a few threats."

"I'll have a try at taking it," said Georgine drearily. "There isn't much else to do."

"I shan't be far away."

"You won't go into the stairwell? Will you promise?"

"I promise. My poor love, it's about time you had your innings."

She heard him quietly re-seat himself in the hall; she fell
back against the pillows, still weak with shock. It would be
impossible to sleep...

Morning sun made the new leaves a gilded green, outside.
Barby was climbing into the bed beside her, jabbering about
breakfast, and there were voices in the hall.

Mary Helen's: "Oh, good *morning*, Mr. McKinnon. Are
you quite well again? You know, I had such a queer night, I kept
imagining people whispering in the hall and going up and down
the front stairs. And I could have *sworn* I smelled a cigarette."

"I was slightly delirious, Mrs. Crane," Todd responded
gravely. "I came to at dawn, out here, to find that I was reading
Elsie Dinsmore aloud by candlelight."

Horace's soft tones, muffled and booming in the enclosed
stairway, "Hey, who left this mop down here?"

"Mop?" Todd was courteously interested.

"Yeah. Wedged into the banisters, right across the stairs.
Great God!" Horace sounded aggrieved. "If a fellow had come
running down here in the dark, he'd have tripped on it and
broken his neck."

Georgine sat up. "Yes, darling," she said in a low voice to
Barby, "you get dressed now, as fast as you can. We're going
home—pronto!"

"Today? Oh, Mamma, I haven't half finished looking at
those old things in the trunks."

"But we must go some time, dearest. You can't stay out of
school forever, and Betty Dillman's party is on Saturday."

"Well—I just wish we could stay a few *minutes* longer.
Maybe if I went up right after breakfast?" Barby suggested
with overwhelming charm.

"*No.* No, Barby." Georgine took her child's shoulder in a
firm grip. "I don't want you to go near that attic again."

"But wh—"

"Don't ask me why. I know, I know, I've always given you
a good reason; but just for this once, you're not to do it because
I say you mustn't."

"Oh." Barby turned away. The back of her neck was heart-rending as ever, but this time her mother was not softened.

After a polite but rather silent breakfast—"If you really must go," said Nella Peabody, sighing, "you'll be wanting your ration books, of course. They've been such a help; I can't tell you how guilty I feel about letting you pay anything for staying here."

Todd had lighted a cigarette and strolled into the front hall in her wake. "The question of pay," he said gently, "is rather involved, I'll admit. You're an honest woman, Nella, and you have no car of your own."

She turned, the gray eyes wide. "I haven't—"

"So you'd have no use for the gasoline. You're thrifty, too. Don't tell me you poured it all out on the ground?"

The pink triangles burned on her cheekbones. She stood silent, gazing at him and breathing rather fast. Georgine, leaning against the stair rail, thought: I should have guessed it.

Mrs. Peabody's glance fell before Todd's level one. A tall figure showed through the stained glass beside the front door, and she turned as if more than grateful for the interruption.

"I had an early call," said. Dr. Crane in the doorway, "and I thought I'd see the little girl before office hours."

"She's quite well, thank you, Dr. Crane," said Georgine. "We plan to leave this morning."

The doctor frowned. "This morning? After an attack like that?"

Nella's gesture, her intent look at him, were neither quick nor guarded enough. "You fixed this up between you, I presume," said Todd gently. "We can't accuse you of malprac-tice, Dr. Crane. You were just erring on the side of safety when you advised us to keep Barby in bed indefinitely. Mrs. Peabody, too—she's an old patient of yours, I know. You're fond of her and concerned about her health, and you'd see nothing wrong in an innocent conspiracy to protect her." He stood straight and smiling, his hands in his pockets.

"Oh, the hell with it," said John Crane suddenly, with a disarming grin. "I can't keep it up, Nell."

"All right." Nella swung round courageously to face her guests. "I made up my mind I'd go to any lengths to keep you. It—it isn't fair that you should help me so much at the first and then leave when it's—when it's—"

"Only a li'le while before the man comes for the furniture," Todd completed it. "I'm sorry, Nella, but circumstances beyond our control—"

"I know!" She grasped the newel, shaking visibly. "I thought it might not touch you, you're a man, and I did need someone to stand by me—you don't know how much. It was never anything but noises up there, but I knew there was something going wrong upstairs. I'd lie here awake night after night, listening, and wondering how soon that malice was going to come close—to touch me. When you two were here, I felt safe for the first time in weeks, in months. And then to see the end in sight, and have you plan to leave just before—just before—"

The doctor walked casually toward her and grasped her wrist. Todd said again, "I'm sorry. But you had your heart trouble, and your mystery in the attic, and the rest of it long before we came. You have been everything that was hospitable and kind to us. I said I'd do my best for you, and I've done it; there's a manuscript that you shall have before we go. For the rest—I owe rather more to Georgine than to you, and even if it caused you active illness I should have to take her away now."

There was a pause. Then Dr. Crane said abruptly, "I apologize for my part in this—innocent conspiracy, I think you called it."

Georgine's breath fluttered on a laugh. "Think nothing of it."

"I'll be getting back to the office now. *Nella*—"

"Oh, very well," said Mrs. Peabody wearily. "The gasoline is in cans, in the bushes behind the summerhouse. I didn't mean to keep it, you know."

"I'd like to settle your bill, Doctor," said Todd equably, "and ask one more question." With some amazement Georgine watched the two men walking out, apparently in perfect amity. We *were* being used, she thought, and bit down hard on her temper.

Todd turned and came back, waiting until Nella had gone swiftly into the kitchen and closed the door, before he said, "Are you all ready?"

"In two minutes. I had to unpack some of our things."

"I'll save time, then, by doing an errand. It's daylight, and you can stay in the open."

"Where are you going?" Her lower lip went up.

"To the garage, to get that carburetor adjusted. It was acting up yesterday. I'll be back in half an hour."

She went upstairs, in a haste that was almost panicky, closed the suitcases and snatched her hat and coat. Firmly holding Barby's hand, she returned to the front porch. Mary Helen had wandered into the sitting room and now sat in the bay window idly looking through the newspaper, from time to time glancing at the waiting pair. Nella's steps sounded inside the house; Horace came out, made a polite little speech of farewell, and went down the street toward the center of the village.

The shadows moved, and Barby fidgeted on the top step. Georgine thought that nothing was so irritating as to wait like this before the start of a journey. Half an hour, indeed. Get a garage man and a car owner together over a carburetor, and time simply slid by them.

"Did you put my flashlight in the suitcase, Mamma?" Barby said. She was subdued; the general feeling of strain over the departure had not escaped her.

"I can't remember, darling. Probably not, I'd have noticed if you'd let it out of your clutches."

Barby fidgeted again. "I thought—" she began, and stopped to ponder. "Oh, I know. Maybe I left it in the summerhouse, Mamma, I'll just go round and look."

"Very well. Come right back, Todd will be here any minute."

If only he'd *hurry*, Georgine thought, shifting her position on the porch steps and glancing uneasily into the open front hall.

It would be like a rebirth to get away from this house: the strange hatreds and fears and conspiracies of the family, the smell of the past, the feeling of "something that doesn't mean well" all through it, from the olive plush sofa in the sitting room to the walnut monstrosities in the attic. She detested every inch of it. To think that in an hour and a half, two hours, they could be home...

She'd been too hurried that morning to beautify herself for a wedding. Once away, they'd have plenty of time. There must be a hotel near, where the bride could curl her hair and powder her nose.

And I'll need a bouquet, she thought practically—on purpose so Barby can hold it. Oh, dear! I wish I had a free mind for all these details.

Mary Helen tripped across the hall, humming lightly. "I think Nella's crying," she observed to the outer air.

"That's too bad," said Georgine wearily. "I hope she'll feel better before we go."

"Having a little trouble getting started?" Mary Helen leaned against the doorjamb and met Georgine's eyes. There was a queer look about her: was she amused, or resentful, or only impatient to see the last of them?

"Yes, a little." Georgine got suddenly to her feet, on a disturbing thought. Mary Helen was saying something about must they *really* go? and she replied absently, "We're due at a wedding. Barby! Bar-*bee!*" The child had been gone for minutes—much longer than it would take her to run to the summerhouse and back.

There was no answer. She called again, louder and more urgently. Her voice seemed to ring far off, across the empty cellar hole of the Bacon lot, high up to the Tillsit chimneys. "Where is she?" Georgine breathed, swinging round. "She always answers when I call!"

Mary Helen seemed to be barring her way, probably in a laudable attempt to dodge her headlong rush through the door. "I saw her in the yard a minute ago, didn't I? She must be somewhere around—maybe down cellar?"

Georgine thrust her aside and made for the stairs. A whole series of thoughts had arranged themselves in her mind: the flashlight—it had been on the table in the hall, right by the attic door…Those flickers of light Todd had seen in the stair well the night before, Barby getting out of bed to look for her treasure…

She reached the second floor. The doors stood open, the bedrooms bright and innocuous in morning light, and empty. She called again. "Barby!"

That smothered sound was coming from above her, the thumping accompanied by muffled squeaks. "Mamma!" Barby's voice cried out, as if through layers of cotton wool. "Mamma! Come quick!"

Georgine, at the top of the attic stairs, stopped in her tracks; she was smitten by a wave of helpless laughter. On the floor at the far end was something resembling an octopus in a chintz housecoat. It flumped up and down, it rose nearly upright and collapsed again, it grew protuberances that flailed the air in vain.

"Barby Wyeth," said Georgine when she could speak, "how on earth did you get yourself tangled up with that thing?" The zipper dress bag, as it ever was; had Barby lifted it down from the hook and got it over her head somehow? "Lie still, darling, I'll come and get you out." She started across the floor, still chuckling.

"Stand still, right where you are," said a harsh whisper.

Georgine checked herself automatically for a wild glare around the empty room. The last of her laughter seemed frozen on her lips. "What—where—" she stammered, wheeling toward the far end. "What do you mean, stand—"

"*Or I'll drop it on her,*" said the whisper, and like something in a horrible dream the great walnut headboard against the far wall rose slowly upright. A dark object like a muffled hand showed at one side, holding it as it swayed forward and stood poised.

"Barby, roll this way!" Georgine cried sharply. "*No*—no, lie still!"

The octopus had given one mighty heave, directly into the orbit of the great mass of wood with its crushing weight. Georgine took one more step forward, and stumbled over an object on the floor; a hard cylinder. "Stand still, I told you!" The whisper seemed to fill the room. "And no noise. I tell you, I'll drop it!"

Barby was *in* the bag, the zipper drawn up. She was blinded and helpless. The distance between them—Georgine measured it with a frantic eye—was just too great; if she dashed forward now she could not catch the headboard before it came down, down on the little soft body...

"Mamma, get me out!" the strangled tones besought her.

"Make her keep still," said the whisper implacably.

Georgine closed her eyes in one mighty prayer. "In a minute," she said, and years of schooled calm kept her voice low and level. "You got in there, now you can stay for a while." She could not, she must not go to pieces now.

"Just lie *still*, Barby—Who are you? What do you want?" She managed a stage whisper of her own, to reach the person who stood pressed between headboard and wall. "I won't move, I'll do anything you tell me, only don't hurt her!"

She dared not cry out for help. And at the first loud sound, the carved panels would shift and become foreshortened and tilt forward...

She drew in her breath in a shrieking gasp, and put both hands to her face. Behind her was the sound of something bumping, rolling downward from step to step of the stairs. Had she left that door open at the bottom? Oh, dear God, let it be open...No, let it *not* be!

"What was that?" The whisper was threatening.

"Nothing. The flashlight. My foot struck it—oh, what *is* it, what do you want of me?"

"Thought you'd get away with 'em, didn't you?" There was venom in the harshly breathed words.

"With what? Please, for God's sake—"

"Anyone could 'a guessed you'd have the luck to find 'em, up here snoopin' around, and in *her* room downstairs, too.

I knew from the first you never come here by accident. You found out somehow—well, you can give back what you took. You'll tell me where they are."

It hissed and spat hideously into the silence. Georgine thought, if I crept forward step by step, and got there in time to throw my body across Barby's—let that weight down more easily—She slid one foot forward; the whisperer couldn't see her...

But it could hear. "Stop it," the voice commanded. "Every time you move, I'll know it. Anyone comes up the stairs, I'll drop this. I mean it. You or that brat found the six diamonds, and you're going to give 'em to me."

The six diamonds?

I should have known, Georgine thought madly. The jewels on the thin chain, in the picture, that Mary Helen had said were amethysts; the safe-deposit box, and Gilbert's errand, and the small cardboard box in the wastebasket. Hidden, hidden—

A ghastly paralysis seemed to have descended on her. Her throat was dry and she cleared it with difficulty, seeing for the first time a chair on its side at one end of the room, the casters wrenched from the legs so that a round hole showed at the base of each.

"I—I don't know anything about them—"

But if that—that *thing* behind the headboard were convinced that she was in possession of the jewels, and meant to get them—or else let drop the weight that still hung poised?

"Ah-h! Liar!" The whisper was almost a snarl. "Nobody else has 'em, and there's no place where they could be that hasn't been searched. You wanted to get away in an all-fired hurry, didn't you?"

I must think of something. Her heart thundered, she gazed frantically at the small bundle on the floor, which now and then wriggled and gave off a smothered noise like a sob. "All right," she said, "we've got them. They're—in the pocket of my suitcase downstairs. Please—let us go! I'll take my little girl and go clean out of the house, we won't even see who you are, you can go down to my room and get them and go free yourself—you won't be interfered with, I promise!"

The headboard was still upright. If that muffled hand should slip or tire, the weight would be uncontrollable. "Please!" she said again in the whisper that racked her throat. "I'll not say a word, nobody will know this has happened."

And there was a flaw in that. What was to prevent her from raising the alarm, promise or no promise, the moment Barby was safe? The creature behind the screen must see that; it couldn't afford to let her go.

It would wait until she and Barby were both within the arc of the great slab; and then—could she shove Barby out of the way?

She felt her nails digging into the skin of her cheeks, and forced her hands to come down relaxed. If there were only something within reach that could be forced against the headboard as a prop—but she was in the very middle of that long room, and the pieces of furniture were too far away. And if anyone came to help her—she was doubly lost as soon as a footfall sounded on those creaking stairs.

"All right," said the whisper, like a hideous answer to her thoughts. "You can come and get her." There was a rattling noise, and a scraping jerk, from the far wall. A cool current of air swept along the floor, raising a swirl of dust from the boards. Had the door at the foot of the stairs blown open, or was someone there?

She twisted round in desperation. Perhaps if she cried out, "Don't come up!"

Though there had been no sound, Todd was standing at the top of the stairs.

He had come—but he mustn't cross the floor, either! He couldn't help—And then she saw. Noiselessly, with exquisite care, he was picking up the long pole that opened the skylight. He held it poised, rapidly gestured her to silence, and then reached it to her hand over hand.

Swaying with relief, she managed to stretch her arm until the pole could be safely grasped. She thought that minutes must have gone by, but it could have been only a few seconds, for the whisper commanded her sharply, "Wait! If you're lyin' to me—Where'd you find the stones?"

"In one of the hollow balls on the curtain rods, in her room!" It was the first thing that came into Georgine's head, and she was regaining her balance before making her rush with the pole. It must not slip, or it would be useless.

"They were not there, ever! She looked there! You lied to me!" the whisper fairly shrieked; and the muffled hand disappeared from the edge of the poised mass. It tilted, ponderously, and came slowly away from the perpendicular.

Georgine had the end of the pole against the carving; she was not quite near enough, she struggled to get under it and lever the pole against the floor. The weight was still descending. Out of the confusion of sounds and movement she saw Todd's thin wiriness flashing past her, dragging the chintz bundle out of the way with one swift jerk, dodging as the shallower footboard came down with a mighty bang. He twisted his shoulder aside as the weight brushed it; swung round and grasped the edge of the headboard just in time to lower it the last few inches.

She heard her own voice crying out insanely, "There won't be anybody there, behind it!"

There was not.

But there was a thin crack of light, and a thin draft that came through; a door which the standing furniture had concealed. It gave onto the widow's walk, it must, there was no other reason for its being.

Todd leaned against the wall for a few seconds, breathing hard; then with no more than a look for Georgine he thrust at the door with his shoulder and stepped onto the crumbling balcony. She saw him lean cautiously over the rail, looking downward; then his shadow went swiftly past each of the windows, making the complete circle of the walk.

She was aware of this just barely, as if she were coming out of ether. The March sun lay quietly on the bare dusty boards. Georgine sat down beside the dress bag. Her knees would not support her another minute, and she had to clasp her hands tightly before feeling returned to them and she could unfasten the zipper.

I mustn't touch Barby, I mustn't grab at her as I want to, she thought. I'll frighten her to death if I do.

From the welter of Mary Helen's summer dresses Barby emerged slowly, crimson, disheveled, and crowned with the ruin of her WAVES hat. She looked sheepish and indescribably guilty, and she began talking at once.

"You said you'd get me out, Mamma, and it was the longest time, and you didn't until somebody *jerked* me! I don't see what I did that was so bad. I never got in there by myself. Honest, I didn't."

"Somebody put you in, I imagine," said Georgine in grave maternal tones. She folded her arms tightly across her bosom, while the attic went round her in slow circles.

Barby looked away. "I just came up for my flashlight, I knew it was up here because somebody took it off that table, and I couldn't find it anywhere else—well, I know you said not to, but I thought just for a minute!" She glanced at her mother, her eyes large with outrage. "And there was somebody behind that bag, and when I went round to look it jumped at me! I got all mixed up with the clothes and things, and I couldn't get out, and it got zippered!"

"Perhaps somebody thought you were meddling."

"Well—maybe. But I *hat* to find my flashlight!"

Todd came swiftly through the open door. He still said nothing, but he bent to touch Georgine's shoulder as he went by. She heard his feet clattering down the stairs.

"Very well, darling. You were bad, but I don't need to punish you any more, do I?"

"No. I—I didn't like it very much in there."

But she had not known of the danger that had hung over her. Thank heaven, she'd never know.

"Well, go and get washed. Yes, all over again, you're dusty. You'd better change your dress too. All right, all right, put on the new one if you must. Just—*hurry.*"

Georgine was not to have time for a breakdown. She heard Todd calling her from below, urgently, and forced herself to her feet and down past the bedroom floor to the lower landing of the front stairs, where he was crouching. Nella Peabody lay there unconscious, her face a queer grayish color, her breathing barely perceptible.

"Todd!" Georgine said. "What did she—it wasn't *she* who was up there?"

"I don't know." He was frowning, feeling for Nella's pulse. "Whoever it was could have got clear away. I wasn't quite fast enough." His voice shook. "Thank God, thank *God* I heard that torch bumping down the stairs when I came to look for you— and that I listened for a minute before I came up to the attic!"

"How did you manage not to let the steps creak?" said Georgine tonelessly.

"I came *up* the banisters, like the original rat—the one you didn't hear coming down, on Tuesday night. Footholds on that gingerbread carving that's used instead of posts—Look here, my dear, this isn't an ordinary faint. Nella's having a real attack. We'd better get her onto a bed, and call for help."

He raised a shout for Mary Helen; listened, and shouted again. "Never mind," Georgine said. "I'll help, I can take her feet. On your bed? It's nearest."

Edging slowly up the staircase and across the hall with the limp burden, she thought, The *original* rat? Does that mean there were two or more, and the whisperer behind the bed wasn't the person who'd been searching on moonlight nights? It seemed more than likely, come to think of it; the haste, the rashness of this one—up there while the whole household was awake, and in full daylight—and the horrible reality of the threats...

She must have turned pale, remembering this, as she swung Nella's feet onto the bed. Todd glanced at her, and said quickly, "Can you hold out a few minutes longer? Won't hurt you to have something to do in an emergency."

"I guess so. I can—oh, here's Mary Helen. Your cousin's having a heart attack, what does one do for her?"

"Well!" Mary Helen said. "I *thought* I heard you calling me, I was outside. Seems to me she has something in an ampule, that you break and she inhales it. I'll look in her room. You'd better unfasten anything tight she's got on."

"I know, I know! There isn't anything except her belt, and I've done that. Can't you hurry? I don't like her looks."

And then all at once there was nothing for her to do; the doctor had come, Todd had driven to the drugstore and brought back not only the required supplies but Horace, who thought more help might be needed; Mary Helen was in attendance, and so was the ubiquitous Susie Labaré, who had appeared at the top of the stairs in the midst of the confusion, and had at once taken charge.

"What, all of 'em here? The hell you say," Todd remarked as Georgine came out to the hall. His eyes gleamed hard. "That's not bad. I'll have a few words with the person who did that to Barby."

"*No,*" said Georgine, going unsteadily toward her own room.

He looked at her sharply. "You don't mean that."

"Yes, I do. Please, not anything more."

Todd bit his lip thoughtfully. "As you say. These are still your innings. But—"

"She's safe, and that's all I care about. Let's just *leave.*"

Barby was struggling with her coiffure. Georgine sat down in the slipper chair and braided the flaxen wisps with fingers that would barely obey her. Her child was still feeling guilty, for without looking round she remarked, "I washed good and hard, Mamma. The back of my neck, even. See?"

"I see," Georgine said. She dropped the brush, gathered the thin little body into her arms, and burst into wild tears.

After one moment of consternation, "Toddy!" Barby called out. "Mamma's *crying!*"

Todd was in the room without delay, though he did not seem to be perturbed. "Of course she's crying," he said. "It'll do her good. You'd cry too, if you were your mamma. It won't last long." His cool fingers closed firmly about Georgine's wrist.

"Well, how long?"

"Let's see. About two minutes more, I think."

"All over my new dress," Barby mentioned with resignation. "How much longer, Toddy?"

"About forty seconds."

Georgine managed to get a full breath into her lungs, and to fight down hysterical laughter. "Darn you both," she said, releasing Barby and feeling for a handkerchief. "Holding a stopwatch on me!" The tears had not only relieved her, they had drained her of all emotion. She looked at Todd dully, as if he were a stranger.

"We'll go in a minute," his calm voice said. "We can be on our way before you know it. D'you think a nice quiet wedding would take your mind off your troubles—or doesn't this feel like a lucky day?"

"It'll be a long time," said Georgine slowly, "before any day will be lucky enough. Todd, don't hold me, or I can't say what I have to. Don't you see—we can't be married."

She never realized until he grew pale how much color usually underlay the even brown of his skin. He took his hand from her wrist. "Barby, please go into the sewing room and look at your book for a few minutes. Close the door between. Go on, cricket." His eyes were steady on Georgine's. "Now, my dear, what is it?"

"I don't see how I can give you up, but I'll have to."

"Postpone the wedding again?"

"Just about—indefinitely. I never thought—I didn't foresee anything like this, Todd. Of course there's danger in your profession. If you have anything to do with crime, even just writing about it, you're bound to get mixed up in horrors every so often. I could accept that for myself, if I tried. I could take it for you; it's your life, you have a right to risk it. But I never thought of its touching Barby. How can I let her in for this sort of thing? She hasn't the choice; I have to make it for her."

He said nothing, but his eyes were intent. "I know, I know," said Georgine wearily, "she's in potential danger every time she crosses the street to school, or puts on her roller skates. I'm—geared to that by now, as every mother has to be. But I'm not geared to expect violence for her, and I don't know when I ever will be."

"Georgine," Todd said, "you're using the one argument I can't combat. I can only point out that a situation like this may never come up again."

"You can't say that it never will. You can't promise that, can you?"

"No. I can give you the odds: about ten thousand to one."

"Do you think they're good enough?"

"That's for you to say." He leaned against the foot of the bed, his legs stretched out to brace him, and put his hands in his pockets. His face had once more taken on that look of being carved from blond wood. "You don't feel like taking a sporting chance? No, that's obvious. I might have expected this, I suppose." Todd broke off and studied her for a minute. "I'm not so wedded to my profession as all that. It could be changed. Unluckily, at the moment, it's my living. I'd have nothing to offer you for the next few years, while I found some other job that a man like me—half a man, you might say, with that crocked lung of mine—can do decently. That seems like rather a long postponement."

Three days, she remembered dimly, could seem very long. He had thought that this very night would be their wedding night; well, so had she, Georgine reflected, a wave of longing rising in her and dying away. "I didn't say I could give you up forever," she told him dully. "I don't believe I could.

In time I might even get used to this—awful riskiness, and maybe you could go on writing. I know you love it, it's your real work, what you were meant for. But I can't, I can't accept it right away."

"Dear Georgine," Todd said, "can't you manage to get mad, and sail into me? Tell me this is all my fault, that I got you into this and caused you a lot of suffering out of pure self-ishness. I've got that coming, God knows. Then, maybe, when it was off your chest—"

"How can I say that, Todd, when it isn't true? Barby got herself into that mess, and you got her out again. I can't be grateful enough. But it's just the way things are. Let's not discuss it any more, please. We'll drop it for a while; we'll leave right this minute, and just go home."

Todd came slowly to his feet. When he spoke, she looked up at him, startled; his voice had a queer metallic clang that she had heard only a few times before.

"No, by God, we won't!" he said. "There were two reasons I wanted to stay here, and I seem to have wrecked one of 'em pretty thoroughly. That being the case, so help me I'll have a go at the other one."

She sat up. "What on earth are you talking about? Todd, you don't mean—you said you'd never accuse anyone of the murder, or of trying to hurt Barby, there was nothing you could do! You're not going to—not just because I said—"

"Yes, Georgine. And yes, 'just because you said.'" His eyes were flinty. "Leave me a li'le self-respect, will you? Let me finish what I've started in *one* department. They're all across the hall still, I can hear their voices. Get hold of yourself and come over there; I may need you."

"What are you going to do?"

He grinned at her cheerfully. "Try a big bluff and clear some of this up. Stick my neck way out; and if I'm wrong and somebody breaks it for me, at least I'll have tried!"

She sat gazing, stupefied, at the open door to the hall, through which his slender hard body had just disappeared. She heard his voice: "Just leaving, Dr. Crane? I'll have to ask you to stay a minute longer, to make sure your patient doesn't have another attack. There's something it's my duty to tell her—and the family."

Georgine got up and followed him, dazed, into the bedroom where Nella still lay. Noon sunlight lay in a thin bar below the windows, and the beautiful clear mirror above the cherrywood dresser reflected the faces of the room's occupants: Horace, checking over some kind of a list; Mary Helen, looking concerned and watchful, and the doctor, wearing a puzzled frown; the tall gaunt figure of Susie Labaré, still bustling about, passing and re-passing the mirror. The stiff white curtains swelled silently inward on the wind, and collapsed again. Nella Peabody lay motionless, fully dressed but with a cover drawn over her, and looked at the ceiling.

"You are all concerned in this," said Todd smoothly, "either as witnesses or members of the family. I think I must ask you to hear what I have to tell Mrs. Peabody; if you agree, perhaps there is some action that can be taken."

He turned to Dr. Crane. "You told me this morning that your patient's chief trouble, what was causing her nervous heart attacks, was uncertainty; not the fear that her husband had poisoned his aunt, so much as the not being sure. Is that correct?"

John Crane cleared his throat twice before he could speak. "I—I believe so. I'm no psychiatrist, but I think if she could know—one way or the other—"

"Very well." Todd took a sheaf of folded papers from his inner coat pocket, and chose one. He walked round behind the table on which his typewriter had been standing, and laid the other sheets face downward. "I'm going to read this aloud," he observed dispassionately, "in the hope that you will all comment on it or correct anything I have wrong. If it should prove to be accurate, you may wish the person involved to sign it. There would be no more uncertainty, then. Nella Peabody would have no more to fear."

How tall he looks, Georgine thought irrelevantly. He's—frightening, somehow. I never knew he was as sure as this...

Todd lifted the paper and began to read. "I poisoned my aunt, Miss Adeline Tillsit, with a lethal dose of luminal, on the afternoon of June 9, 1940. The candy found behind the head of the bed had nothing to do with her death, nor did the earlier death of Serena Peabody, who died naturally of inflammatory rheumatism. I am solely to blame. A little before two o'clock I left my studio—"

A strangled gasp came from the bed, and John Crane went forward swiftly. "It will be better this way, Nella," he said. "You want it; deep in your heart you've always known."

CHAPTER TWELVE

" ... **A**ND THAT," **SAID** Todd, laying down the typed sheet, "is the case against Gilbert Peabody, made up of bits of information you've all given me. Means, motive, opportunity, character; do they satisfy you?"

There was silence for a moment. Nella had closed her eyes and lay like a waxen figure. Then Susie Labaré said on a long breath, "'Fraid so. I never heard it all put together that way, but—that's how it must 'a happened."

Mary Helen Crane said, just audibly, "H'm. Well, now I hope *Nell* is satisfied. That all?" She rose as if to leave.

"No," Todd said. "That's not all. Sit down, please. There is only one person in this room, besides Mrs. Wyeth, who has not something more to answer for, something rather serious." His somber gaze moved from face to face. "Perhaps you think I haven't helped Nella very much? But she has another source of anxiety that I'd like to clear up." He turned toward the bed. "What made you faint on the stairs, Nella?"

She spoke, her lips barely moving. "Awful crash—in attic. I forgot—I was so frightened I began—running up."

"I believe that's true," Todd said. "You could scarcely have been the person we—encountered in the attic; you hadn't the strength to balance that heavy weight, nor quite the agility to climb down the lattice work from the widow's walk to one of the second-floor balconies." The others were exchanging perplexed glances; he went on soberly, "Did you see anyone as you came up the stairs?"

Her head moved negatively.

"You hadn't a suspicion of who might have been there?" Todd asked her softly. "Yet for months you've known that some- thing was going on up there, some kind of a search, and you never mentioned it to anyone until we turned up—strangers, who wouldn't know about the background of this family. Georgine," he said, lifting his eyes, "I should like a closer look at that identification disk Nella wears. Will you lift it out of her dress—clear out?"

Georgine went to the side of the bed as if she were moving in a dream; she detached Nella's fingers, which had flown defensively to the neck of her dress, and drew out the silver disk on its long chain. Something else followed it; a thin strong cord of silk, flesh-colored, whose connection with the chain had been hidden by the silver plaque. On the end of the cord was a tiny bag like a sachet. Its contents were hard.

Nella's head fell to one side, and she let her arms relax. "Open the bag," Todd said. "We've all guessed what's in it, but we may as well be sure."

There they lay in Georgine's hand, six perfect bluish stones, unset, of perhaps two carats' weight each.

"*She* had them!" Mary Helen cried furiously. "She had them all the time!" She swung round toward her cousin. "You fool, you told me Aunt Adeline said she'd hidden them where no one would ever find them! You—you encouraged me, you helped me—"

"It's too bad, Mrs. Crane," said Todd McKinnon soothingly. "All that trouble you took—coming home on nights when you were supposed to be staying out of town, so that Nella wouldn't necessarily associate the sounds in the attic with you; you knew she'd be too timid to investigate alone, and that she'd call Horace to look instead, and that he'd insist the noise was made by rats. Startling, wasn't it, to find that there'd been strangers in the house on one of the nights you chose to search. I'm afraid Georgine and I ruined your plans. When Horace told you we were here, and you remembered some of the stories you'd told to interest my nephew, it made you nervous—didn't it? You followed us when we came home from Dr. Crane's—"

"I did nothing of the kind," Mary Helen said, with obvious sincerity. "I never knew you'd been to his house."

If Todd was disconcerted by this, he did not show it. He said, "Thank you. I hoped you'd clear that up. It was someone else, then, someone who'd wondered all along how much the doctor suspected about Miss Tillsit's death. But as for you"—his flinty look had never left Mary Helen—"you knew how dangerous it was to continue your search, perhaps you'd have dropped it until after we left, except that Nella had asked me to get the antique dealer up here, and the necessity forced you to take the risk. Dyke might have got back from maneuvers, too, and repeated what you'd told him. Something of a shock, wasn't it, when you got that letter out of Georgine's room and found that he could have given away some unhandy secrets?" Now he was speaking fast and crisply. "And all on such an uncertain premise; the diamonds weren't in the safe-deposit box, nobody knew whether or not they'd been sold, and in spite of what your cousin told you there was always that feeling that you might be too late to find the jewels no matter how hard you looked."

Mary Helen looked at him sullenly, her naïve-seeming mouth closed into a thin hard line. "They were mine," she said furiously. "Aunt Adeline's jewelry was left to me."

"Not quite." Todd smiled gently. "The jewelry in the safe deposit was yours; the contents of this house belong to Gilbert.

You had to find them without Nella's knowledge, otherwise you'd be in for a long legal battle. Get them out of the house, and nobody could prove they'd been here. And Nella," he added, "realized that the same thing obtained from her side. She couldn't let you or anyone know she'd found them."

That was what Nella meant, Georgine realized dimly, when she wanted to tell me everything, but didn't quite dare. We might have thought she was dishonest.

"She could do nothing," Todd was continuing, "until her husband came home to stand by her, because the whole family was in league against her. I think she was wrong, that even Judge Tillsit would have to admit that in law those diamonds belong to Gilbert. A pleasant li'le legacy they'll make, too; it's the way his aunt must have wanted this, when she arranged to keep the stones here. How much would they be worth?"

"About two thousand apiece, when she bought them," said Mary Helen, smoldering.

"H'm." Todd waited a minute before he added gently, "People have been murdered for less than that."

"She wasn't!" she screamed. "I had nothing to do with her death, you can't pin it on me. And now you're trying to talk me out of my property. Just you tell me, Nella, where did you find 'em?"

"Don't come close to her," Georgine said on a sharp breath.

"I'm not going to hurt her! But oh, God, I wish I'd strangled *you* while I had the chance. Where did you find 'em, Nell Lace?"

Nella turned her head, and the gray eyes opened languidly. "We must all have looked straight at them a hundred times, Mary Helen, in those days after Miss Adeline died." A slight smile curved her lips. "They were in one of those cut crystal jars on her bureau, that seemed so transparent nobody would look inside for something hidden. They were stuck there with Vaseline so they wouldn't rattle. I might never have found them myself except that the jar broke."

Mary Helen Crane gave a high-pitched laugh, and looked round at the person next her. "So much for your secret places under marble slabs, and in carvings—and your chair casters! I told you I'd looked a thousand times, but no, you were sure there were places only you knew about—"

"You gone crazy, Mary Helen Jefferson?" Mrs. Labaré demanded sharply. Her black eyes swerved round.

"Indeed she hasn't, Mrs. Labaré," Todd said. He gave one of his silent chuckles. "Quite a li'le rash of conspiracy broke out when we came to town, it seems. You probably didn't know that the jewels were still around somewhere, until Mary Helen told you yesterday afternoon. You wouldn't have warned Mrs. Peabody about the lights in the attic; you'd have been up there yourself, looking. I'll hand Mary Helen this much; she was ready to give up the search if her grandfather had been willing to finance her Hollywood venture, but since he wasn't she turned to you as a last resort. What did she do, offer to split the proceeds? What wouldn't you have done for a share in twelve or fifteen thousand dollars, Mrs. Labaré?" He leaned toward her across the table, and his eyes were ugly and formidable. "I hope you've enough of your capital to live on, because I can't imagine anyone's giving you another job now—when they hear that you threatened to kill a small child in the course of *your* search."

The shock of white hair quivered. "I don't know what you're talkin' about," said Susie, and closed her mouth with a snap.

"Yes, you do. It had to be you who was in the attic this morning. The other persons involved could have been up there searching, and it would have seemed quite natural to Barby, because they live here. But she couldn't be allowed to see *you!* You're strong enough, and you're ruthless enough; witness your leaving that mop across the stairs last night, hoping one of us would trip and be hurt, investigating the creaking sounds that you made by standing under the top flight and pushing up at step after step with the mophead. I think very li'le," said Todd ominously, "of your regard for human life. Would every one of your patients' deaths bear close examination?"

That's a shot in the dark, thought Georgine; and was startled to see Susie's head jerk back as if a whiplash had cracked in her face.

"I wouldn't 'a hurt her," she rasped. "Not on purpose. You can't prove it—takin' away my character..."

Todd took his hands off the table and straightened slowly. "And don't threaten to sue for libel," he interjected into Susie's furious spatter of words. "I only asked a question."

"It's all imagination," Mary Helen said quickly. "He's only guessing, that's what he's done about all of this—"

"How'm I doing with my guesswork?" Todd asked the doctor.

John Crane's long face looked haggard with distaste. "All too well, I'm afraid. There are things I—never mind, this is something I can deal with. And now, there are patients waiting for me, and I must get back. If there's anything more, Mr. McKinnon—"

"Just a minute, doctor, please. Nella may still need your help. Now, this document—" He lifted the yellow sheet from the top of the pile and tapped it with a forefinger. "You must decide, all of you, what's to be done with it. Should the guilty party be asked to sign it, and end all uncertainty?"

"Why not—if he'll do it?" Horace inquired. He had been sitting in a straight chair beside the table, his eyes moving from one face to another, somberly interested. "Not that it'd be of much value."

"Very li'le, only let him know that people are sure of his guilt. He can choose, after that, what course to pursue. What do you all think?"

In his turn he searched each face. "You're agreed, I see," Todd said, and drew a heavy breath. "Very well."

He put down the sheet of paper and slid it gently across the table. "*You* sign it," he said, and raised stony eyes to meet Horace Tillsit's.

"*Me?*" Horace said, startled. "Man, are you off your rocker? Sign that stuff about the studio—"

He glanced down at the typed sheet, and his sentence died in midair. There was no start of muscles; Horace had his body well under control; but the blood came crimson to his neck and ears.

Mary Helen looked over his shoulder incredulously. "More of his fiction?" she said in a high, clear voice, and began to read aloud. As she read, the mocking intonation faded gradually from the words.

"I had prepared a single capsule containing ten grains or more of luminal, intending to give it to Miss Tillsit during the first stages of my grandfather's illness. I was unable to find the opportunity then, but on the afternoon of June 9 I heard, on the party line, a call to Gilbert Peabody which informed him that Judge Tillsit had had a relapse and was sinking, and wished to see him at once. From the rear window of the pharmacy I could check on Gilbert's movements. When he had gone, I caught the cat and shut it up in the prescription room, knowing that it would move about on the shelves and clink the bottles and sound as if I were there. The cat scratched me. If Martin Kinter and Rose Bacon had noticed my twenty-minutes' absence I had another story to explain it; but this was not necessary. My great-aunt had no suspicions of me when I came into the room, wearing, to make her laugh, the nurse's cap which I had taken from the clean laundry at the foot of the stairs. She took the capsule willingly on my telling her that it was a new type of patent medicine—"

"Great God, he *is* crazy!" Horace said. He pushed the chair back and got up with no visible unsteadiness. "Trying to saddle me with this nonsense!" The easy smile came once more to his lips. "It sounds so damnably convincing, you know. I suppose I could have done all that, but why should I? I had nothing to gain."

"Not right then," said Todd placidly; but his face had the wooden look of strain. "Did no one ever figure out how the inheritances would work, eventually? Very simply, after all. If Miss Adeline died first, the Judge got all her real estate—that farm property that's been rising so phenomenally in value for the past few years. If she outlived the Judge, she'd inherit his property, as the eldest member of the family. And to whom would she leave it? To Gilbert, her next of kin. And to whom would the Judge leave it? To his own collateral descendant. You could afford to let him live for a while, Mr. Tillsit," said Todd smoothly, "once he had got hold of the bulk of his sister's property. You knew it would be yours before too long; and you can wait, you can be patient if you're sure things will come to you in the end. That afternoon, though, you had to act, to do your best to insure that Miss Adeline would not outlive her brother."

"That's a perfect tissue of lies," said Horace contemptuously.

"So. Then, let's face facts. Gilbert brought her the diamonds late in the morning. According to your story, the first time you saw her that day was late in the afternoon, when she was unconscious. Just when did your great-aunt tell you that she'd 'hidden the diamonds where no one would ever find them'—unless it was during your secret visit at two o'clock? And if you made an innocent call on her then, why haven't you admitted it?"

There was a brief silence. The uncontrollable red came up again.

"Horace," Mary Helen said in a dreadful whisper. She shrank from him, slowly retreating across the room. "That's it. It was you. I never saw that, I never thought of—"

Todd's eyes rested on her for a moment. "Didn't you, Mrs. Crane?" he said remotely. "Well—I believe you'd better sign that, brother, and finish up the business. You've admitted it's true, you know; not in so many words, but your blood vessels give you away when anyone hits on your li'le secrets."

"Sign?" Horace said. "What kind of a fool do you think I am? Sign my name to your goddamned fictioneering nonsense?"

"People have been convicted of murder," said Todd steadily, "on evidence thinner than any writer would dare to use. I've made out a better case, for instance, than the one against Oscar Slater. D'you know how long he was in prison?"

Horace struck the table with the flat of his hand. "The hell with you and your case. Who do you think you are, talking about prison? You can't do anything to me, nobody can touch me, you suppose I don't know that?"

"*I'm nobody*," said Todd, and his teeth showed white in a taunting smile. "I've touched you, my friend, for now you've admitted your guilt in words."

The crimson flush spread until its color could be seen through Horace's thinning hair. His companions were frozen in silence. He glanced round the room once, and seemed almost physically to stoop under the impact of their expressions.

"You can't pin a thing on me," he said thickly. "There's no proof, there never could be. What if that yarn of yours does come near enough—"

"Confession before witnesses," said Todd, looking far away.

"And what of it? If I signed that thing, if I went so far as to write out a statement in my own words and sign it, you couldn't take it into court! It wouldn't be evidence, and your lies are even less—nothing I've said has—what's a slip of the tongue—"

His voice fell off into silence. He looked terrifyingly like Judge Tillsit at the beginning of a fit. Todd's agate-hard eyes flicked him.

"This case will never reach a court of law," Todd said. "But you'll be tried just the same, by a jury of your peers—the people of this town, where your property and your business are, where you've built your life. Look at all of us here. Even if your grandfather could intimidate the others once more, Georgine and I wouldn't keep quiet about you; Nella certainly won't; and if people believed a mere suspicion about Gilbert, they'll surely believe this."

He tore the other typewritten sheets across and across, and dropped the fragments into his pocket. He was still smiling faintly. "You're free, my friend. You can go anywhere you like in this country, no police officer will ever tap you on the shoulder for this offense. You can stay here if you like and try to brazen it out. Nobody can punish you. But you'll never again be able to lay this crime on the shoulders of a man who's with the Armed Forces in the South Pacific. It's yours to carry, now."

Horace Tillsit swung away from the table and plunged blindly from the room. The door went back against the wall with an ear-splitting crash.

Five seconds later a small startled face appeared in the opening. "You said you were coming back in just a minute, Mamma," Barby said in aggrieved tones. "It's been just *ages*. And somebody knocked and knocked at the door downstairs, and I went to answer it because nobody else paid attention, and it's a man."

Georgine sat down on the bed and moistened her dry lips. "What man, dear?"

"He says he knows Toddy, and he wants to look at a bedroom set. I didn't know what he meant, Mamma, and I'm awful tired of reading."

For the last time in this house Todd stepped inside the door of Georgine's bedroom. Deliberately he got out a handkerchief, mopped his brow and called in low, heartfelt tones upon his Saviour.

"So you didn't really know?" Georgine said wearily. She picked up her handbag and straightened Barby's hat.

Todd shook his head. "For all the proof I had, it might really have been Gilbert, or anyone. I had a confession apiece written out, in case anything broke, and it was just luck that it did. The sight of the diamonds was the only thing that'd shake that remark out of Mary Helen. If she hadn't been mad enough to let it slip, there wouldn't have been a clinching point to my argument. And don't ask me what I'd have done if I couldn't have proved my point. I don't know, I never did know, I lost my own temper and bluffed on a pair of deuces. And so help me, it's the last time."

"Is it?" Georgine could not seem to shake off this all-pervasive feeling of dullness. "Lucky you guessed Nella had the diamonds, then."

"I didn't guess," he said meekly. "I felt 'em under her dress when I picked her up; and I'd have thought nothing of that, either, if I hadn't just learned what the rats were looking for."

"Now it's all clear," said Georgine, "and now let's go away before they see us. You're satisfied, aren't you?"

"With this project, yes," said Todd.

She didn't answer his implication. They went quietly downstairs, they got into the car with no ceremony whatsoever and drove away. She hadn't even the spirit to feel relieved.

"Wait a minute," she said as the car turned into the main street. "Did you pay Horace for all those supplies, the other night?"

"Come to think of it, I didn't. As I said before," Todd remarked, "the question of who owes whom what is a li'le involved."

"Well, we still owe money to his partner," said Georgine in the voice of utter fatigue. "Lend me some, I'll pay you back when we get home. You can double-park here, I suppose."

The car stopped in front of the drugstore. Todd seemed to be looking intently into the rearview mirror, as if he preferred not to meet her eyes. "There's plenty there," he said, handing her his billfold. "While you're inside, how's about buying the cricket a new flashlight? Her old one was broken and I left it behind at the house."

"*No!*" Barby shrieked, flinging herself round in the seat. "I don't want a new one, Toddy, you said you had mine! Cousin Dyke scratched my initials on it! I won't have another!"

"Okay, okay, Barby," said Todd, chuckling. "Don't strangle me. We'll go back, if you insist. Pick you up here in five minutes, Georgine."

"All right," she said, plodding across the sidewalk. She was only vaguely aware of a car, pausing at the intersection of Walnut and this main street, and then drawing up with a squeal of brakes outside the store. "Would you get our bill, Mr. Kinter?" she asked the assistant. "I'm sorry if you're busy, but I'm in a hurry."

Martin Kinter looked astonished. "I think Horace would be the one to know about it, Mrs. Wyeth," he said.

"You find it, please," said Georgine. "Horace may not be in the store for some time."

The other customers looked at her with covert curiosity, but she paid no attention. She had caught sight of her face in the mirrored stand in the rear. No reason for me to look as if *I'd* died, thought Georgine; at least I could put on some lipstick.

The frosted-glass window of the prescription room rose above the mirror. She looked at it briefly. With those two clear peepholes it was almost like an elongated mask.

That disturbance near the door was annoying; she concentrated on smoothing the scarlet paste onto her lips. "Came in here, didn't she?" said a harsh voice. "The other ones drove off round the corner, but—yes, that's the woman. The one paintin' her face like Jezebel. Are you pleased with what you've done, Miss, coming to this town with your fancy man and tellin' lies about my family?"

It actually did not dawn upon her until she saw another reflection beside her own: flabby folds of skin under a mottled chin. She came round slowly, and spoke with an awful deliberation.

"You great lummox, are you talking to me?"

"I am. Women of your sort ought to be denounced in public. Forcing your way in on false pretenses, wagging your lying tongue about matters you never had any concern with, that ought to be left in the past where they belong—and now, *now*, trying your best to ruin my grandson—"

He drew a mighty breath and choked slightly on the intake. Georgine cut in before he could recover. "I'm afraid that was done years ago, Mr. Tillsit. You set up a fine example yourself, grasping at every cent you could get and holding onto it—"

"Shut your mouth," the Judge rasped. "Trying to ruin him, I said, with a pack of lying nonsense that wouldn't fool a child!"

"I'm afraid you're the one that's fooled, if you insist your grandson isn't guilty. You've known all along, haven't you? Why else were you so frightened of eating a meal in the house where he lived, except that you thought it might be your turn next? I wish we'd said nothing, but not because we didn't hit on the truth; because I'd like to see you waiting for a month, a year, two years more for the blow to fall on *you*. Did you think it would save you to let your own sister's death go uninvestigated? I know why you were willing to; because you got her property. You were glad she died." She spoke just above a whisper, her eyes boring into his.

"Have you quite finished, Madam?" the Judge said ominously. "That; that's a sample of what I mean. Just what's to be expected of a couple without a moral to their name, that hasn't any more shame than to drag a child around with 'em to deceive—"

The color of Georgine's eyes would have warned a wiser man. "Mr. Tillsit! Your sort of hypocrisy—"

He broke in on her again; bellowing, this time, to the open enchantment of the customers who still lingered about the front of the store. "By God, if you lived in this town, I'd see to it that there were measures taken—"

"And if I did live here," said Georgine clearly, "do you think I'd be afraid of you, you village Mussolini? Why, you're nothing to me but a low-minded old gaffer with the manners of a Barbary ape."

She waited with quiet satisfaction while he allowed his face to swell and turn purple, while the whites of his eyes showed at the bottom and he clawed at his collar.

"And don't pull one of those fits of yours on me," she added. She kept her voice pleasantly low, but in the deathly hush of the drugstore it was quite audible. "You've been scaring people with them for years, but they're just as phony as your title. 'Judge Tillsit!' You couldn't judge a—a Mother's Sack Race."

"I'll have you run out of town," the Judge bellowed. With remarkable agility he wheeled and plunged toward the front door. Not one of the customers met his eye.

Georgine waited a minute, and then followed him. Martin Kinter sprang to open the door for her as she swept through, his other hand modestly tendering a written statement.

She glanced at it. Five dollars even; she drew a bill from Todd's wallet and presented it with a lordly flourish. Thank heaven she didn't have to spoil it by waiting for change, she reflected as she stalked grandly out.

The Judge's car was still parked at the curb, and Costanza, behind the wheel, was twisted around watching with amazed eyes as her employer bustled on foot down the short block toward the police station. Georgine gave her a pleasant nod in passing, and climbed into Todd's car, waiting in mid-street. Barby's face appeared, bright with interest, at the window; she turned and made some remark.

"Mamma does look pretty," Todd said gravely in reply as Georgine hoisted Barby aside and sat down. "I think she's been getting mad at someone."

"Ha! Have I! Worse, in fact." She glanced down at her child and spoke carefully, in a language which would have baffled any Continental, though Todd, who had also been to an American high school, understood her perfectly. "J'ai juste faite," said Georgine, "un terrible scène en publique avec ce vieux chameau le Juge." She looked round with interest. "He *is* going into the police station. How do you suppose they run people out of this town, with a mounted posse?"

"Is that what he threatened to do?" said Todd, grinning. "What a pity we're just on our way out, anyway."

"I thought of that," said Georgine blithely, "and so of course there's only one thing to do: dodge him somehow and stay here until we've finished all our business."

His head turned sharply.

"Yes, that's what I mean. You've got the ring and the minister and the license all lined up, it'd be sinful to waste them. And, seeing as it's you, Todd, we're willing to take a chance with you—a million times over. Aren't we, Barby?"

"Sure," said Barby, uncomprehending but game.

"Don't let anyone see where we're going," said Georgine, twisting about in the seat. "I can just barely make out what they're doing down the street. Yes, there comes the Judge out, pointing at your car. Somebody's getting into an old sedan. Lead 'em a chase, Todd!"

Todd complied, his face rigid but his mouth now and then twitching faintly. He dallied artistically until the pursuer could see exactly which street he had turned down, and then cut neatly across to another; he shot round corners and had to stamp on his brakes to avoid hitting the police car itself, trundling past in the opposite direction; and after he had followed it unnoticed for several blocks, swung sharply into an alley and came to rest, the car almost hidden by thick bushes, at the back door of the Rectory.

"We'd better hurry," he said, rushing the bride and the maid of honor through the kitchen, past an astonished housekeeper. "Is the Rector here? Good luck. I'll do the explaining." He stepped into the next room. "You see, Father Patton," his voice floated out, "the police are after us."

Georgine was laughing as she started to follow him. She caught a glimpse of a startled kindly face over a clerical collar, and thought, It's my *wedding*...

All at once she was enveloped in a sort of emotional fog that nearly overwhelmed her. But this is absurd, she told herself just before her mind went blank; I've been married before, I shouldn't be acting like...Then her hands and feet went cold as ice; dimly she heard Barby expostulating, dimly felt a peculiar sensation as of something laid in her arms and then taken away. That must be her own voice, miles away, muttering some kind of response to urgent promptings. Someone was gripping her hand, steadying her...

"—man and wife," said another voice through the mist. "And may I wish you every happiness? Perhaps you'd like to sit down, Mrs. McKinnon."

Her vision cleared. She looked down at the sapphires on her left hand. Yes, she must have got married. Her head turned and she caught sight of Barby, who stood blissfully clutching an armload of pampas grass. "They had it right here in the parlor, Mamma," Barby said, "and you didn't have a bouquet, but you promised me I could hold yours when you got married, and I—"

"I see, darling. That's enough, now." Pampas grass, thought Georgine wildly, and me in an old jersey dress I've worn six days. Something dignified and lovely—a simple ceremony that we could remember always. Well, that last part was true enough.

There was something else missing from this scene; could it be the bridegroom? Yes, there he was, outside the window. He must have left her the second the knot was tied.

He spoke earnestly to a lanky gentleman who stood beside a battered sedan; he made a restrained gesture toward the window, and his companion's eyes followed. Georgine saw the strange face split by a slow, broad grin.

Todd reappeared in the sitting room, his friend in tow. "You know Ed, of course, Father Patton? And Georgine, may I present my good friend Ed Talcott? Ed, my wife."

"I'd like to shake you by the hand, if you don't mind, Mis' McKinnon," Ed said rapturously. Georgine complied in bewilderment. "Now, lookit, Mac. I've got to make like I'd lost you on the edge of town, see? But if you should happen to go back down the main street, I'd arrange to be way over on Cottonwood about that time, and nobody could prove I hadn't been watching the approaches, see?"

"I do see. A fine idea," said Todd heartily. "We'd better make it snappy, though, so you won't get into trouble. Father Patton, I can't thank you enough for realizing the, uh, nature of the emergency. Finest wedding I've ever been to."

"And, Mamma," said Barby breathlessly as they climbed into the car, "that nice man said I could keep the bouquet, that you ought to have it. Now I've got everything, because, look!" She snapped open the glove compartment triumphantly. "My flashlight was in here all the time. Toddy just forgot that he'd brought it along after all."

Georgine looked round slowly at her bridegroom. "Toddy just forgot," she repeated musingly. "Todd McKinnon, did you see the Judge coming with fire in his eye, and make up that excuse to leave me alone and drive off, so that he'd get after me?"

"Dear heart," said Todd placidly, "you haven't begun to plumb the depths of my depravity." He swung the car into the main street, and kept it to a sober pace.

The Judge was standing on the sidewalk in front of the police station. He watched the bridal car go by. With growing incredulity, with visible horror, he goggled at the three beaming faces turned toward him, and his mouth dropped slowly open.

Barby gave a squeak of sheer delight, and turned to her parent, "Oh, Mamma, lookit his face!" she said. "Could I count that as a Big Red Object?"

"Just for this once, you may," Georgine told her.